WE BURY NOTHING

Copyright © 2025 Kate Blair
This edition copyright © 2025 DCB, an imprint of Cormorant Books Inc.
This is a first edition.

No part of this publication may be reproduced, stored in a retrieval system or transmitted, in any form or by any means, without the prior written consent of the publisher or a licence from The Canadian Copyright Licensing Agency (Access Copyright). For an Access Copyright licence, visit www.accesscopyright.ca or call toll free 1.800.893.5777.

The publisher and the author expressly forbid the use of this book in any manner for the purpose of training so-called artificial intelligence systems or technologies, and reserve this title from the text and data mining exception in accordance with the European Parliament directive.

Canadian Heritage Patrimoine canadien

Canada Council for the Arts Conseil des arts du Canada

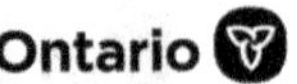

We acknowledge financial support for our publishing activities: the Government of Canada, through the Canada Book Fund and The Canada Council for the Arts; the Government of Ontario, through the Ontario Arts Council, Ontario Creates, and the Ontario Book Publishing Tax Credit.

Library and Archives Canada Cataloguing in Publication

Title: We bury nothing / Kate Blair.
Names: Blair, Kate, author
Identifiers: Canadiana (print) 20250166011 | Canadiana (ebook) 20250166038 | ISBN 9781770868021 (softcover) | ISBN 9781770868038 (EPUB)
Subjects: LCGFT: Novels.
Classification: LCC PS8603.L3153 W42 2025 | DDC jC813/.6—dc23

United States Library of Congress Control Number: 2025934234

Cover and interior text design: Marijke Friesen
Manufactured by Friesens in Altona, Manitoba in August 2025.

Printed using paper from a responsible and sustainable resource, including a mix of virgin fibres and recycled materials.

Printed and bound in Canada.

EU RP eucomply OÜ
Pärnu mnt 139b-14, 11317 Tallinn, Estonia
hello@eucompliancepartner.com, +3375690241

DCB Young Readers
An imprint of Cormorant Books Inc.
260 Ishpadinaa (Spadina) Avenue, Suite 502, Tkaronto (Toronto), ON M5T 2E4, Canada

Suite 110, 7068 Portal Way, Ferndale, WA 98248, USA

www.dcbyoungreaders.com
info@cormorantbooks.com / www.cormorantbooks.com

To all the authors whose books are getting banned.
And to those who seek out banned books,
and read them anyway.

CHAPTER ONE
June 20, 1945

Not for the first time, George wondered if things were easier on the other side of the barbed wire. Inside, it was lit up like midday. The prisoners of war gathered together in the warm huts, out of the unseasonably chilly rain. They had each other, friends and comrades, even in defeat.

The other guards — mostly old-timers, unlike George — searched inside the site, where they'd no doubt find the missing POWs. In the meantime, he limped around the perimeter in the dark. They were playing their silly games again, hiding under a hut or in the laundry to throw off the roll call. He'd hoped they were done with this nonsense once Hitler shot himself. Couldn't they just send them home now? Why were they still keeping German soldiers in Canada, feeding them and taking care of them? Hadn't they taken enough?

He paused to swallow the grief.

The no-man's-land between the two fences was empty. No cut in the wire he could see. He trailed the flashlight along the ground, looking for disturbed earth or any sign of a tunnel between the camp and the woods. The light highlighted only the curtain of water slashing down and puddles convulsing with the fierce rain.

Naturally, he had been given the perimeter search. The other guards all suspected what he was, although no one said it. He was never included in the beers in the main guard tower.

Sod this for a game of soldiers. At least he'd be leaving it all behind tomorrow — all the whispers and the sneers. He wouldn't give them any excuse to send him out again. He'd check carefully, casting his light in sweeping waves to the left and right, water from his useless, peaked cap dripping in his eyes.

He was so used to the view, so used to the monochrome of mud, the slick darkness of the ground, and the lopsided rhythm of his steps, he almost missed it: a lump, right at the treeline.

He hurried over. Perhaps the Jerries had dug a tunnel after all, and this was a mound of discarded earth. But as he got closer, the flashlight brought out the color in the lump. It was a chap in the gray POW uniform with the red circle sewn on the back that the prisoners detested. He was face-down. George knelt next to him and rolled him over.

His eyes were open, but he was gone. His soft features were familiar, cheeks rounded with youth: Erich Stein.

Dammit. Why did it have to be him?

Erich had almost succeeded in his escape. He was right at the trees. What on earth had he been thinking? Why hadn't he listened to George? He was fixing Erich's mistakes! All he had to do was sit tight. George's plan wasn't perfect, but it was the best he could do in a world like this, the best for all three of them. Stupid, stupid boy!

George knew he shouldn't care. Erich was just another dead man among millions — one of the enemy, too. But how had he died? George looked him over. He thought he saw blood on his head, but it could have been the wet of rain. And how had he got out of the camp? There were too many questions. George needed to blow his whistle, to call the other guards and show them what he'd found. He'd have to tell Daisy.

The tears came and they wouldn't stop until he was weeping, back shaking, kneeling over the still boy.

What was the point of any of this?

CHAPTER TWO

I first heard of Erich Stein on a true crime podcast.

The podcasts were to distract me on those long waits in the hospital while my dad slept away most of his last days. The story stuck in my mind as it was local-ish, my province of Ontario featured among farther-flung mysterious murders. But the episode itself was a disappointment. The podcaster came to no conclusion on the all-important question of whodunnit.

I'd preferred historical true crime then. The distance in time, the fact that there was no one left to mourn, made the deaths less brutal. I once believed history was a refuge, a quiet place where the hurts of the present couldn't touch me. It never occurred to me that it was alive and angry, that it could reach its claws into the present and rip the world apart.

If I'd known, I'd never have applied for the summer internship program at the museum. Perhaps if I'd left well enough alone, everyone would still be alive.

I could imagine how the German prisoners of war felt as the stifling, whitewashed room that was my home for the summer pressed in on me: alone, far from their families, consumed with worry and unsure of what would become of them in this small Canadian town.

But, unlike those enemy soldiers eighty years ago, I'd chosen to come. I'd worked hard on my application after the school counsellor told me about the program. It had felt like a sign. As if the universe was giving me a chance to resolve some of the uncertainty of those awful hospital days by solving Erich Stein's murder myself. Listening to the podcast had given me a head start, but I'd thrown myself into the research, and had beaten stiff competition to be there.

The room was just big enough for a single bed, a desk, and a battered, old, wooden wardrobe. The light spilling out through the grimy window barely made it to the first pines of the forest outside. The branches rolled in the breeze like waves.

The Heritage Site manager, Sarah, had said this was a guard's room, not a cell, back when the place was a prisoner-of-war camp, but it felt like a cell, especially in the solid humidity of a summer evening. The retrofitted air conditioning was weak in this old wing of the building and there was a soft, sweaty smell I hoped wasn't me.

I yanked on the hem of my black shirt-dress, wondering when I should head to the welcome reception. Was it the kind of thing you arrived at on time or fashionably late? My outfit had seemed perfect when I bought it: neat and formal while not being too try-hard, but it had crumpled in my backpack and lumped weirdly on my stomach.

The museum that was once Camp 43 sat on the edge of town. There wasn't even the comforting hum of passing cars, which were a constant in my part of Toronto. Cicadas buzzed, and the electricity line running down the road to town hummed. I didn't like the quiet. It let the doubts swell in my mind until my skull felt like it would burst.

It was easy to be crazily ambitious in my application when it was just theoretical. I cringed, remembering my arrogant claim that I'd have a good shot at solving an eighty-year-old murder mystery.

Perching on the edge of the thin mattress, I pulled my Camp 43 file from the desk drawer and thumbed through the notes I'd made. I'd hit a wall with the online sources and outdated books at the reference library, in spite of all the time I'd spent there after school. I hoped there was more information in the camp archive. But what if there wasn't? Would they send me home if I couldn't find anything?

There wasn't much known, really. None of the guards had noticed anything unusual until evening roll call on June 20, 1945, when two prisoners, Erich Stein and Rainer Schmitt, didn't show up. A panic ensued as fears of escaped Germans led them to check the camp perimeter, which is why Erich Stein's body was found first. He'd died just outside from a head wound. The other body was found in one of the barracks. Rainer Schmitt had a head injury too, but was in much worse shape, with multiple other injuries, including a broken arm and broken ribs. The prisoners had clammed up, claiming none of them had seen anything. Schmitt could easily have been beaten to death by at least one of the other POWs, but why had Stein been found outside the camp? One explanation was they'd hidden in the hut's attic during roll call and somehow fallen, but Stein's injury hadn't been immediately fatal, and he'd tried to escape on his own, perhaps disoriented. Or maybe the two had fought and Stein, mortally wounded after killing Schmitt, had fled.

The real mystery was how Stein got out. He had a history of escape attempts, once trying to flee the farm where he was on work duty. But climbing the two barbed-wire fences would have been impossible even if he was uninjured. The guards insisted he couldn't have escaped between the inner and outer fences, which had twelve floodlit feet of open land between them, watched at all times. There were no signs of holes in the fences or tunnels beneath.

It had seemed like an exciting angle for my application when I'd first started reading about the camp. Now that I actually had to solve the mystery, it felt like I'd boxed myself into another kind of cell.

I dropped the file and stared at the white wall. It was clammy with condensation as the humid day cooled into evening. Since the Camp 43 days, the site had served as a school, an agricultural college, and a meditation retreat before they finally got the funding to start making it into a museum. It had that impersonal, institutional feel, like the hospital room where we spent so long with Dad, holding his limp hand as he slid away from us, just over a year ago.

At least I hadn't put his death in the application. Mom had wanted me to mention him. She'd said I deserved a break, deserved something good after all we'd been through. Maybe I did. But I was sick of those looks of sympathy, sick of everyone asking if I was okay. I knew the museum summer program was competitive and I'd worked damn hard for it. I didn't want to wonder if I'd gotten it out of pity.

I had to get out of my head. I should knock on the doors of the other three students, see if they were ready to go to the reception. I could use some friends, some normality.

The iron knob was damp, the door swollen with the humidity. It only opened a crack before it stuck. I was about to yank it hard when I heard the voices of two of the other students down the passage — I recognized them from when we'd met earlier: Ephram's deep tone and the light, sing-song cadence of Ruth.

There was an edge to Ephram's voice that stopped me pushing the handle harder.

"It's not right."

"Are you going to tell Sarah?" Ruth asked.

I moved close to the tatty whitewash of the door, keeping my ear back from a painted-over splinter on the frame.

A long silence. "You should, Ruth. You don't belong here."

"This is exactly where I belong. You know nothing about me, okay?" She sounded on the edge of tears.

Ephram sighed. "Fine, I won't tell. But it doesn't mean I think it's okay."

"Yeah, you made that clear."

The gentle clack of Ephram's leather shoes on the hallway tiles faded, and all was quiet. I barely had a moment to wonder what that was about when a cheerful rat-a-tat on my door made me jump. I wrenched it open.

Ruth wore a low-cut, green dress and heels. Her red hair was up in a smooth chignon, and I felt a thousand times worse about my crumpled outfit and ballet flats.

She entered without waiting to be asked. "What's that?" She made a beeline for the file and picked it up. She peered at the title, then dropped it like dirty laundry. "Keira, are you doing homework?"

If I hadn't heard the argument, I'd have thought nothing had happened.

"No. I mean, I was just looking at it. In case anyone asks about my project."

"Relax. Tonight's a party! You got in, so you must be smart. You," she pointed right at me, "don't need to prove yourself to anyone."

Her approval felt special. Perhaps it was her utter confidence. It was like getting an award and it drove all my questions about the sort-of-argument I'd heard out of my head.

"What's your project?"

She waved a hand. "I said I'd do something about relationships with the locals." She jumped onto my bed, shuffling herself back so she leaned against the wall, legs straight out in front of her, crossed at the knee. "So, what's your take on Ephram and Asha?"

"I ... They seem nice."

"They seem rich."

"Asha's rich?" Ephram was totally obvious — he'd arrived in an actual suit, pushing a high-end, silver, four-wheeled suitcase that glided over every surface. But Asha's clothes looked like they'd come from a thrift store.

"That dye job? Must have cost hundreds. You saw the vintage convertible Beetle in the parking lot?"

"The one painted with flowers?"

"Hers."

"Oh."

I didn't know anyone else our age with their own car. Everyone back home was stuck on public transit, although a lucky few got to use their parents' cars once in a while. Even my mom didn't have one. She'd had to borrow my uncle's to get me to Westonville.

"So, it's agreed. Us unrich kids will stick together?"

I didn't want to take sides. It felt particularly wrong since we were the only white students; Asha was South Asian and

Ephram was Black. But Ruth was magnetic. She pulsed blood-red with life in my tiny room. She pushed herself off the bed in one smooth motion.

"Time to party."

"Shall … shall we get the others?"

She shook her sleek head. "Asha went early and Ephram just left."

I was a little hurt that Asha hadn't waited for us and didn't know what to say about Ephram, so I followed the surgical click of Ruth's heels down the tiled corridor, past the other bedrooms and the small kitchen/common room, and out a side door. It was even warmer outside, with the soft touch of a breeze on the bare skin of my arms and legs.

The site looked gray in the dark, as if the color had been sucked out. I wasn't used to a world without light pollution and I imagined the stars would be amazing if it wasn't so cloudy.

The two-storey museum building was a boxy heap crouched in the night. The windows at the side were dark: empty eye sockets. The reception was in the new gallery at the front and our rooms were in the unrenovated bit at the back. The caterers were set up in between, which is why we'd been told to go around the outside.

My shoes crushed the dry grass, each step a whisper. To our right, the panels of a wire fence separated the part of the museum that would be open to the public in the fall from the unfinished area. The graffitied and unrestored hut beyond loomed out of the shadows. The obscenities sprayed on the battered walls seemed more threatening without the sun to neutralize them. I wondered if this was the hut Schmitt had died in. I wondered if the site was haunted: decomposing Nazi revenants stalking the dark in threadbare uniforms, heads caved in.

Another sound came over the rasp of wind through grass: the hiss and snap of something coming toward us — footsteps on the other side of the hut. Ruth's eyes widened as she heard too.

A figure rounded the corner.

For a ridiculous second, I wondered if he was human. There was something wraithlike about him: black hair over a pale face, the slash of high cheekbones. But the Ramones T-shirt and jeans didn't exactly gel with the spirits of my imagination. One eyebrow went up slightly, his only sign of surprise on seeing us.

"Summer students, I presume." He approached the fence, moved a panel out, and slid through the gap before replacing it. His gaze fixed on my face, eyes dark and intense.

"And who might you be?" Ruth's voice was a casual drawl, like she ran into people in the out-of-bounds section of old POW camps every day.

"What were you doing there?" I said, accidentally speaking over Ruth.

"Max de Jong. I'll be working with you. This is a shortcut from my place. Shall we?"

"I thought there were only four of us," I said.

"Just a volunteer. Got to polish up those university applications, right? I'm guessing you're Ruth and Keira, since neither of you look like an Ephram or an Asha."

"I'm Ruth."

"Keira," I said. "How old are you?" I cringed even as the words came out. I'd wanted to impress him and instead I'd come out with a total middle-school question. But he did look older than us. I wasn't sure if it was just the shadows on his face or the way he carried himself.

"Eighteen."

That killed the conversation, even if it cleared things up. Only a year older, then.

I felt better about my ballet flats as we made our way around the main building. Ruth stumbled more than once, her enviable grace impaired by her heels on the hard, uneven ground.

The parking lot out front brimmed with cars, light spilling from the glass of the modern extension onto bumpy rows of windshields and hoods. I caught sight of myself in the reflection on the doors before they opened automatically with a hushed hum: brown hair forming a frizzy halo around my pale face. I should have worn it up, like Ruth. I felt young next to Ruth and Max. They were just so much more together, more confident. We stepped inside. Air conditioning chilled the sweat on my skin as I blinked in the bright entrance.

An older man sat behind the reception desk with name badges arrayed in rows. It looked as if there had been dozens at one point, but only a handful remained. The low murmur of a crowd came from the gallery beyond.

"There you are!" Sarah, our manager, had changed into a shiny blue shirt tucked into neat black trousers, paired with kitten heels.

"We made a friend on the way," Ruth said.

Sarah ran a hand through her pixie cut. "I see you've made an effort for the *formal* reception, Max."

"What? This old thing?" He perched his fingers on his T-shirt. "You're too kind."

She grabbed our name badges and shoved them into our hands. "Thank you, Randall," she said to the older man, who ignored us. I struggled to attach the magnet to the back of my badge through the fabric of my dress as she hustled us into the main gallery.

I immediately felt horribly out of place.

Most of the women wore cocktail dresses, but a few long gowns swept across the polished pine floors as middle-aged and elderly adults clustered and chatted. Even the waitstaff were better dressed than me: the women wore black shirts, pencil skirts, and heels as they moved through the crowd balancing morsels of sculpted food and flutes of champagne on their trays.

Ruth seemed to sense my discomfort, perhaps because I was repeatedly trying to smooth my dress down over my stomach like a crazy person. "Don't worry. You look great."

Max nodded, giving me a smile that made my mouth suddenly feel dry.

Sarah pointed at a waitress circulating with drinks. "I know none of you are nineteen, so don't even think about it."

"Hadn't crossed my mind. Frankly, I'm insulted." Ruth put her hand on her hip.

The gallery walls were plastered in spotless white and still smelled of fresh paint. Empty museum cases were scattered throughout the space and a string quartet played in the corner. The women leaned into their golden-brown violins and cellos. The delicate rise and fall of the music mingled with staccato laughter.

Ephram and Asha stood off to one side. Ephram wore a neat black suit, different to the one he'd arrived in. His head was tilted at a curious angle as he watched the crowd. That seemed to be a habit of his, like he was slightly confused by the world. His glasses glinted as he took a sip of water.

I saw what Ruth meant about Asha's hair. I'd been impressed by the rainbow cascade down her back earlier. It did look professionally done, with no trace of brown at the roots. Not at all like last year when I'd decided to dye my hair blue, and it went a kind of swampy green. She wore a turquoise shirt that slid off one shoulder, flashing a purple bra strap that matched her long skirt and the Doc Martens that peeked out at the hem.

Asha gave us a grin and Ephram nodded as we approached.

Ruth whistled. "If the museum can afford all this, they should be paying us loads more."

"This isn't coming out of my budget. The reception is sponsored by his uncle." Sarah waved a hand at Max.

Ruth angled her whole body toward him. "Who *exactly* are you?"

"I told you: Max de Jong. I also have the misfortune to be related to Peter Hopper. Don't hold it against me."

I tried to place the familiar name.

"This is his party?" Asha sounded disgusted.

"Is he here?" Ruth glanced around.

"Peter's chair of the museum board. He and Julia are over there." Sarah pointed across the room. "They lobbied for years for the site to be a museum, and they matched the government funding so we could run this summer program with a decent honorarium for our students."

As I saw him, it clicked. Peter Hopper was a politician. He was an important minister of something. I couldn't remember which party he was with. I never really kept up with the news and I'd stopped reading it altogether once my dad got sick. Things had been depressing enough.

Peter Hopper was old, probably in his late fifties. He wore a perfectly tailored, navy suit. The brunette clutching his elbow was at least a decade younger, in a halter-neck, teal dress cut low in the back, her upper arms personal-trainer toned. She spotted us and tugged at his arm.

Sarah took a breath as they strode across the room. "Peter, Julia. Such a lovely party."

"Absolutely our pleasure," Julia said in a British accent. "We're so excited to finally have our students here. We had to make a bit of a fuss about it all."

"Thank you so much!" Ruth practically vibrated. "I'm Ruth Kowalska."

"Peter Hopper." His voice was low and rich, accent somehow extra Canadian in contrast with his wife's. "You're quite the genius, from what I've heard. All kinds of awards and the most glowing references, Sarah tells me."

Ruth looked awkward for a moment. "You're too kind."

Julia swooped in on Ruth, pressing her into a hug. "Call me Jules. We're very informal. You'll be focusing on the relationships between the camp and the local population, right?"

"You have an amazing memory, Jules."

"That stood out to me too," Peter said, "because my own father was here then. My grandfather was the camp commandant for a while."

Ruth's eyes widened. "Is your dad still alive? I'd love to talk to him about it."

"He's well into his nineties, and his memory isn't what it used to be, but if you'd like to try, I'll put my assistant in touch with you."

"That would be wonderful!" I half expected her to curtsey.

Peter turned to Asha. "You must be our artist prodigy, already exhibiting in galleries while still in high school."

"I have to go to the bathroom," Asha muttered, and she disappeared into the crowd.

Max watched her go, an odd smile on his lips. "I'll get a drink." Then he was gone too.

Unfazed, Peter Hopper offered me his hand. "Keira Martin, I presume. The sleuth."

"I suppose. I mean, I'm going to try to look into things."

Weak. I was better with books than with people.

I shook his hand. He clasped his other on top, turning the handshake sideways, elongating the moment and holding eye contact in what was probably meant as an authentic attempt to connect. It felt super weird.

"I'm sure you'll do great, Keira. True crime is all the rage these days, so I think it'll make a fascinating addition to the exhibitions. Sarah said you did an extraordinary amount of research for your application. You can't go wrong with a work ethic like that."

As soon as he released me, Julia moved in for her hug. I wasn't sure what to do and found myself patting the warmth of her bare back. It felt way too intimate.

"And Ephram Annah, another overachiever!"

"Anyah," Ephram corrected gently as he shook hands with Peter.

"Anyah, sorry. I hear you proposed a well-thought-out and ambitious original research project. University-level stuff."

"Thank you."

Julia leaned toward Ephram, but faced with his stiff demeanor, seemed to change her mind on the hug and shook his hand instead. "Lovely to meet you, Ephram. What a team! Exceptional students chosen from hundreds of applications. The crème de la crème."

That made me feel worse. How disappointed would they be if I came up with nothing?

"Anyway, now you're all here," Julia said, perhaps not noticing that Asha hadn't returned. "We have an itty-bitty announcement to make."

Peter nodded. "You may have heard about the Hopper Scholarships."

I hadn't, but I was all ears.

"We've been happy to support a number of students throughout their university careers —"

Julia interrupted him, bubbling over with excitement, "— and this year we decided to ring-fence a scholarship for one of our four museum students!"

I wasn't sure what "ring-fence" meant, but my breath caught anyway: a scholarship. A chance to get through university without crippling debt. Maybe even help Mom out with rent a bit.

Ruth actually clapped. "That's so kind of you!"

Now her sucking-up made sense. She must have known about this already but hadn't bothered to mention it. So much for us unrich kids sticking together.

"It's our pleasure! Now, you must circulate. It's a fabulous networking opportunity."

As soon as Peter and Julia stepped away, they were accosted by an elderly couple. Our little group sank into an uncomfortable silence. I had absolutely no idea how you were meant to "network." I spotted Asha and Max standing close together on the other side of the room, deep in conversation, and felt a childish kind of jealousy. *I saw him first.* Although I had to admit, if I had a choice of Asha or me, I'd pick the hot, rich, successful artist with super-cool hair as well.

I'd been desperate for a good summer after the awful year I'd had. Perhaps stupidly, I'd been hoping it would be like summer camp, with extra history. But Ephram and Ruth seemed to hate each other already, Asha and Max had apparently paired off, and in spite of Peter and Julia's generosity, her "itty-bitty announcement" had taken a group of potential friends and turned them into rivals.

Waiters circulated like dancers, twisting between groups, pausing, offering their trays. The quartet played, the two violinists turning their sheet music in perfect unison. Lights shone in the museum's glass cases, highlighting empty space waiting for exhibits.

I tried not to think about how much that scholarship could help — not just with money, but with getting accepted to the University of Toronto like Dad had wanted. I had a twenty-five percent chance, in theory at least. All I had to do was solve an eighty-year-old cold case.

No pressure, right?

CHAPTER THREE

February 10, 1943

The train juddered through the spotless white of the landscape. Erich Stein wiped the frost from the inside of the window with his sleeve. The chill sliced through his replacement uniform and greatcoat, though they were a darn sight better than the tattered Afrika Korps fatigues he'd been wearing when he'd been captured in Tunisia.

He'd spent most of the voyage to Halifax terrified of their own German U-boats sinking them. The cabin had stunk of vomit, but it was so cold on deck his breath froze, stiffening the scarf wrapped around his face until it felt like icy cardboard.

As they arrived, Leutnant Hofmann slid down the sea-ice laden mooring ropes, dangling dangerously before dropping down to the docks. He apparently made it halfway across the city before he was caught. Returned to the echoing cold of the processing hall, Hofmann was greeted by cheers and backslapping, breath rising in puffs over his laughing comrades.

Erich wondered how Leutnant Hofmann had been taken prisoner in the first place. No doubt he'd showed out well when the chips were down. Not like Erich, so lost in the scouring grit of a sandstorm, he'd surrendered pathetically to the first soldiers he found, begging for water.

What was it the Führer said? *Those who do not want to fight do not deserve to live.* Something like that anyway.

Since Halifax, it had been an endless train ride across an empty land. Days of nothing but the white undulation of fields and forests occasionally punctuated by a snow-capped farm or the mournful blare of the train's horn as they crossed an empty road. The few cities they stopped in were small, undamaged, and free of the frantic bustle of troop movements and the industry of war. Canada felt eerily quiet compared to England and to home.

Some soldiers drew maps of their route, noting the placenames of the towns they passed, already planning the next escape. But they'd laughed at Erich when he'd tried to help, excitedly reading "Bovril" from a wall. It turned out to be an advert for a hot drink, not the name of a Canadian city.

A few of the other Germans were dozing and a couple of their elderly guards too, snuffling and snoring. Gefreiter Klein coughed at the front of the carriage, a wet hacking sound that had been rising in volume and desperation, his eyes red and streaming.

Across the aisle, three of Erich's comrades played with an old pack of cards, cupping them behind their tatty-gloved fingers so the well-known creases and dog-eared corners didn't give their hands away. The fourth, Obergrenadier Walter, stared blankly at the floor as his knee jiggled and his head twitched — a man constantly in jerking, trembling motion.

A cigarette dangled out of Offizieranwarter Fischer's mouth

as he peered at his cards, smoke streaming toward the ceiling in a gray line that wobbled with the jolting of the carriage. Erich watched hungrily. Like most of them, he'd long ago finished the pitiful few smokes they'd been issued back in Halifax.

Opposite him in the little bay of four seats, Oberfüsilier Meyer leaned in.

"I bet you when we pull up there's nothing there but a big pit. Then," he mimed a machine gun, "rat-a-tat-tat. These doddering guards will cover us with dirt and head back out east to pick up their next batch of victims."

Erich felt just as sick as he had on the boat.

"Or there's mines and they work us to death in the freezing cold. Either way, we're never going home." He gave a self-satisfied sniff and sat back, folding his arms over his gray blanket.

Erich turned back to the glass. Ice crystals were creeping back into the space he'd cleared in the arched window. He slipped a hand into his pocket and felt the smooth wood of the good-luck charm his mother had given him against his fingertips. He blinked back the tears that threatened.

He was nineteen, too old to miss her this much. He was a soldier.

"I don't think you need to worry about that." A deep voice from Erich's right. He'd thought Feldwebel Schmitt was asleep. He glanced at Meyer opposite, and from the sheepish look on his face, it was clear he had too.

"Would they be giving us so much food if they're planning on killing us?"

It was true, they'd feasted ever since they'd arrived. Thick pieces of bread richly spread with butter. Generous slices of beef marbled with fat, and real coffee, not the acorn *ersatzkaffee* he'd gotten used to, and it came with actual sugar and cream. Apples and tinned peaches or pears with every meal, dripping with sweet syrup. The soldiers hadn't had so much fruit in years. It showed, too. The train toilets were a mess. The guards wouldn't let them close the doors for fear of escape attempts and the stink stole into the carriage.

"They're hardly acting like men ready to commit cold-blooded murder, are they?"

The old guards had been quite chatty with those who spoke English, which surprised Erich as they must have fought in the Great War. A few even knew a little German. His time in Canada so far was nothing like his stay in England, where they'd been on minimum rations and he'd been shouted at and spat on. And anything was better than the temporary camp in Tunisia, with the filth, flies, sweat rashes, and scorpions.

"The Canadians know the way the wind's blowing. Once we've taken England, we'll come for them. And how merciful do you think the Führer will be if they've been slaughtering our brave boys?"

Erich felt the tight clench of his heart loosen a little. Things made more sense when Schmitt explained them. Obviously, they wouldn't be slaughtered like animals. That was the kind of defeatist thinking that had cost Germany the last war. If the Canadians tried to kill them, they'd take on the ancient guards, wrestle their guns from them, and escape.

He thought of Franz von Werra. He'd taken his chances in the snow after slipping out the window of these trains and made it back home via America, Mexico, and Brazil, having amazing adventures on the way.

Of course, that had been a few years ago. Things had changed. America had been neutral then. It was the enemy now and von Werra had since sunk to a watery grave in the North Sea. But maybe Erich could still show he was a real German, like von Werra and Leutnant Hofmann.

He had to get back to Germany, or at least get away from their guards so he could be ready when the Wehrmacht arrived on Canadian shores. He'd prove he not only deserved to live but was good enough to be in the vanguard of their glorious march across this vast, empty continent.

He had to escape.

CHAPTER FOUR

The Hopper Scholarship was generous, it turned out, covering tuition entirely for a full degree. But three weeks into our summer program, I was certain I wouldn't win it.

We'd sunk into an awkward rhythm. Sarah and Max were in constant motion. They bustled around with boxes, stumbling up and down the stairs with signage and lumbering around with large text panels as the main gallery took shape.

Asha's sculpture formed on the field to the south of the main museum: stones made to form grave-like shapes in a camp-style enclosure, the whole thing half-covered by a tarp. She said it was going to be called "Dead/Buried" and was about the loss of life during World War II and the ambivalent nature of the town's relationship with the men who had been a part of it.

Ruth spent all her time with her new BFF: Peter Hopper's father and Max's grandfather, Bertie. She was interviewing him on his experiences as the son of the site commandant and reported that he insisted on her calling him "Gramps" and had adopted her as an honorary member of the family.

That just left three of us in the museum office. It was set in the eaves of the main building and smelled of the new flawless cream carpet I was terrified of spilling my coffee on. One half of the room was given over to the office, the other half to a small meeting room.

We each had our own desks, Ephram, me, and the old man who'd been sitting with the name tags at the reception: Randall Clifton, the museum's vice-chair. Sarah insisted we "not bother him," and his presence was a weight on the room, enforcing a heavy silence. He glared at his computer, fingers moving painfully slowly as he jabbed at the keyboard as if he were angry with it, an irregular rhythm that burrowed into my skull, blocking out all thought.

Ephram flicked through books and documents, the rustle of each page-turn unnaturally fast. When he typed, his fingers produced an impossibly quick clatter on the keyboard, which made me feel worse about my glacial progress.

Each morning, a square of light shafted down from the sloping window. It crept across the floor until, when the sun was at its zenith, it climbed onto my desk to focus on me, like I'd done something to annoy it. Sweat prickled on the back of my neck as I stared at my screen, chin in one hand, scrolling with the other. I worked through endless scanned documents looking for clues and only found receipts for milk deliveries and notes on extending the septic tank.

In the evenings, Ephram mostly stayed in his room on video calls with his girlfriend. His parents picked him up and took him home for weekends. Asha drove her Beetle into town each night, where she'd apparently found more interesting people to hang out with. Sarah returned to her own apartment in Westonville for a couple of hours each evening for dinner, returning for curfew.

She had to stay at the museum overnight to supervise us for the duration of the summer program. She normally lived at the apartment in town that she and her best friend rented together. They had moved out from Toronto, hoping that their frugal, rural lifestyle would help them save enough for a down payment on the Millennial dream: home ownership.

I'd long since realized that would always be out of reach for me.

Our wing was creepy at night, the museum isolated out beyond the edge of town. Whenever I was alone, I remembered that men had been murdered here: one beaten to death, the other killed mysteriously in the darkness outside. I was terrified that one night I'd glance at the window and see Erich Stein staring back at me.

I messaged Mom a lot, but she often worked evenings and took ages to reply. And my group chats with friends back home were full of summer plans I wasn't a part of. To be honest, I'd felt a little cut off from them ever since Dad had died, anyway.

It was hard not to think of him when I was alone.

I was deeply grateful for Ruth's comforting presence. We hung out together in our kitchen/common room, watching ridiculous reality shows on Netflix on Ruth's laptop on the nights when the Wi-Fi worked well enough, which distracted me from my failure to find any clues at work and from the ghosts I imagined outside.

I had no idea Westonville held real things to fear.

I survived on the salty blandness of ramen and Kraft Dinner, trying to save as much of my honorarium as possible. Plus, I kept running out of fresh food; the grocery store was in town, vegetables and fruit were heavy, expensive, and went off super quickly. I twice left my half-and-half on the counter in the morning and, without Mom to put it back in the fridge, it was unusable by the time I was done work. I got used to taking my coffee black.

Ruth normally ordered in. She alternated between Thai and pizza, each delivery lasting her a couple of days. The fridge was full of Ephram's passive-aggressively labeled but delicious-smelling stews that he brought in a cooler from home at the start of each week. We tried to remember to wash our dishes right away, as Ephram made a big deal about plates in the sink, sighing loudly and clattering them unnecessarily as he moved them in the morning.

I wasn't sure if Ruth sensed my research-related desperation or was running out of conversation, but I was embarrassingly grateful to her on the day she invited me to meet Bertie.

We set off together, cutting through the main gallery. The cases were filling with objects. I peered in as we passed, reading the labels. We wandered by toy soldiers whittled out of wood; threadbare, khaki-green Veterans Guard uniforms; and fake Iron Crosses that were made by melting down candy wrappers and sold to gullible guards.

Max was placing a small number next to a delicately rigged ship-in-a-bottle. Once he was done, he locked its case and chucked the keys to Sarah.

She caught them smoothly. "Ruth, a quick word please?"

"We're just heading out to see Bertie," Ruth said.

"Perhaps we should step into the education room."

Ruth shrugged and wandered over to join Sarah, leaving me standing next to Max.

"How's the mystery going?"

"Plain sailing. Just like the *Titanic*."

He grinned, a wry smile that lit up his dark eyes. "Well, if it was simple, they'd have figured it out at the time, right? Like the Medicine Hat murders."

"The what now?"

"You know. Up in Camp 132."

Great. Of course he knew more than me about my own project.

"Where the Nazis murdered two of their own and were executed?"

"I really haven't looked into what happened at the other camps." Which seemed stupid, now I thought about it, but there had been so much to read on the Westonville camp. I'd spent weeks poring through books and old documents at Toronto Reference Library for my application. It had been nice to immerse myself in the history of the camp, to learn as much as I could and not think about Dad so much. They'd even had an original menu from the camp at the library, and you had to sit in a special glass cubicle to read it. Apparently, some of the German soldiers had been renowned chefs before the war began.

"There're books on it in the office. Check it out when you get a chance."

"I will, thanks." I tried to think of something else to say, some way to pretend I wasn't a complete idiot, when I noticed the murmur of Sarah and Ruth's conversation in the next room. It rose in volume. Ruth's higher voice was fast and angry. Sarah's deeper tone was calmer.

Max raised one dark eyebrow. "Someone's in trouble."

"Why?" I whispered.

"Isn't it obvious?"

The door to the education room opened, and Ruth's voice was clear. "It's not up to you anyway." She strode into the gallery. "Come on, Keira. We don't want to be late."

Sarah stood with her arms crossed. Ruth kept walking, and I hurried to catch up. It was clear she wasn't about to fill me in on this argument, either.

Max joined us. He fell into step next to me as we headed through the reception and out into the solid heat of the late July day.

"Where are you going?" I asked, as he stayed by my side.

"With you two, of course. We can hang out with my granddad together."

I glanced at Ruth, wondering if she knew about this.

She gave a slight shrug. "It's a free country."

"It's my house," Max countered.

"You live with your grandfather?"

He shoved his hands in the pockets of his ripped jeans as Ruth led us down the side of the main building. "When my mom decided to go live in Europe a couple of years ago, they wanted to send me to boarding school. But he suggested I move in with him instead."

There was so much weird rich-family stuff to unpack there I didn't know where to start. Max continued as we stepped out onto the field at the center of the site.

"We take care of each other. It's a pretty good deal, apart from having to live next to my fascist uncle, of course."

"What is your problem with him?" Ruth asked.

"Apart from him being the actual worst?"

Ruth rolled her eyes. "He and Jules seem super nice to me."

"What do you think of them, Keira?"

"I'm not really political. But they've been very generous."

He sighed, as if I'd disappointed him. "Everything's political."

That stung. I used to care about politics. But after my dad got sick, it got harder and harder to see beyond the bubble of my family, to see beyond the next treatment, the next scan. The news was full of other people's suffering, and I could barely carry my own. Then after he died, everything else slid into irrelevance for a while.

No, worse than that. It was like the world was mocking us, continuing with its usual business, when everything should have stopped, like it did for me.

The only thing that had got me moving, got me doing my homework and research for my application, was knowing that if I didn't, I'd be letting him down. He'd wanted me to go to the University of Toronto. I couldn't bring him back, but I could do that for him. And there had been comfort in the library, a quietness in immersing myself in the history of the camp. It was like being pleasantly underwater, distant from the jarring noise and too-bright light of the surface.

The splotches of beige on the main lawn of the site were spreading as the summer went on, swallowing what little green was left like bacteria in a petri dish. I took a breath and oriented myself, trying to conjure the remaining bones of the camp into the living thing in my mind.

Sarah had said the restored hut to the east of the main building was where Rainer Schmitt had died. But Erich Stein's body had been found outside the fence on the west side. Only one skeletal guard tower remained, looming over the grounds to the northwest, but there would have been a dozen surrounding the barbed wire with their watchful gaze.

Max opened the fence to let us through.

"We're going this way?"

He smiled. "I told you when we first met. It's a shortcut."

Beyond the graffitied hut, the land dipped slightly. The grass rose above my bare knees, the dry stems shushing us as we waded through. I tried to imagine this with a close-cropped lawn, tried to fix the broken barracks in my mind.

"The fence must have been about here, right?" I waved an arm, both to clear a cloud of midges and indicate where I meant.

"So this must be near where Erich Stein was found."

Ruth gave a dramatic sigh. "Don't you ever stop working?"

"It's interesting. There was nothing between his hut and the fence on the east side. Stein must have crossed the whole camp with a head injury to get here. It's farther than I thought."

"This side is nearer the road. This whole area is full of swamps, bogs, and little lakes. It makes sense he'd escape on this side. It was his best hope of getting anywhere," Max said.

"I want to ask your grandfather some questions about it, if that's okay."

Ruth gave a frustrated huff. We both ignored her.

"He was only seven back in the war," Max said. "Just a little kid. I doubt he'll know anything. Sorry."

We traipsed on in silence through bushes and then trees — a young wood that had filled in the space in the nearly eighty years since the camp closed. Max grabbed my arm, keeping me upright when a root, hidden under the tangled sprawl of ivy and Virginia creeper, tripped me. Even after he let go, I could feel the touch of his fingers on my bare skin.

I'd expected a fence or something to mark the end of the museum's land, but when the ground rose a while later, a gabled Victorian house peeked out of the branches ahead of us, the side covered with a rotting old trellis with a withered plant of some kind still clinging to it. We stepped into what was obviously once a well-tended garden that now held a desiccated lawn and flowerbeds sprouting dry stalks. Max led us to the front, dark hair shining as he stepped out from the shade of the trees. A muddy, silver BMW was parked in the turning-circle driveway.

"Home sweet home." Max led us to the veranda and held open the front door.

The hall smelled of furniture polish, and the wooden steps and gleaming banisters of a wide staircase led upstairs. Wood was definitely the overwhelming motif, with dark wooden floors and wooden paneling reaching halfway up the walls.

"This way." Ruth strode to the staircase, as if it were her house. I followed her up and into what appeared to be an upstairs sitting room.

The surfaces were cluttered with pictures of babies and small children, a couple of which were adorable little versions of Max and some that had to be the Hoppers' two daughters. Mingled among the photos were an arrangement of what looked like schoolchildren's crafts: a painted mug saying "World's Best Grandpa," a lumpy clay cat, a badly carved pig, and a crocodile made out of an egg carton covered with green-painted bubble wrap.

Bertie sat in a tan La-Z-Boy-style chair that didn't match the elegant wine-red sofa and armchair set. An oxygen tank leaned against the wall behind him. He was thin and pale with wispy white hair. His gray eyes lit up as he saw us.

"Ruth, my sweet girl! And you … brought my grandson and a friend!"

Ruth hurried over, bending down to give him a kiss on the cheek.

"I'm sorry. I'd usually … stand to meet you, but I'm having a little issue with my leg at the moment." He seemed to have trouble with saying more than a few words at a time, pausing to breathe in between.

"That's totally fine, please rest. I'm Keira Martin."

He held out his hand. "Albert Hopper … call me Bertie." His skin was soft and moved under my fingers as we shook, loose on his bones. He gestured at the sofa.

"Keira's super smart," Ruth said. "She's another intern. You'll like her. I do."

I sat on the sofa, smiling at the compliment. Max settled next to me, so close I caught his distractingly pleasant, minty pine smell — some kind of expensive cologne or body wash, no doubt.

"Did you come … to talk about the camp?"

"Do we have to?" Ruth moaned, shoulders sagging.

"I mean, it would be great if we could. Did you spend time there?"

Ruth scowled at me, but I was desperate. I'd got nowhere with the archives.

"Yes, in the offices. I spent time with the guards, but not … the main camp. My father was careful to keep me away from … the Krauts. He knew how dangerous they … could be."

I wanted to ask if he needed his oxygen, but that might have sounded patronizing.

"Did you know any of the guards? Like George Wright?" He was the man who'd found Erich Stein's body.

"Of course. He was my … brother Harry's best friend."

"You actually knew him?" I said, shocked at my luck. "Can I … Can I record this?"

"Go ahead." He waved a liver-spotted hand.

I pulled up the voice memo app on my battered old phone, started recording, and put it down on the side table. I expected Ruth to object, but she'd wandered over to the family photos.

"This is Harry." She clutched a black and white photograph of a handsome young man in a Navy uniform. "The whole of Westonville adored him. There's a memorial to him in the churchyard."

"So, Harry was best friends with George Wright?"

I'd directed the question at Bertie, but Ruth answered. "George would have done anything for Harry, from what Bertie's told me."

There was something pointed in the way she said it.

"They were inseparable," Bertie continued for her. "He was … a year older than Harry. He'd broken his leg badly as a child and it healed shorter. His limp meant the army didn't … want him. That's why he became a guard. Most of the others had seen action in the First World War, so he didn't really … fit in."

"Tell her what happened to Harry," Ruth prompted.

Bertie's thin chest rose and fell slowly in his beige shirt.

"My brother signed up as soon as he turned eighteen, desperate to … see action. He died in a U-boat attack … weeks out of training. The HMCS *Esquimalt* sunk within … sight of Halifax. Hitler shot himself fourteen days later."

Ruth lowered her head respectfully, red hair falling in her face. It was the first time I'd seen her animated about anything to do with the camp. "It was a huge shock to everyone."

I could only imagine. "That must have been hard on your family."

"Mother was never … the same again. She died in her forties. Cancer, but I think the … grief brought it on."

The clack of the front door came from downstairs, then two pairs of feet climbing the staircase. I glanced around. "Is someone else coming?"

Max scowled. "My uncle has an office here. He pays a little rent. Not enough, but it helps toward cleaning and nursing costs."

The footsteps went to the room next door, followed by the low murmur of conversation, a man and a woman's voice. I focused on Bertie.

"Harry was a … hero. He died fighting … the worst evil our world has seen."

He coughed, wet and phlegmy. Max leaned forward, but Bertie waved a dismissive hand.

"He sounds amazing," Ruth said. It made my stomach turn to see her so obviously sucking up to Bertie, just like she did with Peter and Jules. It felt totally cringe with them, but full-on manipulative with the old man.

The conversation next door had either grown louder or moved out onto the landing.

"… best if you just go. We can sort out the details later."

I tried to ignore it. "Do you have any theories on how Erich Stein escaped?"

His laugh turned into a cough. "Not much of an escape … was it? He only made it a few … meters."

Ruth had put the photograph back down and was straightening it lovingly.

"Any idea how he was killed?" I asked.

Bertie shrugged. "No idea. But he and that other one got … what was coming to them. Do you know how many Canadians were … killed in the war?"

To my shame, I realized I didn't.

The voices came from the hall again. "… sorry. But with the leadership run —"

It was totally distracting. "Forty-four thousand. Forty-four thousand … good men like Harry."

A woman's voice spoke outside now, "… everything you wanted —"

Bertie coughed again, a hacking bark. He pulled a handkerchief from his pocket and put it to his mouth. Max had his hands on the knees of his ripped jeans, ready to jump out of his seat.

"Maybe we should stop," I said.

"I'm fine," Bertie said softly. "I wanted … to sign up too. But I was just a child."

Peter's voice came from outside, talking over Bertie. "… that's not a bad thing, is it?"

"I … don't want to tell Sarah how to do her job," Bertie continued, "but … maybe you should focus more on the Canadians, and less on the … Jerries."

The voices outside finally seemed to be done. Through the crack in the door, I saw a woman in a suit, her sleek, dark bob swinging as she hurried away. One set of footsteps clicked back down the stairs. But Bertie began coughing before he could say anything else, a deeper, longer cough this time. His body shook as he spluttered, and the pale white of his face turned pink.

Max leapt up, hurrying to the oxygen tank. Bertie shook his head, but Max picked up a clear tube and, with gentle care, put it over his grandfather's ears, positioning it carefully at his nose. As he stepped back, Bertie's coughing fit subsided.

Sadness stole through me. We were losing the last of people like Bertie, who lived through the war, who felt it and knew it. Our grip on history was slipping until it was just stories.

"You know I … hate having that on when we have guests."

Max put a tender hand on his grandfather's shoulder. "We need to go now anyway. We have to be back at the museum for a meeting."

Ruth opened her mouth to point out that no such meeting existed but caught a glimpse of Max's expression and stayed silent. It was obvious Bertie needed rest. I stopped recording.

"Thank you so much."

"Thanks, Gramps." Ruth leaned in for a kiss. Max gently squeezed his grandpa's hand.

Bertie pushed Max's black hair out of his eyes. "You really should … get that cut."

Out in the hallway, I almost walked straight into Peter Hopper. He was leaning on the banister and looked startled to see me.

"Sorry," I said.

He quickly recovered, smoothing his already-neat gray hair. "Keira, Ruth, Max. Good to see you. Working on your projects?"

Max crossed his arms, but I nodded.

"Your father is so helpful," Ruth said.

"Glad to hear it. I am so sorry if I disturbed you. I was dealing with an HR issue. A private conversation I wouldn't have had if I'd known you were here. Did you hear any of it?"

We all shook our heads.

He smiled at me. "Ah, U of T, my old alma mater. Is that where you're going?"

For a moment I wondered if he could read minds, then I realized I was wearing a thrift store University of Toronto shirt over my denim skirt.

"Yeah. I mean, I'm hoping to. My dad worked in construction. He helped build the Bahen Centre before I was born and always dreamed of me going there."

"Good choice." He clasped his hands together in front of his perfectly ironed blue shirt. "As it happens, the Chancellor's a friend of mine. I could put in a word for you. And I'm glad I ran into you. Jules and I are throwing a little shindig tomorrow. We'd love it if you would come."

"Nope," Max said at the same time Ruth said, "That sounds lovely!"

"Great," Peter said, ignoring his nephew. "It starts at six. We'll see you there."

"Thank you so much," Ruth said.

My jaw clenched at her simpering. Other than spending every spare minute with Bertie, I wasn't sure if she'd done anything on her project. She obviously saw her route to the scholarship as being directly through the Hoppers themselves.

Well, two could play that game.

"Can't wait," I said.

CHAPTER FIVE
October 28, 1943

Erich bit his lip to stifle a laugh.

They stood in ruler-straight rows on the muddy sports field in front of the low-slung wooden barracks, each of the nearly six hundred men at ease. Stabsfeldwebel Schneider's arms were clasped behind his back and the silver buttons of his uniform gleamed in the sun. He looked every bit the Lagerführer: the camp leader, a paragon of German strength. All the prisoners in the camp answered to him, not their Canadian captors. He had to know about the game they were playing today, but his poker face was much better than Erich's.

The old guards traipsed through the sludge re-counting each row. They hadn't spotted the two dummies hidden among the men, supported by soldiers on either side. At a glance, the *ersatzmänner* even fooled Erich. He tried not to look directly at them. He tried to focus on the sharp, peeping call of a bluish-black bird perched on the wire to the left.

The heads were papier mâché. The men had glued their own hair trimmings on the bald skulls and tufts of brown stuck out from the caps on top. They'd ordered a soft pink lipstick from the Eaton catalog to draw around the mouths, claiming it was for the plays they put on in their small theater. The bodies were spare uniforms stuffed with fabric and newspaper and the legs were jammed into black boots.

Once again, the guards counted the puppets among the men and shook their heads, wondering where their extra two prisoners had come from.

The hint of a giggle escaped Erich, earning him a sharp glare from Feldwebel Schmitt, his hut leader. He squeezed his lips together and looked toward the trees beyond the wire. A few brown leaves still clung to the branches at a broken-necked angle. They whispered like old parchment when the wind rustled them into life.

"Back to the barracks," one of the Canadians shouted. "We'll count them in there."

The men waited for the same order to come from Stabsfeldwebel Schneider, whether or not they understood the English. Once it was given, they saluted their Lagerführer and marched to their huts, closing ranks around the dummies to hide them. The nearest Canadian guard shouted at them to hurry, so they slowed to an amble as he huffed and threatened.

Once inside, they rushed to stuff the fake soldiers under a bunk, then everyone scuffled to their places. By the time a guard rapped on the door, each man stood stiffly by his bed.

The room was normally perfect — a testament to their feldwebel's discipline. But they'd trampled mud onto the rough wooden floor and there were smeared footprints clustered around the hiding place.

The scout entered, hair gray under the khaki-green of his Veterans Guard of Canada cap, old enough to be the father of any man in the hut. Their captors were a mixed bunch. Some had been in German POW camps in the last war and sympathized with them in their captivity, while others nursed old resentments. Some used the barrack searches to help themselves. Krause had his prized close combat badge stolen.

Erich could see the smeared muck out of the side of his eye. It tugged at the corner of his vision as the scout walked by each of them, counting. Once he'd passed, boots heavy in the quiet hut, Erich allowed himself a quick glance. The mess seemed too obvious. The scout had to notice.

He turned back to find Feldwebel Schmitt's glare fixed on him, shocking in its ferocity. He stiffened and kept his eyes to the front. The thud of the scout's step paused. He began counting again from the back of the hut, double-checking.

Erich held himself still. He tried not to look at the expression on Schmitt's face.

The guard reached the front. "I make it seventy-nine. You have one in the camp hospital, correct?"

Schmitt gave a curt nod.

"Then everything seems right here."

Erich felt no desire to giggle. Schmitt's anger had shocked that right out of him. He had no trouble holding his face neutral as the guard sighed and left. He couldn't join in as the other men relaxed, laughing when they imitated the stiff march of the guard as he thumped up and down the hut.

Erich slumped onto his bed, reaching underneath for a cigarette from the box there. His hands shook slightly as he lit it. He'd let his comrades down again.

He wanted to pull out one of his mother's letters. But it wasn't done to pore over the letters of a parent the same way the other men pored over the words of their sweethearts.

He wanted to be in the kitchen back home, before all of this. He wanted his mother bustling around him, wiping the surfaces while he ate home-baked bread and smoked ham with the morning sun streaming in the window. Her pride in him showed in the way she paused to watch him eat, head tilted and smiling.

No one was proud of him here.

He was so sunk in his own misery, so focused on the soft crackle of the glow of the end of the cigarette as he inhaled, he didn't notice Feldwebel Schmitt approaching until his thin mattress shook as he sat next to him. Erich gave a hasty salute.

"You almost gave us away there, Stein."

Erich squeezed his eyes shut, afraid he'd humiliate himself and cry. "Sorry, sir. I mean, I didn't think it was that important. We were just messing with the guards."

"We need ways to throw off the count. When we get men out, the longer it takes the Canadians to realize they're missing, the better their chances."

Erich felt even more stupid.

"You've said you want to be part of an escape?"

He nodded vehemently. "I've been learning English and memorizing maps. I've been saving chocolate and made some fishing hooks. I'll help with digging or anything you need."

"I need you to grow up, Stein. A sniggering schoolboy isn't going to get far, is he?"

Shame washed over Erich, thick and cloying. "I'll do better, sir."

Schmitt did not look convinced. "I'll be watching."

CHAPTER SIX

The worst night of my life actually started well.

Ruth and I got ready for the Hoppers' party in her tiny room. The air was so thick with her floral perfume I could taste it in the back of my throat. She insisted I borrow her green dress, even though I didn't have red hair, just a hint of auburn in my boring brown. She'd sent me a link to a shampoo she said I really should buy to bring out the color and to help with the frizz. I'd taken one look at the price and decided to stick with my drugstore discount brand instead.

Ruth laughed a bit too hard at my attempt to walk in her absurdly high heels, finally agreeing I should stick with my black ballet flats.

She posed in front of the mirror, turning her head from side to side. "Didn't Harry have great cheekbones? Do you think mine are as nice as his?"

"You do have great cheekbones." Ruth's were prominent, emphasized with perfect makeup. When I'd tried a YouTube contouring tutorial, I looked like I'd smeared mud on my face.

No doubt Max had inherited his impressive cheekbones from that side of the family.

I hoped he wouldn't hate me for going to his uncle's party. His contempt for his family seemed to have rubbed off on Asha. She was throwing an "art party" up on Crown land north of the museum. She'd invited us, knowing we couldn't come. I still felt bad about missing it.

"Did I tell you my great-grandparents were from Westonville?" Ruth said.

"You mentioned it. Did Bertie know them?"

"My great-grandmother, Margaret Fortin, lived on a farm just outside town. She moved away after the war and died in '95."

"And your great-granddad?"

"Her husband died a few months before her."

It seemed an odd way to phrase it. "That's so sad. She couldn't live without him."

She flicked her red hair over her shoulder. "Perhaps. I never knew them."

I decided to broach the unspoken. "So, what was that all about with Sarah yesterday?"

Her jaw clenched. "It's my business, okay? And she has her own secrets, too. I can't imagine the Hoppers would let her keep her job if they knew the truth about her, eh?"

"What truth?"

Ruth sighed. "I don't want to talk about her. We're going to a party. How do I look?"

The topic was clearly closed. She spun, white dress brushing against the walls as it flared out. Her hair was loose in soft red waves down to her shoulders.

"Lovely," I said honestly.

"Then come on! I think we're fashionably late enough. The party awaits!"

Peter and Julia's house was the other side of Max and Bertie's. Apparently, Bertie's father had bought his when he became camp commandant, and Peter Hopper had bought the house next door many decades later.

Peter and Julia's house was a three-storey, white mansion with green shutters on the many windows. The driveway was filled with unnecessarily large cars: Mercedes, Yukons, and Land Rovers that spilled out down either side of the road beyond.

People flowed to the grounds at the back. And they were grounds, not just a backyard — large enough for a full-on garden party with a marquee tent and stations serving food and drink. A stone terrace protruded from the back of the building forming a kind of stage, with semi-circular steps descending to the garden. A band played jazz. Guests chatted in small groups, women in expensive dresses, heels sinking into the soft grass. Men stood in shirt sleeves, suit jackets slung over arms, shadows stretching out behind them.

Ruth looked unsure for the first time. "Do I look okay?"

"You look like you belong here."

She grinned as if that was the best compliment I could have given.

I scanned the lawn for the Hoppers. I kept seeing people who looked like them, but each time they turned out to be yet another perfect middle-aged couple — total *Where's Waldo* vibes. The light from the lowering sun faltered as an amber-edged cloud passed overhead.

"There they are," Ruth said.

I was impressed at her rich-people differentiation skills.

We hurried in their direction, but they were moving away from us. As we approached, they headed up the steps to the stone terrace. The band stopped playing, and Peter and Julia Hopper took their places by two microphones, spotlights sharpening every edge of their perfectly cut clothes in the encroaching dusk.

We'd ended up in the front row for whatever speech they were planning. Other attendees were drifting over, filling in the space around us.

"I'm so glad to see so many of our good friends here today," Julia said, "and some new friends, too." She directed that at Ruth and me. Ruth beamed.

As people hemmed us in, Peter Hopper thanked God and talked about His plan and His will, and I felt awkward.

Several video cameras, with the CBC and other logos on them, stood discreetly off to the side, pointed at the stage. I'd heard someone saying Peter was running for party leadership, but I hadn't paid much attention. Clearly this was a political event, not some casual garden party.

I wished he'd warned us. I had no interest in getting involved in politics.

Peter talked about the Canadian way, job creators, preserving our traditions, and the need to deal with rising crime. It was all the usual vague stuff. I kept my head down, staring at my black shoes, draped in the shifting shadows of the bodies around me.

"For so long," he said, "our wonderful small town has been free of the kind of divisiveness and extremism we've seen in the cities. Sadly, it seems it has finally reached us. There's a drag event coming to the library here, and it's aimed at our children."

I snapped my gaze back to him as discomfort prickled up

my neck. My friend Sadie and I had taken her little sister Adiva to a drag queen story time in Toronto before my dad got sick. It had been innocent fun; a performer in fabulous make-up, a full brown beard, and a pink soufflé of a dress had read *The Book with No Pictures* to a bunch of giggling kids. Adiva got things adorably wrong and called her a "dragon queen."

Peter continued, "I was at the library last month for a community event and was shocked to find a Pride display with books full of sexualized content in the children's section."

News about 2SLGBTQ+ book banning in libraries and schools had pierced even my bubble. I knew that kind of intolerance was big in the US. I'd never really thought of America as a foreign country, until recently. I'd always thought we had more in common than we had differences. But that had all changed lately. I just couldn't understand what was going on down there anymore.

And yes, I knew some of it had been creeping up to Canada, too. But I'd assumed Peter Hopper was one of the usual dull politicians Canada bred, fighting over the details of boring stuff I didn't understand, like "fiscal policy," whatever that was. But this wasn't just politics. This was Politics with a capital P.

"Maybe we should go," I whispered to Ruth.

"No. They'll see us."

Of course she was thinking about the scholarship. I should be too. I swallowed.

"Woke extremists are pushing their agenda onto our children: a perverted agenda that has no place in the kid's section of our libraries."

Maybe America wasn't so foreign, after all.

The dark eye of one of the TV cameras swept over the audience. I turned away. Which was worse, being recorded here or being seen walking out? Perhaps I could tell the Hoppers I was claustrophobic. It wasn't completely untrue. People pressed in tighter behind me and on my sides. Strangers' shoulders shifted against mine.

"We really should get out of here."

Ruth shook her head again.

Peter pounded a hand into his fist. "Enough! We need to stop this now. We need to protect our children, protect Westonville. We need to clear out this corrosive influence."

The roar of the crowd jolted through me. Someone's breath was hot on my hair as they cheered. A body bumped against mine, pushing me forward.

I didn't decide. I just turned and began to push through the crowd. Muttered apologies slipped from my lips as I tried to keep my panic under wraps. I stumbled out, down the side of the house to the main road. I leaned my hands on my thighs and sucked down deep breaths.

Bulky cars surrounded me, listing like turning ships, one set of wheels up on the sidewalk. I could still feel the closeness of the crowd, hips and elbows buffeting my body. Wild applause echoed from the back of the house: more a rally than a garden party. Not my thing. Never mind. There was an actual party I could go to, at least.

I had no idea how horrific the evening was about to get.

CHAPTER SEVEN
May 30, 1944

At the camp, there were classes in English, agriculture, physiology, music, navigation, engineering, and railroading. In the summer, blackflies drove them mad as they tended their gardens to make the place look presentable for Hitler's inevitable arrival. In the winter, the cold crept into their bones as they shoveled snow and hauled coal for the barracks' stoves. They celebrated the Führer's birthday, the harvest festival, and *Heldengedenktag* with games and contests. At Christmas, they decorated trees with ornaments made from the tin foil that wrapped their cigarettes. Together they sang "Stille Nacht" and "O Tannenbaum" and dreamed of spending the next Christmas at home.

None of it stopped the boredom.

Erich borrowed English books from the camp library and strained to make sense of the American and British films they screened: *The Maltese Falcon, Random Harvest*, and *How Green Was My Valley.* Bit by bit, the words resolved, foreign syllables reshaping themselves, sentences untangling on the page.

He played soccer and took part in marches and runs, ensuring he would be in peak physical condition when the Fatherland needed him again. He refused work outside the camp. If there were plans inside the wire, he wanted to be on hand to join in.

His opportunity to prove himself came the following spring.

The hut was always full for mail call. It was the one time when, for a moment, Germany inched closer to Canada. Parcels arrived from home and North American friends and charities, wrapped in brown paper, containing cigarettes and chocolate, socks and sausages; Canadian cash was concealed in double-bottomed tins of pumpernickel and radio crystals were baked into bread. Letters from loved ones came with pictures to be pined over, then positioned over bunks. Like many of the men without sweethearts, Erich stuck Varga girl pin-ups carefully cut from *Esquire* above his bed to keep him company.

Some men rationed their letters, reading them a miserly line at a time over days. Some gulped them down greedily, even if several arrived at once. On the days no mail came at all, the men were more likely to pick fights, to snap at each other and sulk in their beds. Feldwebel Schmitt would encourage them out of the hut, reminding them of their duty to keep themselves ready to fight for the Reich. Reminding them that Germans did not allow themselves to fall apart, as other races did.

Lately there were more days with no mail. New POWs told tales of unexpected defeats. Erich knew they'd retreated from Stalingrad and it had been hard to get reliable information on the Eastern Front since. No one trusted Canadian propaganda and those captured there never ended up in Ontario. Dark rumors swirled about their fates at the hands of the Bolsheviks.

Lübeck had been firebombed before Erich was captured, and Hamburg had been hit, but such attacks had been rare. Now there were whispers of wave after wave of bombings, of proud German cities pummeled into rubble.

Schmitt told them that temporary reverses were part of the reality of war and the Fatherland stood like iron. He said Italy changing sides was a good thing. The Italians were weak, a liability. They would betray the Allies, too.

Tactical retreats were nothing to worry about. They made the enemy lower their guard, and while lines got entrenched in warfare, the Wehrmacht were right on the verge of a breakthrough. Germany's Thousand-Year Reich would soon take its rightful place astride Europe. The corruption that had weakened the Fatherland would be purged and everything good, everything right, would be restored.

When Schmitt talked like that, Erich felt better. Yes, things were hard right now. But Hitler would fix everything. The future was bright for all of them.

But occasionally, letters brought bad news. Some nights, sobs were stifled with pillows. Mannerheim went to the schoolroom right after getting mail one gray Thursday. When he didn't show up for the evening roll call, he was found there, hanging from his belt.

Erich's own letters had taken a more ominous tone. The black marks of the censor hid whole paragraphs, but his mother claimed she was "making the best of things." She cheerfully told him of old friends and schoolmates that were "still alive" as if this was the best possible news she could convey. She kept asking how the Canadians were treating him, though he'd often reassured her about the excellent conditions of the camp, of mouthwatering meals of boiled beef with onion sauce, chicken with gravy, roast mutton, steamed fruit pudding, and apple fritters.

He wondered how much of his own letters were escaping the censor's pen.

It had been six weeks since her last letter had arrived. He told himself he didn't need to worry. There had been delays before, stutters and pauses in word from home. Schultz received eight letters at once after some snarl-up in the system. Allied ships were often brought down by their U-boats, drowning the cargo of letters in their bellies. The fact there was less mail was a sign of German strength. It was surprising that any got through, really.

His mother was fine. She had to be fine.

He perched on the edge of his bunk each day at mail call, rubbing the smoothed-down bumps of his wooden good luck charm as the names of the fortunate were read out.

"Lang, Karl; Wagner, Hans; Krause, Oskar."

Each hurried up eagerly and returned to their beds with their eyes fixed on their envelopes, lost in their own anticipation.

"Richter, Ludwig; Werner, Leopold; Schultz, Horst. That's it, I'm afraid."

Erich slumped back, staring at the bottom of the bunk above as the other unlucky men filed out to get back to playing baseball or rehearsing in the camp theater.

There was a creak from above. Erich glanced around, but the upper bunk was empty and he couldn't work out where it had come from. He felt drained. The longer he didn't hear from his mother, the harder it was to find the energy to go to his English lessons in the schoolroom hut or to join in with the soccer games, no matter what Schmitt said.

He became aware of footsteps on the wood floor. Karl Lang crouched down next to him.

"Still no mail, huh?"

Erich shrugged. "What did you get?"

"Just from my uncle."

"Everything okay back home?"

"I think so." He held up the zebra-patterned paper. "Apparently, he had a lovely walk with his wife. The censor decided I didn't need to know what happened after that."

Lang folded up the letter and slid it back in the envelope. "You'll get word soon, I'm sure. Just tell me you're not going to spend all day in bed."

Erich sighed.

"We just got our wages. Let's get beers from the canteen and drink them in the sun. The flies aren't bad today." Lang pulled a few blue tickets of camp currency from his pocket.

"Fine." Erich rolled out of bed and straightened his shirt. "But only if you're buying."

The room was almost empty. A couple of other men reclined in their bunks. Erich opened the door for Lang and waved him through to the yard beyond. Above Erich, the odd creak came again. He paused, still holding the door, curious as to the cause.

The ceiling collapsed on him in a thunder of wood and earth.

CHAPTER EIGHT

Finding Asha's party wasn't easy. "Crown land north of the museum" was frustratingly vague. She'd said there was a path to the left of the road about a kilometer past the museum turn-off, but I'd stumbled out of the front of the Hoppers' house instead of taking the usual route through Bertie's and Max's land. I headed down the unfamiliar road, tramping through leafy residential streets that faded into farmland, at which point I realized I'd got turned around. I pulled up Google Maps and retraced my steps.

It was getting dark by the time I was on the lonely road north of the museum, and the night crept in from the forest on either side. Even the cicadas were falling silent. It felt like they were abandoning me.

Had I overreacted by leaving the Hoppers like that? Why hadn't Ruth come with me? She didn't want to be a part of that, did she?

I didn't know her well enough to be sure. She had a ton of secrets, after all. She hadn't told me why Sarah was so mad at her, and I still didn't know what had happened with Ephram. A similar parental income apparently wasn't enough to base a deep friendship on.

I started to notice how alone I was. There were no streetlights, no passing cars to cast their headlights on the road. The air felt cooler, leaving me clammy. It was quiet, too, other than occasional croaking from the undergrowth, and the cry of a whippoorwill.

There was something else, too, just on the edge of hearing. A low noise, repeating. It took a while for my distracted mind to work out what it was.

A beat: a steady, bass beat.

The party. Thank God for that. I just had to follow the sound.

I turned on the flashlight on my phone and cast it at the trees to my left as I walked. After a while, I spotted what I hoped was the path Asha mentioned. It was little more than a rut between trunks. Trees reached toward me with branches like claws. Small twigs tugged on my dress and scratched at my face. In a forest at night, it was obvious that fairy tales were horror stories, originally. The old ones were full of gore and butchery. We cleaned them up and filled them with flowers, but woods are malicious. I almost twisted my ankle. I thought of dead Nazis, will-o-wisps, and false paths through the wilderness, and cursed my own stupid imagination.

An orange glow finally appeared between the trunks, flickering as the wind caught and released the flames. The trees petered out, shriveling down to scrubby groundcover that opened out to flat rocks, where the bonfire had been built. The dark mass of a lake lurked beyond the firelight, oily black in the night. I could make out vocals over the bass now: mainstream hip-hop, sounding tinny. Probably playing out of a Bluetooth speaker.

The partygoers were silhouettes against the fire, but I was able to pick out Asha in her big boots and a short dress. As I approached, my eyes adjusted and I saw Ephram sitting off to one side, casual in a long-sleeved white T-shirt and jeans and talking to someone I'd never met. There were other figures too, although I didn't recognize any of them.

Max came barreling around the side of the fire. "Keira! You have graced us with your presence." He was a bit louder than he needed to be, probably due to the wine bottle in his hand. "How was the other party?"

"I shouldn't have gone."

"Well, at least you finally figured that out." He glanced around. "Where's Ruth?"

"Still there, I think. Although, I got lost, so it took me ages to get here, and she might have left since."

I checked my phone, wondering if she'd messaged. I had reception, but there were no notifications. My battery bar was alarmingly low.

Max shrugged. "But you're cool now, right? No more fraternizing with the enemy?"

"I definitely won't go to another of their 'shindigs.'"

"Then let's celebrate!" He ran over to a couple of boxes at the side of the bonfire and came back carrying a full bottle of wine and a corkscrew. "Setup for my uncle's events is always a bit chaotic, and I managed to spirit away three cases without anyone noticing."

He stuck the bottle between his knees and opened it with a flourish. A little red wine splashed on the rock, dark as blood in the night.

"Sadly, I didn't have as much luck with the food," he said as he handed the bottle to me. "They didn't do trays of canapes this time. They went with staffed 'food stations' instead, and they'd probably have noticed if I tried to carry one of those off."

I took a swig and looked around. Most people had their own wine, apart from Ephram, who was drinking from his usual water bottle.

"Traitor!" Asha swooped down on me. I braced myself, but Max held his hands up.

"Keira has seen the error of her ways!"

I nodded. "Sorry. They were going on about a drag show at the library being inappropriate and stuff. It wasn't cool. I didn't know they were like that. I didn't know it was a political event."

"Hmm." She didn't sound convinced. Her bottle was almost empty. "But no art for you."

"What?"

"Art. This is an art party." She waved a hand at the side of the bonfire. "Everyone else can draw something they regret, or write a poem. They whisper a confession to the fire, then we burn the paper. It's called Fire/Forgiveness. But you're not allowed. You'll have to do something more to atone."

"Like what?"

Asha stuck a hand on her hip and looked me up and down. "I'm not sure yet."

I took a gulp of my wine, not liking the expression on her face. I suspected my "atonement" would be rather more demanding than whispering to a fire.

"Sorry I'm late!" We all turned as Ruth appeared out of the trees.

Asha gave a snort of disgust and turned her back on her.

Ruth sighed. "This is about the Hoppers' party, right? Let's not make a big deal about it. I don't want to take sides."

Max shook his head. "Don't you know what my uncle stands for?"

"Just because you don't share his beliefs doesn't mean he's evil, you know," said Ruth. "Can I have some of that?" Before I could say anything, she took my bottle and had several large gulps. "Having strong Christian beliefs isn't wrong. Is it, Ephram?"

She raised her voice and beckoned to him.

"What are we discussing?" Ephram asked as he came over.

"Christianity," Ruth said. She swayed slightly. "I was saying that just because the Hoppers have strong Christian beliefs, it doesn't mean they're evil, right?"

Ephram shook his head, hard. "Don't lump my faith in with theirs."

He backed up, face grim, and returned to where he'd been sitting. How had I never realized he was a Christian? I tried to remember if I might have taken the Lord's name in vain in front of him or something. He always did have a slightly put-upon air about him, which made a lot more sense if people were always making assumptions about him, like Ruth had.

"I'm just open to different points of view." Ruth directed this at me, as if I'd challenged her. "There's two sides to everything, you know, and there's no harm in listening."

She was beginning to get on my nerves. "This is all about the scholarship, isn't it? You're sucking up to them for that."

She laughed. "Why would I want leftovers?"

"Leftovers?"

"I'm not after the scholarship, Keira. If you want it, I might be able to help. I should have some sway with the Hoppers. I'm just waiting for proof about a family rumor. And if that fails," she leaned in a bit, even though she was practically shouting, "I do have a nuclear option in my back pocket, from my meetings with Bertie. But I want to avoid using that. Even though it would totally help out *some people*." She put real emphasis on the last two words.

I rubbed at my ear. It hurt from how loud she'd yelled in it. She'd got some spit in there too. "What are you talking about?"

She took another big swig of my wine.

"All should be clear in two to four weeks. Once I have proof, it'll change everything."

I snatched my bottle back.

"You should have stayed at the party. The food was amazing. Especially the desserts. They had these mini-tiramisu things and little donuts filled with chocolate cream, and people going around with wine who weren't checking ID."

That explained why she was swaying.

"It was a really good time, in spite of my little fight with Jules."

"You had a fight with Jules? What about?"

She waved a hand dismissively. "It'll get sorted out."

"Was it over what they said about the library?"

Her face crinkled. "Why would I fight with Jules over that?"

My expression answered her.

"They aren't saying it's wrong to be gay, you know. They're just saying that stuff shouldn't be shoved in children's faces."

"But …" The stress of the day clouded my head, or maybe it was the wine. "That's not —"

Max interrupted, his empty bottle of wine now replaced with a full one. "Keira, I need to speak to you for a moment, if that's okay."

Deprived of my wine, Ruth grabbed Max's. He made a feeble effort to get it back, but she held it out of reach. "You can have it back when you bring my friend back."

Max sighed and nodded to me. "Come on."

He led me to the other side of the fire where the lake lay in the shadows. There were a couple of people swimming, only visible as dark bobbing heads in the center of circular ripples cast orange by the firelight.

"You looked like you needed rescuing," Max said.

"I guess," I said, even though I felt awkward about it. I wanted to argue with Ruth, wanted her to understand why she was so wrong. But a part of me knew it was useless. She'd made her mind up.

I glanced back over. Ruth was already chatting to a guy I didn't know. She was laughing, head back. She took another swig of her stolen wine.

"You shouldn't think about her too much. Come on." He pointed to another group. "I'll introduce you to some nicer people."

Max really tried to cheer me up, and I was touched at the effort. We chatted with a few locals our age, although their names slipped out of my mind as soon as he was done. He stayed at my side the whole time, a couple of inches too close in a way that felt softly exciting. I gave him my bottle, since Ruth had stolen his. I didn't want to get wasted anyway.

It was hard to look away from him. The firelight suited him, bringing out those cheekbones and glinting in his dark eyes.

"You know, most people can't admit when they are wrong," he said. "It's a rare thing, what you did tonight."

"I hate their politics," I sighed. "But I could really use that scholarship."

I wondered if they'd seen me leave. If so, I could probably kiss that goodbye. But would I want to take their money anyway?

"That's their MO. They use their money to get to people. It's amazing what people will go along with if you promise them a bright future."

On the other side of the fire, Ruth was still drinking, most of the way through her bottle. But she stood on her own now, a worried expression creasing her brow. She glanced around as if she was afraid of someone in the crowd. I got the impression I'd missed something important.

I caught her eye and she gave me a small, nervous smile. She looked so scared that I forgot my annoyance for a moment, and I found myself smiling back.

"Do you think Ruth's okay?" I asked Max. "She looks … odd."

He sighed. "You want to check on her, don't you?"

I nodded and we wandered over. "You okay?" I asked.

"Fine," she said, looking over my shoulder. I turned around. There was no one there. Ruth's eyes looked weird. Like they were wider than they should be.

"Are you sure?"

"You don't look okay. Maybe we should walk you home," Max said.

She shook her head, blinking. "Nah. Just the fire playing tricks on my eyes." She looked down at her free hand and turned it over a couple of times.

"Let's walk you home. We were going anyway, weren't we, Keira?"

I picked up on the hint. "Yeah. It's coming up on our curfew."

Ruth shook her head, as if she were clearing it, checked her phone, then took another swig of wine. "There's, like, nearly an hour until eleven."

Max took his bottle back from her. There wasn't much left. "Maybe slow down a bit?"

"You're the one who brought the wine." Her smile wavered, and she glanced back over to the fire. She didn't try to snatch the bottle back. Maybe she'd finally realized she'd had enough.

"We could wait for you," Max said.

"Just go. I'm having fun!"

She didn't look like it.

"Come on, Keira," Max said. We headed for the whispering trees. "Did she seem high to you?" he asked once we were out of earshot.

I felt stupid as soon as he said it. Of course she seemed high. That was clearly what had happened while I was distracted. I hadn't seen her join the group of smokers by the fire, but it seemed obvious. She was high and probably a little paranoid.

"She totally did. What do we do?"

"Well, she won't come with us. I'll speak to Asha and Ephram, ask them to make sure she gets back to the museum okay."

I waited by the trees while he traipsed off to speak to both of them. Ephram looked put out and Asha argued, but they both nodded in the end. I considered staying with her, but the idea of walking home through the dark alone with Max made excitement fizz in my belly.

"Done," he said on his return.

The wood didn't seem so threatening with Max there. I was massively aware of how close the two of us were, alone in the dark on that narrow track, using his phone to light the way. My battery had died completely, so we had to stay close to share the light from his phone. More than once I had to squeeze right by him, brushing against his chest as he held back branches for me. His face was mostly in shadow, but the strong jaw and the dark hair still looked good.

Not my type, I told myself. And he hadn't chosen to be alone with me anyway. He'd asked Ruth to come too.

It was almost a relief when we stepped onto the main road, and I was able to get a little distance from him. But still, only a meter or so opened up between us. When one of us ambled farther away for a moment, it was almost as if there were elastic there, pulling us closer again.

There were no streetlights and no moon, but the sky was dazzling, a blanket of stars, some bright, some dull, but so numerous they formed a kind of mist in the night sky above. The road was a gray path carved through the heart of the wilderness.

"Is Ruth okay?" Max exhaled through his teeth. "Like, mental-health wise?"

"I think so." Although again, how well did I know her? "She's quite … intense."

"I mean, I'm not big on judging people for their drinking or drug use, but she seemed to hit both pretty hard tonight, and that worries me."

We walked in silence. He was right, and I felt out of my depth. My feet dragged on the gravel of the road.

"I thought I knew her. But I've obviously been way too focused on how much she's been sucking up to your family. I've not been looking out for her."

Max drifted over toward me again. His arm brushed mine. The wind in the trees grew to an excited hiss, as if the woods were whispering about us.

"Don't be too harsh on yourself. My uncle has been doing his best to get his claws into her. If you're not used to getting attention from important people, it can be pretty dazzling."

I opened a little gap between us. Not too much. "Why is he so focused on Ruth though? I mean, what can she do for them?"

"They want my granddad's house, but he's promised it to me. They've been trying to convince people he's got dementia, making a big fuss about him losing a toothbrush or forgetting a word so they can apply to take control of his estate." He kicked a stone.

"With all the time she's spending with him, I think they're hoping they can get her to say something, maybe make something up, so people think he needs to go into a home."

I shook my head. "Ruth wouldn't be a part of that." Although I wondered why I felt so sure about it. After all, everything had proved that I didn't know her well at all.

"I hope not." He turned a smile on me. "I don't want to be alone."

"What do you mean?"

"Mom is off being a bohemian artist in Europe. My dad didn't even stick around long enough for me to be born."

"Oh, that sucks." It felt like a stupid thing to say. Max seemed so cool, so calm. But his own aunt and uncle were trying to kick him out of his home and steal his only real family away.

No wonder he hated them so much.

Sarah was still up when we got back. She raised an eyebrow when I walked in with Max.

"He just walked me back," I said quickly.

Sarah kept looking between Max and me. He stood too close. The tension between us felt super awkward now we had an audience.

"Right," I said, a little abruptly. "I should be going to bed. Thanks for walking me back."

"Okay. See you at the museum." Was it my imagination, or did he look disappointed?

"Yeah. See you then." I hurried down the corridor to my room. Behind me, Sarah asked Max a question I didn't hear, and I felt my face heat.

I was still awake when the others came back. I'd tried to sleep, but my thoughts had been chasing each other through my mind ever since Max had left, trying to work out if there was something there, or if he was just being nice and I was completely delusional.

I heard the side door click open then close again. I checked the time on my phone, which had recharged enough to turn back on. It was spot on eleven and I'd missed a couple of messages that had come in about ten minutes earlier from Asha.

Is Ruth with u? The first one said. The next read: *We have 2 come home now anyway.*

The murmur of voices came from the common room. I listened carefully but couldn't hear Ruth. I crept out into the hall. Four of them stood talking, all still in their day clothes. I was surprised to see Max still there and felt totally exposed in my sleep shorts and bra-less tank top.

I crept down the hallway to see what was going on. My bare feet were soft on the cool tiles, but they all turned as I approached.

"Oh, it's you," Sarah said. "You haven't seen Ruth, have you?"

"I thought you guys were going to walk her home," I said to Asha and Ephram.

Asha gave a dramatic sigh. "I wasn't happy about that, first of all. But we would have, if she hadn't disappeared."

"Disappeared?"

Ephram answered. "I was keeping an eye on her. She was right by the fire, and then she wasn't. I only looked away for a minute, but I have no idea where she went."

"We were hoping she was here," Asha finished. "I messaged and called but got no reply."

"Sorry. My phone died."

"A fire? Where were you all?" Sarah asked.

There was some shuffling and looking at shoes before Ephram spoke. "At a party. On the Crown land to the north of the museum."

"With some locals," Asha added, probably to avoid admitting it was her party.

"And alcohol, presumably?"

No one said anything, which was enough of an answer.

"Come on, guys. I'm meant to be looking after you. I don't want to ground you." Sarah pulled out her phone, dialed a number, and pressed it to her ear. She paced as she waited. "Her battery's probably dead too. Or she's off with a boy." She gave me a look as she said "boy," and I felt awkward all over again. "But you can get lost on Crown land. It can be dangerous, especially for city kids. Was she drunk?"

Again, we exchanged glances. I was the one who finally spoke, feeling like a total traitor.

"A bit, but she was being kind of off, too. Like maybe she could have been … high."

Sarah froze. "Drugs?"

"I don't know," I said quickly. "Maybe she was just in a weird mood."

"Definitely seemed high," Asha said, obviously happy to chuck Ruth under the bus.

"Oh God." Sarah cast her gaze around the room as if there would be an answer scrawled on the scuffed white walls. "It better have only been weed. Okay. I'll drive you all back to the party, and we'll look there. I don't want to get the police involved just yet. Get changed, Keira. We'll be having a very serious talk once Ruth is back here, safe and sound."

CHAPTER NINE

May 30, 1944

Erich came to on his bunk, his clothes a mess of earth and blood. His head echoed with a blinding ache. He moaned and tried to sit up. Agony jolted through his leg, excruciating as an electrical shock. He cried out, and a hand clamped over his mouth.

Feldwebel Schmitt's face came into view.

"Quiet, okay?"

It took a few seconds for the pain to subside enough for Erich to nod. He knew he should salute, but it didn't seem to be the time. Schmitt let go of his face. The hut was a flurry of silent activity. Men swept up the earth that covered much of the floor. Tins had appeared from somewhere and were being quietly filled with dirt. Three prisoners stood on boxes, two holding a beam, the other gently tapping nails in with a hammer, using a delicate, fast motion more like sewing than construction. One man's face was bright red, the muscles in his neck standing out like bars as he held the weight of the wood.

The hush and hurry of it all felt like a dream.

Schmitt removed his hand. Dirt was smeared on his cheek, and he kept glancing at the door. "I'm sorry, Stein, but we need everyone to stay as quiet as possible."

The pain in Erich's leg, the effort to keep from screaming, fractured the scene into jigsaw pieces that didn't fit: the impossible amount of earth indoors, the strangely silent soldiers.

"What ... happened?"

"We're digging a tunnel. We were storing the spoil in the attic. But we used some of the hut's beams to reinforce the tunnel, and it seems the weight of the earth was too much."

Even through the agony, Erich felt the snub. He hadn't been told, hadn't been trusted. All those times Schmitt had contrived to get them all outside for exercise, exhorting them in the name of the Reich, it was so his loyal few could hide earth above Erich's unsuspecting head.

"But we must be silent. If the guards discover this, they'll search the site until they find the tunnel, and we're close to the fence." He glanced down at Erich's leg. His trousers were wet with blood. Schmitt pulled up the fabric carefully, inch by inch. Erich kept his eyes up, focusing on the splinters in the slats above his head. He bit his lip, tried to breathe through his nose. Tried not to whimper.

"Hmm," Schmitt said.

Erich glanced down. There was a gash below his knee, half a foot long and a finger-width wide, so deep the blood looked black in the shadow of the bunk above. He squeezed his eyes closed, dizzy.

"I'm sorry," Schmitt said, "but we can't send you to the camp hospital. There would be too many questions. But we can stitch and dress that here."

Erich hadn't realized Karl Lang was there until he leaned over. "Couldn't we ask Dr. Bauer to pop by and do it, sir?

Obviously we can't let the Canadian doctors and nurses know, but he might even be able to smuggle some morphine out from the hospital hut."

Schmitt shook his head. "We can't trust Dr. Bauer. But it's a minor wound, well within the capability of any of our field medics. And don't worry, Stein. We'll give you alcohol. You won't feel a thing."

He straightened up. "Come on, let's put that still from hut thirteen to good use! Bring me the strongest stuff you have."

It wasn't even close to true that Stein didn't feel a thing. He drank the moonshine they gave him, but he was woozy before it touched his lips: dizzy and a little nauseous. He'd not had any of the moonshine before. It smelled like varnish and tasted no better. The spirits burned his throat and he almost threw it right back up. They poured more, and he drank that too, trying to force down his gag reflex.

And still it came, clear liquid in the bottom of a tin mug, being held in his face, tipped into his mouth, even when he tried to murmur at them to stop, to give him a little break for a breath. They did pause, but never for long enough. The alcohol kept coming and he had to swallow or let it spill over his face. He gulped as best he could between the spluttering and retching. Who would drink this stuff for fun?

When yet another cup was done, someone slid a piece of wood between his teeth. He gagged but kept it in place.

"Bite down if it hurts," someone said.

Stinging agony stabbed through his leg as something poured onto it. He clenched his teeth hard as the pang of it convulsed through his body.

"I'm just disinfecting it."

As the pain ebbed, Erich felt the cool of the alcohol spreading into the bedsheets around his calf, smelled the chemical reek of it. His leg did hurt a little less now. Or perhaps he was just cut off from it a bit, cut off from the room, too. The words of the other prisoners were confused, and he couldn't put them together enough to make sense. He wasn't sure who was talking to him and who wasn't. He closed his eyes, but felt as if he was falling backwards, as if he was going to be sick.

Then the torture began in earnest. Erich focused on biting the wood. Focused on the bulge of the mattress above him as it pushed its way through one of the slats, heavy with the earth that had fallen from the ceiling. He tried to block out the agony in his leg as someone tugged and pierced the skin of his wound. Tried so hard not to scream, not to give them all away.

Afterwards, they gave him yet more to drink.

At roll call that evening, Erich was the dummy, slung between Karl Lang and Oskar Krause. Lang answered for him as he struggled to keep his head upright. They carried him back to the hut and laid him out on his bed.

Schmitt was at his side, although Erich hadn't heard him approaching. Hadn't even known he was in the room.

"You did well today, Stein," he said.

Erich leaned over the side of his bed and vomited on the feldwebel's boots.

CHAPTER TEN

Sarah's old Toyota bumped along the dark road. I stared out, hoping to see Ruth wandering back, carrying her heels, lifting the hem of her white dress so it didn't trail in the dirt. But the branches we scrolled past held nothing but darkness.

"Where?" Sarah asked.

Asha leaned forward from the front seat, squinting. Eventually she pointed out the track into the woods. We piled out and stumbled back along the narrow path, single-file with our phones out for light. Max was in front of me, but he didn't hold the branches back this time. Like all of us, he was in too much of a hurry, too focused on finding Ruth.

The bonfire was barely visible now, just a low orange glow. A couple made out near the treeline, although in the dark, they were just a weirdly moving lump with too many legs. They looked up when a phone flashlight picked them out, and one of them swore. Neither was Ruth. I recognized a couple of guys next to the fire as people Max had introduced me to but couldn't remember their names.

"Ruth!" Sarah shouted. "Has anyone seen Ruth Kowalska? About so high," she held up a hand, "with red hair."

The couple broke apart and headed into the woods, obviously in search of more privacy. I could tell by the disgruntled expressions of the guys by the fire that even if they had seen Ruth, they weren't about to narc on anyone.

"Okay," Sarah said. "We have to search this whole area in case she passed out somewhere. Stay in pairs. I don't want to lose any more of you."

Max and I drifted together, and we searched around one side of the fire. Ephram pointed out a spot people had been using as a bathroom, behind a stand of trees. It absolutely reeked in there, but there was no sign of Ruth.

We shone our phone lights into the woods, but it felt pointless. It was a deep tangle and unless Ruth was within a few meters of the clearing, we'd never find her.

"What's that?" It was Asha who asked, and she wasn't looking into the trees but pointing at the black shadow of the lake. I followed her gaze and saw it too. Something in the water, a few meters out from the shore. A floating lump, like a pale backpack, breaking up the smooth shine of the dark water under the starry sky. As I got closer, cold prickled through me.

On some level I already knew.

Sarah ran into the lake, splashing wildly toward the thing. Ephram followed, and they grabbed it. They stumbled back up to dry land. I knew what it was, but I couldn't let myself think it, not even when they began CPR.

"Call an ambulance!" Sarah screamed.

I couldn't move, so Asha did it.

It was too late, of course.

The last of the party stragglers melted into the night before the ambulance arrived. They'd kept their distance, and once it was clear nothing could be done, they'd crept away, obviously afraid of their parents finding out where they'd been. I heard a girl crying softly as her friend led her through the trees toward the road. A part of me wished I could go with them, wished I could walk away and pretend none of it had happened. But I was stuck in the nightmare as it unfolded.

I tried not to look at Ruth. Her eyes were closed, as if she was asleep and could wake up at any point. Sarah kept up CPR for a painfully long time. Ephram moved onto the other side and they took turns for a while, Sarah's voice counting to thirty over and over as we stood there, waiting for something, anything.

When the ambulance finally came, the paramedics took over, but it was no use.

The police came after that. There were only a couple of them. They took names, numbers, and home addresses of everyone who stayed. They asked questions and made notes. We told them she was drunk. Told them she might have been high. They nodded solemnly. One of them disappeared after a while, called away by the static of his radio muttering about a crash on the highway. The other stayed, waiting for someone to come and get "the body."

We were allowed to go, but they said someone might contact us again.

The dark and the lights from our phones made the walk back to the car disjointed. My view of everything was jumpy and incomplete, like a found-footage movie. I couldn't feel sad, because a part of me was sure there had just been a terrible mistake, and things would be undone by the dawn when we'd all be able to see clearly again.

We were quiet on the ride back in the car. When we got to the museum, Sarah sent Max home and the rest of us to our rooms.

I tried to sleep. The bed creaked as I moved, unable to get comfortable, the mattress digging in to my hip, the pillow too lumpy at the side of my face. Occasionally, the low hiss of a car came from the road. Perhaps it was more police, or whoever else came at a time like this. Electrical wires hummed. Crickets creaked, as if nothing had happened.

Inside, the quiet was oppressive. I'd often been able to hear Ruth moving about next door as she got ready for bed. I'd always found it comforting.

That night, the silence from her room deafened me.

CHAPTER ELEVEN
May 31, 1944

Erich woke the next morning to a clean hut. There was no trace of earth or splintered wood on the floor. The other men moved slowly, limbs loose and relaxed, released from the frantic activity of the day before. Erich carried the only evidence of what had happened, the weight of it in every part of his body.

The morning sunlight split his head open. Nausea wracked his body. His leg couldn't hold his weight, but he tried to hide it, tried to limp outside alone for the morning's roll call before admitting he needed Lang's support. The wound on his calf heated his whole leg, and every movement, every beat of his heart, sent pain thrumming through it.

It was a relief to return to the hut once they'd been counted, to lie back on his bed. Krause, the field medic, brought more moonshine and coaxed him to drink. Erich swallowed again and again, trying not to inhale the disinfectant stink, feeling the sharp heat of it as it slipped down his throat, the strange cold of it in his gut. He tried not to gag, but it was no use. He liked beer, but for the life of him, he couldn't imagine why anyone would get blotto on moonshine by choice. He managed to keep it down.

Krause waited for it "to kick in." Erich lay back on the bed and felt his head cloud, felt the world tip and spin. He let himself detach, let himself lurch into a muddle of disconnected thoughts. Krause pulled up Erich's trouser leg, ready to remove the dressing and clean the wound.

He'd barely tugged on the fabric before he had to stop and find another wood chip for Erich to hold between his teeth.

By the third day, Erich's whole body burned. Each twitch sent a convulsion of agony from his leg through his body, yet he couldn't stay still. He shivered and trembled, chills and sweats fighting it out within. His pulse was a racing metronome, his heart pounding on his ribs. His wound radiated heat, dominating Erich's thoughts, sucking all his attention: a yawning pit of pain. He couldn't keep down the alcohol. A bucket had been placed next to his bed, but it was now as empty as his stomach.

"Can't we take him to the hospital now, sir?" it was Lang's voice, but it felt distant. Like a memory, even though Erich could see his friend right there, at his bedside. "It's been days, and the hut's mended. They won't work it out."

"It would be difficult to explain, particularly now he's been stitched up. And his fever will break soon." A hand clamped on his shoulder. Erich flinched. A face floated above him. Schmitt's face, latching itself onto his voice. "You don't need to go to the hospital, do you?"

Erich wasn't sure if he shook his head or shivered. Either way, Schmitt smiled.

"You're a credit to the Reich, Stein."

To Erich's surprise, his mother turned up at roll call that evening. He was just as hot, but the shivers had stopped and the pain was at a distance, for once. Still, Lang had to support him.

The man in front of him swatted at a cluster of mosquitos. They didn't seem to be bothering Erich. Usually, he was covered in itchy white bumps. Perhaps they didn't like the stink of alcohol that oozed from his pores. Or perhaps the pain in his leg kept him from noticing any other discomfort.

His mother moved through the men, weaving between the neat rows. He kept catching glimpses of her, slipping in and out of the lines like the light from the setting sun. She was looking at him but wouldn't come any closer, as if she were playing a game. He knew to acknowledge her was against the rules somehow. He stood as still as he could, shoulder braced against Lang, and followed her with his eyes.

Eventually, she stood in the Lagerführer's long shadow as he watched the Canadian guards marching up and down their rows and counting the prisoners. The Lagerführer's gaze fell on Erich and he tried to stand up straighter, to lift his weight off Lang. The Lagerführer gave a soft nod, and Erich felt a rush of joy. The Lagerführer knew about his injury. Of course he did — he knew everything in the camp. The Lagerführer himself appreciated his effort.

But the Lagerführer didn't seem to know about Erich's mother. Or if he did, he was ignoring her too. The sun was in Erich's eyes, too bright, cleaving into his head, and it was hard to see her through the dazzling pain. He blinked fast, only catching glimpses, and in those strobing seconds, she looked as if she were pulling faces behind the Lagerführer's back, ridiculous schoolyard expressions: tongue stuck out, cheeks puffed, cross-eyed.

"I don't want to play," Erich muttered under his breath.

"What?" Lang asked.

Erich shook his head, embarrassment at her behavior creeping up on him. She shouldn't be mocking the Lagerführer.

He tried to wave an arm, subtly, to signal to her to stop it.

"Are you okay?" Lang whispered.

"I just want her to stop."

"Who?"

But his signal had worked. She'd stopped pulling the faces. For a moment, she looked sad, regretful. She drifted toward him, the sun behind her, turning her into a silhouette, a shadow moving across the field, and Erich was afraid that if he lost sight of her, she'd be gone. But it was hard to look at her, framed by the setting sun. His eyes streamed, blurring her shape.

He'd offended her. She was going to leave without talking to him. She was already growing indistinct. He lifted his weight from Lang, who reached for him. Erich brushed his arm away and stepped out of his row, toward his mother.

"Please," he said. "Please."

But she had already gone.

The other men watched as Erich Stein collapsed in the mud, weeping.

CHAPTER TWELVE

I woke to the sun streaming through the grime of my window. I checked my clock: still early. I'd only been asleep for a few hours and a part of me hoped the scene at the lake had been a nightmare, in spite of the remorseless logic of the evening.

I crept out to the hall. I stepped as lightly as I could, listening to the other rooms, hoping no one would emerge. If anyone else woke, it would break the strange spell I moved under, the hope that if I just made it to her room with no one seeing me, I'd find Ruth asleep in her bed.

I paused at her door, screwing my eyes tightly closed and wishing as hard as I did when I was a child blowing out birthday candles. I turned the handle, and it opened with a soft scrape.

I stepped into a still life. The night before frozen in time: makeup on the desk, day clothes crumpled on the floor, her floral scent in the air. But no Ruth. She had spun here just yesterday, showing off her white dress. She'd been frustrating in some ways, but she'd been the only person who'd wanted to hang out with me. She'd stopped me from being totally creeped out by my ridiculous imagination each night. She'd been so vibrant, so alive. It seemed impossible that she was dead.

How could everything have gone to hell so fast?

The duvet and sheets were piled up in a heap on the bed, and for a moment, I hoped they might hide her. But the blankets were soft and gave way beneath my hands. The hard knot of her body wasn't there. It was in a morgue somewhere, cold.

I should have made sure she got home okay. I knew she was drunk. I suspected she was high.

I'd still left her.

I drifted around her room, as if I were the ghost, not her. Her washbag perched on the side of the desk, filled with the usual: toothbrush, toothpaste, shampoo, and conditioner. I stared at it all for a long time. She'd never use it again.

Some packaging lay behind it: a small cardboard box, ripped open. A genetic test kit.

I leaned closer, vague ideas about an investigation into Ruth's death and fingerprints keeping me from touching anything. I couldn't read much on the mangled packaging, and the information sheet under it, but one phrase jumped out.

Results in two to four weeks.

Stuttering fragments of the night before drifted back. Ruth had said something about having sway with the Hoppers, and something about two to four weeks. She said she'd learned something from Bertie that gave her a "nuclear option."

A garbage can stood against the desk. Among the usual things — an old toothbrush, screwed up paper, and used tissues — I saw more packaging with the same logo as the kit. She'd presumably used the test and sent it out. She must have done so recently, hence the two-to-four-week comment last night.

Hair stood up on my arms. Ruth had discovered something about the Hoppers, something genetic. But what? I wasn't sure how much genetic test kits cost, but they weren't cheap. This must have been important to her.

A creak came from down the hall. I wasn't the only one awake. But I was the only one snooping around a dead girl's room. I hurried to the door, slipped back out to my own room, and collapsed back onto the bed.

I couldn't save Ruth. I couldn't go back in time and fix my stupid, selfish mistakes. But maybe I could find out what she knew about the Hoppers. Maybe I could finish what she'd started.

I just had to make sure I got to the mail first every day, starting in two weeks.

CHAPTER THIRTEEN

June 5, 1944

When Erich woke, the bed above him had disappeared. He stared directly up at the beams of the ceiling, wondering if the weight of earth had brought it down again, taking the upper bunk with it this time.

There was warmth in his body, but not the burning of his fever: a softer warmth that spread through to his fingertips, that bloomed through him. A restful, gentle warmth, like a fire down to its embers on a cold day.

The hut sounded different, too. A man coughed on the other side of the room, the noise clear and unmuffled. Shoes shuffled along the floor, but there was no murmur of conversation. Erich pushed himself up on his elbows. His head spun, and he almost fell back on his pillows. He was aware of a tug in his leg, the soft ache of receded pain.

This wasn't his hut. There were no bunks, and each bed was an island, adrift in its own space. Erich's was against a wall, the white blankets pulled taut over his body.

He was in the hospital hut.

Shame lurched through him. He'd failed, somehow. He'd given the game away. He tried to remember what had happened, how he'd ended up here, but he could only clutch at the last wisps of the dream he'd awoken from, of walking alone along a street of houses with no front doors, only windows through which he looked at smiling families, unreachable in their cozy living rooms.

The man in the next bed fiddled with his hair, rubbing the ends of it between his fingers, neurotically. It was already matted into peaks, making him look like a nervous hedgehog. In the bed beyond that, a man in an airman's uniform read a paper, mustachioed face visible through the rectangular holes cut by the censor.

"Aha, our sleeping beauty awakes!" A male voice, accompanied by the clack of shoes on the wooden floor. "I'm Dr. Bauer."

He wore a white coat and a large grin. Erich had heard something about Dr. Bauer. Something important. Something Schmitt had said.

"So, what happened to you?"

That they couldn't trust Dr. Bauer. That was it.

"Hmm?" Erich said, playing dumb.

"You've been in and out for five days. That was quite the state your leg was in. I can't imagine how painful that must have been without morphine. I bet you feel better now with some of that in your system, eh?"

That topic seemed safe enough. Erich nodded.

"Good. I've cleaned it all out, and hopefully we've dealt with that infection. That was an awful attempt at stitches. Who did that?"

"I did, sir." It seemed the safest approach. He had to assume that everyone in the hut had claimed ignorance, and if he took responsibility, no one else should get into trouble.

Dr. Bauer's eyebrows went up. Erich couldn't tell if it was with surprise or skepticism.

"That would explain why they were such a mess. Why on earth didn't you come to the hospital?"

"It was just a scrape. I decided to handle it myself. I'm a soldier, sir."

"This isn't an interrogation, Stein. And this isn't a battlefield, either. You don't have to dress your own wounds. Especially when you are evidently so bad at it."

"Yes, sir. Sorry, sir." Erich leaned back on the pillows, pleased with his lie.

A few hours later, Feldwebel Schmitt himself came by. Dr. Bauer hovered nearby as they talked.

"I heard you'd woken, Stein. Gave us quite the scare there, you did."

"I'm sorry, sir."

"What happened to you? How did you get that leg wound?"

Erich had had a little time to think, so his story came out smoother this time. "Fell while running, sir. Scraped it on a rock. I didn't think it was that bad and didn't want to bother anyone, so I stitched it myself. I realize now how foolish that was."

Schmitt was facing Erich, his back to Dr. Bauer, who couldn't see when the feldwebel gave Erich a warm smile. "Yes, that was foolish indeed. You should have come to me. But it seems all is well now, so no harm done. I hope you'll recover enough to return to the barracks quickly."

Erich inhaled, swelling with pride.

Dr. Bauer stepped over. "I'm afraid he'll be with us for a while. He came perilously close to dying, and he's lost a lot of weight.

He needs time to build his strength back up, all of which could have been avoided if he'd just come here in the first place."

The feldwebel looked irritated. "Well, we'll await your return impatiently, Stein."

"I really don't feel that bad. I'm sure I'll be back soon, sir."

"Excellent."

Erich managed a salute as Schmitt left. Once he'd gone, Dr. Bauer lowered himself onto the corner of Erich's bed. His voice was soft, and he looked at the floor as he spoke.

"You don't feel so bad because you have a lot of morphine in your system. It would be dangerous to leave the hospital early. Almost as dangerous as waiting so long to come here. It's lucky you collapsed at roll call, lucky the guards brought you to me. I doubt you would still be with us, otherwise."

Erich shivered. "Sorry, sir. I shouldn't have tried to deal with it on my own."

The doctor met his eyes. "I'm glad to hear no one knew you were injured. Glad to hear it was just boyhood foolishness that kept you from the hospital, Stein. It would have been awful if other people had known and discouraged you from coming here, given the state you were in. Those would be terrible men, you understand. Men who would let a good lad die for no reason."

The doctor stayed on the corner of the bed, staring at him for a long moment. Then he stood, smoothing out his white coat. "It is good that we do not have such evil men in this camp."

And with that, he walked away, shoes clicking on the wooden floor.

That night, the camp alarm woke Erich. The other patients sat up in bed, rumors coursing among them like electricity under the rising and falling wail of the siren. Guards entered, counting, searching under beds. The bustle of their movements leaving a vacuum as they hurried back out again, leaving them in stillness.

The next morning, Erich's fears were confirmed by the muttered murmurs between the other prisoners when the nurses were out of earshot. Five men were missing and the tunnel had been discovered. The news animated the patients, the usual moans and splutters of the hospital hut smothered by whispers and laughter. Erich lay frozen under his blanket.

He'd proved himself, hadn't he? So why hadn't Schmitt waited for him?

Perhaps that's why he'd come by the day before, to see if Erich was up to breaking out. Perhaps if he'd been stronger, if he'd got out of bed there and then, he could have gone with the other men.

Or perhaps he'd been afraid that Erich would blab to the doctors, to the guards, whether through delirium or disloyalty, and he'd wanted to use the tunnel before Erich had a chance.

The day kept on, gray and useless. As if to rub things in, there was a mail call. Two of the other patients got letters, while Erich got nothing. He thought of his hallucinations of his mother, of her familiar form moving between the men, just out of reach. He turned toward the rough wood of the wall.

Lang came in to see him later, his only visitor since Schmitt had been by.

"You weren't part of the escape?" Erich said quietly.

Lang shook his head with a smile. "Nope. Was as in-the-dark as you until you caught the ceiling with your head. But I wanted to bring this. Found it on the field near where you collapsed."

In his hand was Erich's little wooden good luck charm. Some dried earth stuck in the dents, but it was otherwise unblemished.

Erich held out his hand, and the familiar weight of it fell onto his palm. He closed his eyes and felt the smooth surface under his skin.

"Knew you'd want it."

"Thank you so much."

Lang didn't meet Erich's gaze, but he leaned in, making sure the rest of the room couldn't hear. "I'm sorry. I should have gotten help for you."

Erich shook his head, wondering if Lang had spoken to Dr. Bauer. "It was my choice. I wanted to do my bit."

"I should never have let things get that bad," Lang said. "And I won't let that happen to anyone else."

There was a determination in his look that made Erich feel uneasy.

Two days later, another patient was brought in, slung between two guards, arms over their shoulders, body dangling between them like some ghastly parody of a crucifixion. The toes of his shoes dragged on the wooden floor, catching in the gaps between the planks.

His face was grotesquely swollen, eyes purple, lips puffy and cracked. Spidery lines of dried blood hid what little was left of his features. Erich wondered if this was an escapee, caught and brutally beaten by the Canadians. But instead of greeting him as a returning hero, the other men turned away as he passed.

Erich leaned toward the nervous hedgehog in the nearest bed. "Who's that?"

"Meyer," the man replied.

Erich vaguely remembered the doom monger he'd been sitting opposite on the train. "What happened to him?"

"He's a communist," the man said, resuming his hair twisting.

Erich nodded, as if that explained everything. Which it did, he realized.

Earth above his head, escapes behind his back, beatings in secret. He felt like a man watching a play between the scenes with the lights down: sensing rather than seeing the moving scenery, the reshaping of the world around him.

The escaped Germans were found hiding in a barn. Erich heard the cheers through the hospital windows as they were brought back through the camp on their way to solitary — the wild applause and whooping of the prisoners gathered on the main field to welcome them. It sounded as if they were celebrating the surrender of the Allies, not an escape attempt that failed in less than two days.

Erich's leg ached constantly, and it seemed impossible that he would ever get comfortable again. His appetite didn't come back. Sometimes he felt the edge of hunger and was able to force down a few bites. But each day at mail call it receded, replaced by the twist and tip of nausea. Food stuck in his throat. It was too rich, too much. Erich kept thinking of his mother and wondering if she was okay, if she was starving, if she was rotting in the ruins of their bombed-out home. He'd seen men dying in pain and pieces, but he'd managed to shut that part of himself down, managed to not feel it. But when he thought of the same thing happening to her, he felt as if he would suffocate with the horror of it all.

From his sick bed, Meyer whispered about a big defeat. He said the papers were full of it; he claimed the Allies had launched an invasion of France. The rest of the hut ignored him, refusing to listen to propaganda and the rumors of an ostracized, defeatist traitor.

Erich wondered if Meyer's stories were what had gotten him beaten up. His whispers got to Erich, further turning his stomach, even though it couldn't be true and he tried not to listen. He found it harder to find the strength to walk to the bathroom, harder to find the energy to move at all.

When Dr. Bauer wandered down the rows of patients a few days later, Erich struggled to sit up. His whole body was infused with exhaustion.

Again, the doctor perched on the corner of his bed. "You haven't been eating."

Erich shrugged. "I haven't been hungry."

"Part of that will be nausea from the medication. I've been reducing the morphine. We'll see if you can do without it, although I expect it will be unpleasant for the first few days. But that's not the only problem, is it?"

Erich shrugged again.

Dr. Bauer fixed Erich with a piercing stare. "Have you had bad news from home?"

Erich exhaled, glad he'd asked about that and not about his leg or Meyer's mutterings. He shook his head.

"Really?"

"No bad news at all. I haven't even heard from my mother in … a while." His voice caught on the words.

"Ah. I see." Dr. Bauer took a deep breath. "Do you have other family at home?"

"No. My dad's dead."

"No sweetheart, either?"

Erich shook his head. Girls had never seemed to notice him. Not that he'd had much of a chance to meet them around the compulsory Hitler Youth meetings that had led right into his national service and military training.

Dr. Bauer sighed. "There are slower, less deliberate ways to do what Mannerheim did."

Erich sat up straighter, appalled. "I'm not trying to kill myself."

"The result is the same, if you don't eat."

"I'm just not hungry."

"If you give me your address, I can speak to some of the camp visitors, to the Red Cross and the Swiss, and see if we can get any news about your mother from them."

"You can?"

The doctor pressed the pads of his fingers together. "I can't promise it will be good news, and I don't want to lose another young man if we only confirm the worst. This camp is …," he shook his head, as if he couldn't find the right word, and his gaze fell on Meyer's bed, "not a healthy place right now. But I might be able to help with getting you out of here."

Erich felt the rush of excitement, his dreams of escape, of being cheered like the other men suddenly vibrant in his mind again. "What do you mean?"

"All the enlisted men will be expected to do work duty soon. And I've heard of a farm nearby that I think you'd be perfect for, as soon as you've recovered. You'd spend the days with the family and come back to the camp at night."

Erich sunk back in his bed. Many of the other men worked outside the camp — logging, in paper mills, or at farms. They got a little pay for it on top of their German army salary, but it would have meant giving up his English lessons, vowing not to escape while working, and not being on hand when the call came.

But the call had come and gone without him.

"They only need one person, and they want someone reliable, a young man they can trust around their family. I could put your name forward."

"I don't know."

"You need to be reminded that there is a world beyond this barbed wire. I'll speak to the Lagerführer."

CHAPTER FOURTEEN

Mom came to pick me up later that day. We were given a few days off to go home, and the option to leave the museum program altogether. I thought the police would bring us all in for a proper interrogation, but I only got a short phone call to confirm what I'd already said. It seemed Ruth's death was a pretty open-and-shut case. Nothing unexpected was found around the lake or in the autopsy.

We didn't see Ruth's family. They didn't come to the museum, just the morgue. Sarah packed up her room and shipped her stuff home while we were away. None of us were invited to the funeral. No doubt her family didn't want the people responsible for her death to come.

I couldn't blame them.

I expected lectures from my mother about the party, but I think she decided that losing a friend was a bigger lesson than any she could bestow. She asked me if I'd taken drugs myself. I promised her I hadn't and even offered to take a drug test, which seemed to satisfy her.

I wandered around our tiny apartment in a daze. Mom had moved into my room while I was away. She offered to take the pull-out couch as usual while I was home, but I insisted that she stay in my bed. I saw the way she winced as she stood and bent down. Her back was worse than ever.

It seemed impossible that Ruth was gone. I hadn't known her for long, but we'd spent every evening together for weeks. It was as if a hole had opened out of nowhere and swallowed her. The world seemed fragile, untrustworthy. If someone as alive as Ruth could just disappear from existence, how could anything ever feel safe again? It had been bad enough when Dad died, but there had been plenty of warning then.

Not that it had made anything easier when we lost him.

Our apartment, with the soulless beige paint and the uneven parquet floor, seemed less real than the darkness that lurked behind it — the darkness that had snatched Ruth and Dad out of the world. We'd moved after Dad died, and his presence didn't infuse the place, like it had our last home, anchoring us to him. There was no memory of his deep laugh in the kitchen, his calloused hands clutching his cutlery. His astonishingly loud snoring had never awoken us at the new apartment, and he'd never left his keys dangling in the outside door by accident. The place was too full of the two of us and too empty of memories.

Home used to be something I felt bone-deep. Now it was just an absence.

I met up with some friends, when they weren't working or otherwise sunk in a holiday routine that didn't involve me. We'd been drifting apart anyway, and they had new in-jokes I didn't get. Plus, it was super hard to talk to people who didn't know Ruth and now never would.

She'd drowned. That was no surprise. She did indeed have drugs in her system — LSD, as it turned out. She also had a very high blood alcohol level. She'd been caught on the cameras at the Hoppers' rally after I'd left, and the association between a pretty, dead girl and a rich, political family meant she'd made it into the papers, which is how I found out about the results of the autopsy.

It didn't hurt the Hoppers though. They obviously weren't to blame, and the news cycle moved on to the Hoppers' speeches about "corrupting" books in the children's sections of Canadian libraries, and their campaign against the upcoming drag queen story time at Westonville Library.

I told Mom about the scholarship. I didn't mean to, but it came out somehow when I was telling her about Ruth.

She stiffened, clutching the cloth she'd been using to wipe the table. "A full scholarship, Keira. Just imagine what that could do."

Like I hadn't been doing exactly that. "I don't think I want their money."

"Why? Would you rather it went to someone who supports Peter Hopper?"

That stopped me. It wasn't something I'd considered.

"How will it help anyone for you to drown in debt while someone terrible takes the money instead? Wouldn't it be better if you got a good start in life and they didn't?"

I shook my head. "I'm not going to get it anyway. I've got nowhere in my research."

She folded the cloth and draped it over the edge of the sink. "The summer program isn't up yet. I believe in you. And so did your dad. Think about it, Keira."

Dad had believed in me. He was sure I could do anything I "put my mind to." But the world didn't work like that. Dad was also sure he could beat the cancer. He was sure he had enough money saved. He was sure he wouldn't be off work for long.

He was sure he wouldn't die.

Mom wandered across the room and sat on the edge of the pull-out bed, pushing my heaped comforter out of the way and patting a space next to her. I hadn't yet folded it back up into a sofa like she usually did as soon as she woke.

"I need to tell you something."

I joined her and sat obediently.

She pushed her lips together for a moment. "Keira, you know how expensive it is to live in Toronto."

"I'm saving most of my honorarium. I can help out a bit."

"I'm getting less agency work. I've had to take more time off for my back."

"You didn't tell me that! I'll get another weekend job as soon as the summer's done."

Mom shook her head. "Your Aunt Jess says they're desperate for seasonal workers near her, cashier roles and other jobs that won't be such a strain. It would pay less, but rent is cheaper there, and I could get EI in the offseason."

Cold slipped into my stomach. "You want to move to Nova Scotia?"

"Not 'til you're done high school," she said quickly.

"But ..." I didn't need to say it. The plan had always been for me to go to U of T. And I'd assumed I'd have a place to live, here with Mom.

"There are universities in Nova Scotia. I hear Dalhousie is nice. You could live with me if I found a place between Halifax and Jess. It wouldn't be a great commute for either of us, and you'd still have to cover tuition and books and all that, but it's probably doable."

"Dad didn't help build Dalhousie. It wasn't his dream for me to go there."

"I'm sure he'd understand. Things have changed, and he just wanted you to be happy."

"I'd be happy at U of T, like he wanted. And Toronto is home!"

"You could still go! With that scholarship and an evening job, you could rent a cheap room in a shared house. If you were careful, you could graduate without too much debt."

She didn't need to state the obvious. Without the Hopper Scholarship, I definitely couldn't afford Toronto. I'd owe more than I could ever pay back.

"It's worth going for, right? It's not like taking their money means you agree with them."

My shoulders fell. "I guess not."

The Toronto Reference Library was where I'd researched Erich Stein's murder, so it was inevitable I'd end up back there, the curve of the red and orange balconies cradling me, the soft buzz of low conversations oddly calming. It was the best place to start unraveling everything that had happened in Westonville. There was still so much I didn't understand about Ruth's death, although I was totally clear on my role in it.

I'd fought with her. I'd left the party without her. I should have been there to save her, and I wasn't. I owed her.

She'd also fought with Ephram, Sarah, and Julia, and I still had no idea why. I couldn't bring her back, but maybe if I understood more about her, I'd understand why the dark had taken her.

In spite of the fact I'd actually seen a DNA test in her room, it took me way too long to think of checking ancestry websites.

I had to sign up for a free trial but soon found the great-grandmother she'd mentioned: Margaret Fortin. But when I saw her great-grandfather's name, my breath stopped.

Ruth's great-grandfather was George Wright, the guard who found Erich Stein.

I stared at the name on the screen for a long time. Margaret Fortin became Margaret Wright. Why on earth hadn't Ruth told me?

I leaned back on my wooden chair, feeling disconnected from the quiet bustle of the library, the hum of the glass elevators, and the soft muttering of a couple at the next table.

Ruth had never shown any interest in my careful research, even though it involved her own family. I shook my head. Had she not been listening when I mentioned George Wright? No, she definitely had. She'd immediately talked about Harry and how close he was to George. She'd said George would have done anything for Harry.

Our conversation on the evening she died came back to me, her spinning in the white dress. She'd said that her great-grandmother's husband had died a few months before her great-grandmother did. She hadn't called him her great-grandfather. I'd thought it was an odd way to put it at the time.

I remembered her later in the dark by the lake, the same white dress soaked and clinging to her still body. I shook my head, trying to clear the image.

Margaret Fortin and George Wright had married in Toronto on June 25, 1945. As Ruth had said, they'd died a few months apart in 1995. Ruth's grandmother was born in Toronto on December 30, 1945.

Something was off. I checked the marriage and birth dates again.

It was possible that Ruth's grandmother was premature, or her parents were just too into each other to wait for marriage. But Ruth had mentioned a family rumor.

It didn't take much to put it together. She'd even asked me if her cheekbones looked like Harry's. If Margaret Fortin got pregnant by Harold Hopper in March or April 1945, and he died before he could make an honest woman out of her in the judgmental 1940s, no doubt she'd have been looking for a husband as soon as possible to hide her shame. They were beyond uncool about unmarried mothers back in those days. Her life, and her child's, would have been incredibly hard in a small town like Westonville.

Ruth had said that George would have done anything for his friend. Perhaps that included looking after his best friend's lover and unborn baby. Moving to Toronto probably prevented any questions about the timing of the birth.

Ruth clearly thought she was a Hopper and was waiting for DNA proof. No wonder she called the scholarship "leftovers" at the party. No wonder she said she might have some pull with the Hoppers. She thought she was one of them, perhaps even entitled to some of their money.

She'd also mentioned a "nuclear option." What was that?

I got no further with the ancestry sites. There's only so much you can learn from lives stripped down to bald dates. I could imagine Ruth's on there now, just two of them: her birth seventeen years ago and her death last week.

She was so much more than two numbers.

She was, officially at least, George Wright's great-granddaughter. That totally changed things. I'd only focused on the reports of him finding the body, and now everything about him mattered. As soon as I got back to the camp, I'd read everything I could find on him.

Was I insane to feel there was a connection with Erich Stein? He'd died five days before George and Margaret got married. Was that just a coincidence? George had no doubt handed in his notice before Erich's death, so it probably was. Or maybe finding the body was what had made him quit. What motive would George have for killing a prisoner, when the war was over and he was about to move to Toronto and marry anyway?

Erich's death felt more urgent now. While most of the documents I needed to look into him and George were back at the museum, there was somewhere I could start investigating, right here in Toronto.

I found books on the Medicine Hat murders at Camp 132 that Max had mentioned.

It was Canada's last mass execution. It took a while for me to get the gist of what had happened, since it was all a bit confusing. I'd already known that some of the POWs were Nazi fanatics, while others weren't so all-in. All German men eighteen and up had to join the army, and some just went along with things, out of fear or a lack of alternatives, in spite of the horror of what they became a part of.

Like the POWs themselves, some camps were more extreme in their beliefs than others. In Camp 44 in Quebec, they were so extreme that they planned a full-on suicidal terrorist attack they intended to launch if they felt the war was lost. Hundreds of them were going to break out, fight their way to the nearest city, and murder as many people as they could before they were stopped. Luckily, the plan was discovered and the prisoners dispersed to other camps before they could carry it out.

On the other hand, there was a camp in Sorel, Quebec, where they sent the German POWs who were clearly anti-Nazi, partly for their own protection. Most of the other camps, including Westonville, were "gray" camps, somewhere in the middle.

Medicine Hat — Camp 132 — held a ton of extreme Nazis, who murdered their own countrymen after deciding they were "disloyal" to the Reich. One of their victims, August Plaszek, had been telling everyone that the Germans were going to lose the war. The fact that he was totally right didn't make any difference. He was beaten and strangled to death by his own comrades. Three men were put on trial for it, and one hung.

But that wasn't the last of the murders in Medicine Hat. Events in Berlin made the Nazis on Canadian soil even worse. There was an assassination attempt on Hitler by a group of conspirators with various motivations: some who were anti-Nazi, some who wanted power themselves, and others who knew defeat was inevitable and didn't want to prolong everyone's suffering. The one thing they all had in common was wanting to get rid of Hitler and negotiate peace. They'd apparently been trying for a while, but on July 20, 1944, they almost succeeded.

I paused in reading, looking up at the yellow wood of the stacks, the books shelved in rows of vertical colors. A man coughed on the floor below me, the noise echoing up. A woman with headphones on a work call at the next table kept making "mmm" sounds in agreement with whatever the faces on her screen were saying.

I wondered what the world would have been like if they'd actually killed Hitler. How many had died in that last, pointless year of war, when the Nazis destroyed so much just to try to cling to power? Bertie's brother, Harry, for one. Rainer Schmitt and Erich Stein might have been home safe instead of dead in

Westonville. And I couldn't bear to think about all the men, women, and children who had gone into the concentration camps in that last year, all because Hitler was shielded from the bomb's blast by a table leg.

So many lives stolen. Each of them ripped out of the world like Ruth and Dad. The fabric of so many families tattered and torn.

Hitler retaliated. He had five thousand people executed in Germany, and gave a speech to his faithful followers worldwide, telling them it was their duty to get rid of any traitors in their midst.

It seemed the Nazi POWs in Medicine Hat had done just that.

They came after Karl Lehmann, who had apparently been reading Canadian newspaper reports and also dared to speculate about Germany losing. They hung him on September 10, 1944, and those who murdered Lehmann were put on trial by the Canadian authorities. They died at the end of a rope, just like their victim.

That was a motive, at least. Perhaps Schmitt and Stein had dared to suggest something as ridiculously outlandish as the idea that Germany might not win the war. Perhaps they weren't fully Nazi and so were sentenced to death by the camp Gestapo for their disloyalty, like Plaszek and Lehmann. Perhaps they were both attacked and Stein managed to flee, somehow getting out of the camp, only to die from his head wound.

They weren't the only victims of Nazi so-called courts of honor in POW camps, either. They also attacked men suspected of being gay. They had their decorations stripped from their uniforms and were viciously beaten. The Canadians barely treated them better, with the defense lawyer in the Medicine Hat trials attacking an apparently gay witness for the prosecution. He used his "homosexualist" nature to undermine his testimony, claiming that someone with a "perverted mind" could not be relied upon.

They'd also given dishonorable discharges to gay members of the Allied military, kicking them out of the army to spend the rest of their lives labeled as "sex perverts."

It was all so gross, but it was a possible motive, too. Could Schmitt and Stein have been lovers, caught together and murdered by the Nazis as punishment?

One last aspect of the Medicine Hat murders grabbed my attention. There were rumors of an "order" given to kill all traitors and make it appear to be suicide.

I leaned back in my chair, my unfocused gaze blurring the students hunched over their laptops and the homeless seeking respite from the summer heat.

Rainer Schmitt and Erich Stein hadn't been the only men to die at the Westonville camp. I'd seen the incident reports for at least one deadly accident and a couple of suicides, but they'd seemed unconnected so I'd barely glanced at them. A few more men had died in the camp hospital from disease and cancer.

As soon as I got back to the museum, I'd have to check them all carefully. Perhaps they weren't what they seemed.

I had a plan now: read up on George Wright; look up the camp death reports; speak to Ephram, Sarah, and Julia about why they'd argued with Ruth; and wait for the results of her DNA test.

It wasn't much, but it was a start.

CHAPTER FIFTEEN
June–July 1944

Schmitt did not visit Erich again, although Lang came by often and filled him in on the news from the camp. Meyer's beating injuries were superficial, and he was soon well enough to leave the hospital and go to work in a logging camp. Other men were brought in, aching with cancers and broken limbs or wheezing with pneumonia, the sound of their labored breaths making Erich's own chest feel tight.

Without the morphine, Erich's leg throbbed with every pulse, but the pain wasn't as sharp, and the heat was gone. His appetite slowly returned. Dr. Bauer didn't ask him about the escape and didn't mention the rumors of Allied advances. Instead, he encouraged him to eat the rich stews and sausages made by their own German camp chefs. He brought Erich extra cakes and pastries from the mess: spongy and sweet *apfelkuchen*, honey-glazed *bienenstich*, and crumbly and moist *streuselkuchen*. He sat with him each day as mail call came and went with no word from his mother. He talked about growing up in Berlin in the twenties, a life so different to Erich's regimented upbringing — a life of meeting friends and girls in coffee shops and bars. No endless training, no Hitler Youth, no war.

Erich listened warily. After all, Schmitt had said the doctor was not to be trusted. But he never said a word against Hitler, or the Nazi party. Indeed, he often spoke of the shortages of the twenties, of the unemployment and hunger. Yet Erich found himself yearning for the freedom Dr. Bauer had grown up with.

He remembered a couple he'd seen from the train as they'd sped through one of dozens of interchangeable Canadian stations on the way to Westonville. It had been such a simple scene, yet it had stayed in his mind. The two of them were bundled up in long coats and hats, not the ubiquitous uniforms of Germany, watching curiously as the train passed. The young man's red scarf was thrown back by the wind, and there had been something so carefree and thoughtless in the way he'd reached for the girl's hand. Something so unguarded and open about it all.

Erich wondered what it would be like to live like that: to decide where he wanted to go and who he wanted to be with, instead of an adolescence of drills and exercises, national service and military training, followed by war and imprisonment.

Erich was in the hospital for a month. Schmitt welcomed him back to the hut on his return, but there was a stiffness in his manner. Erich guessed he'd taken too long to recover. He hadn't been strong enough, German enough for the feldwebel.

He was beginning to suspect he never would be.

The hut was mostly empty during the day now. Men had been sent out to satellite camps to work on farms and at paper mills. While Schmitt protested the work orders, he claimed they were yet another sign that the Canadians were losing the war — that their men had been slaughtered in such great numbers that they now needed Germans to toil for them.

On the day he was due to start at the farm, Erich joined the work parade to the camp gate. It was hot already, a solid, humid heat that held him in his place in line, trying to stay still and cool. He didn't want to arrive sweaty; he would be representing Germany. Other men shuffled as they waited, boots scuffing the hard dirt. From the distance came the intermittent tattoo of an unseen woodpecker.

"First time working out of the camp?" A voice from behind.

Erich turned. A heavy-set, older man stood behind him, nose thickly spread across his face.

"Neumann," he said, holding out his hand.

"Stein." Erich shook it.

"It helps, you know? It feels more normal. I didn't want to at first, but I got a letter from my boss about stuff back home." He stuck a finger in his ear and twisted it. "Turns out they've hired someone to do my job, and that was it, you know?"

Erich didn't know, but he nodded anyway.

"Hurts, doesn't it? The world going on without you. Like you died instead of being captured." He had a faraway look in his eyes. "You need to prove you're still here, show you're useful, right?"

Erich thought of how quickly he'd surrendered in Africa, of everything he'd done to try to prove himself in the camp since. But the war and the escape had gone on without him anyway. He hadn't been useful to anyone.

"I suppose so."

"That's right. Good lad." Neumann clapped a hand against Erich's back so hard he stumbled forward. "Plus, the pay helps, right? I send back stockings to the missus. You can order them from the Eaton catalog, and she loves them. Don't want her to forget about me. Would hate to find out I'd been replaced in that department too, eh?"

There was paperwork at the first gate, each man checked and noted down; Canadians stood by, bayonets leaned against shoulders. They were taken to the second gate, where there was yet more paperwork. Erich signed a promise not to escape while on work duty and he, Neumann, and another German were signed over to a young guard whose limp had obviously excluded him from the Canadian army.

Erich saluted him, as they did with all the guards, but the young man shook his head.

"George Wright." He held out a hand.

"Erich Stein," Erich said, shaking it. George's grip was firm, but he didn't make a competition of it, like some men.

"Do you speak much English?" George asked.

Erich paused, feeling that he should only give his name, rank, and serial number, but the other two men seemed at ease with the conversation, and he'd seen prisoners chatting amicably with the guards and scouts in the camp. Still, it wouldn't do to give too much away.

"A bit," Erich admitted.

"Great. Since you're new, why don't you ride shotgun? You're my last drop-off anyway." George waved at the passenger seat of a battered, gray truck. Erich was confused by the word *shotgun* and wondered if he'd misheard, but the gesture made it clear what George meant. The other two men were already climbing into the bed at the back.

"Lucky boy," Neumann called out in German. "Much less bumpy in the front."

Erich climbed onto the cracked and tattered leather of the bench in the cab of the truck and pulled the door closed. It didn't shut properly.

"Try again," George said, as he slid in on the other side. "It takes a good yank to get it shut." He mimed tugging at the door hard.

Erich slammed the door as George started the engine. It felt odd to be sitting next to a Canadian: one of the enemy. The vehicle shuddered and then lurched into life, jolting through the ruts in the hard earth toward the gate. A clipboard was passed through the window, George signed it, the gates opened, and then the old truck was bouncing along the dirt road.

The window was open and the warm air blowing in felt like freedom. The countryside bounded past, green wheat bowing and bending in flowing waves across the fields. Erich could imagine the hiss of the growing stems in the breeze, although he couldn't hear it over the growl and rumble of the old engine. They passed fields of horses, of cattle, and of corn, and Erich was struck by the peaceful plenty of it all.

He'd been out of the camp before, of course — on marches, and occasionally to go swimming at the lake a few kilometers north. But he'd never been out of the camp without his comrades and superiors, without the careful discipline of the Wehrmacht.

"You'll like the Novaks," George said. He glanced at Erich to check he understood. Erich nodded.

Novak was a Czech name, wasn't it? He might be working for Slavs. He stared out of the window as he digested that fact. Should he be ashamed?

"First stop," George said after a while. He pulled up in front of a gate by the road. The two other men jumped out of the back of the truck and opened it in what was obviously a familiar ritual.

After they drove through, the men swung it shut and jumped back in. They rumbled slowly down a long, straight, rutted track that ran next to a roughly made, wooden fence. To the left, pigs wallowed in a field of drying mud, or slumbered under low corrugated-metal arches that reminded him of the bomb shelters he'd seen in England.

They pulled up in front of a brick farmhouse, with a gabled roof. A man stood outside, shirtsleeves rolled up to his elbows. The two men in the back jumped out again and went to join him.

"Stay with me," George said, getting out of the truck and slinging his rifle over his shoulder. Erich followed as George pulled out more papers, and the farmer signed.

"See you later!" Neumann said as the farmer led the others away across the fields.

At the gate this time, it was Erich's job to open and close it to let the truck through, before he got back in the truck and they bumped along the dirt road together again.

Erich leaned an elbow on the door, angled out of the open window. He stopped himself from sticking a hand out to feel the flow of the wind over and between his fingers. He was a soldier, not a schoolchild.

It felt strange. It felt normal. He could almost imagine he had the freedom Dr. Bauer had grown up with — the freedom of the young couple at the station. He could pretend he and George were just two friends out for a drive on a summer day.

But when he glanced down, he saw the gray of his POW uniform and thought of the big red circle on the back. The other prisoners joked that it was put there as a target that even the most doddering guards couldn't miss. The countryside around them wasn't German, either. The fields were too wide, there were too few houses. And there were no arms factories, no army trucks or marching men.

It was about another twenty minutes' drive to the Novaks' farm. The rolling fields petered out as trees rose in patches around them: pine and spruce. The land was wilder here, lumps of granite pushing out of the forested earth on one side, reed-filled bogs appearing on the other, the road the only clear way between the two. It grew rougher as they went, pitching the truck in a rolling motion. George's knuckles were white on the wheel, holding their path steady as the potholes and furrows tried to yank the truck to one side or the other.

Finally, they approached another gate, at what appeared to be the end of the road. Erich clambered out to open it when George asked, gazing ahead at the farm itself, so different from the comfortable land where they had dropped off the other men. A few scant fields had been snatched from the wilderness. Erich could see why he'd been trusted to work here alone. There was no prospect of escape from the farm except for the road itself, unless he wanted to risk being lost forever in the forests and marshes that surrounded it.

The farmhouse was close: a small clapboard building. A truck, even more battered than the one he'd arrived in, was parked in front. Pigs snuffled in a pen to one side of the house, and chickens squawked and scratched in a mud run.

The front door opened as George turned off the engine, and a barrel-shaped man came out of the house, supporting himself with a stick on one side, where the bottom half of his leg was missing. He frowned at the truck.

"Come on," George said. "You'll like Joe. I promise."

Erich got out obediently. Joe Novak looked him up and down. Erich stood straighter. He was shorter than most and still skinny from his accident. He doubted he was the *übermensch* Joe had been hoping for to work on his farm. He'd probably been expecting someone more like his two stocky comrades already laboring in the fields up the road.

But Joe nodded, and there was approval in his gaze.

George limped over to meet the man, and, once again, there was paperwork. Erich didn't catch all that was said between them, but he heard his own name, and George waved him over.

"Joe Novak," the man said, and he held out his hand.

Erich shook it, noticing the callouses. "Erich Stein." He nodded at the man's leg. "The war?" he managed in English.

"No," the man replied. "An infection, about a year ago."

The door to the house creaked, and a head peeked out. A thin young woman with limp ginger hair and wearing a faded floral dress peered at the three of them.

Joe turned around. "Stay inside for now, Daisy," he said, not unkindly. "My stepdaughter," he explained as the face disappeared and the door shut. "You'll meet her at lunch. With me." There was a warning in his voice.

Now Erich understood why he'd passed muster. It wasn't in spite of his size, it was because of it. Joe hadn't wanted an *übermensch* around his daughter. He'd wanted to know that even with one leg he could still defend her against the enemy who would be working at his farm.

He was used to being "the enemy." He'd been "the enemy" for years, ever since he was captured. He'd been despised in England and kept under careful control in Canada. But that wasn't about him, it was about all of them. It was strange to imagine that anyone might think that he, Erich Stein, was "the enemy." But on this isolated farm, it made sense.

The trees swayed at the edge of the cleared land, leaning in as if they wanted to reclaim what little space the Novaks had.

"Your wife is here too?" Erich asked in English, trying to be polite, but Joe shook his head, looking sad.

"Died three years back."

"Oh. Sorry."

George nodded at both of them. "I'll leave you to it, then. I'll be back at four."

The truck jolted and bumped its way back to the gate. Erich considered running over to open and close it, but didn't want that to be misunderstood as a dash for freedom, so he watched as George climbed out and did it himself. The truck disappeared in a haze of dust between the trees.

"Come on then," Joe said in English with a wave of his hand. "I'll show you what needs doing."

He headed toward the small barn near the treeline, half-hopping, half-swinging himself forward using the crutch. Erich was impressed with the speed of his rolling gait, using the stocky power of his upper arms as he propelled himself forward across the hard earth. There was a fluidity to his motions that Erich found surprising in a man who had only lost his leg a year ago. Joe was clearly not the kind of man to let things get in his way.

It was hard to see him as inferior, even though he had a Slavic name. He was taller than Erich and stronger, in spite of his age and injury. Perhaps he had Germanic blood after all.

It soon became obvious that Erich's job was to take care of the tasks that required two hands while standing or up a ladder. He spent the day fixing parts of their roof and guttering, and chopping wood. It was tough, physical labor, more than he was used to, and he still felt the weakness of his injury.

But watching Joe drove him on. Joe fed the pigs and shoveled their muck one-handed, while leaning on his crutch. He collected the chickens' eggs and weeded their vegetable patch, on his hands and knees. He helped Erich drag the larger logs into place for chopping. Every so often, Joe would glance at Erich's work and give an appreciative nod, which pushed Erich to work harder.

Not long after midday, the door to the house opened, and the ginger-haired girl called out.

"Lunch is ready!"

Joe nodded toward the house, Erich laid down the axe, and they headed up together. The muscles in Erich's upper arms burned, and the skin of his hands was hot. He wondered if blisters were forming. But it felt good.

Neumann was right. It was wonderful to be useful again.

He felt the softness of some of the boards on the front deck underfoot and found himself working out how to replace them. He was no carpenter, but Joe had probably done such fixes before, and between the two of them, it wouldn't be that hard.

Joe opened the door for him. Erich paused on the threshold, hit by a wave of vertigo.

For a moment he felt like he was looking at himself from a very long way away. As if he was his old self from the start of the war, wondering how he had come to this. How could he be happy to help a man the Fatherland was at war with? Happy to enter his home as a prisoner, a servant? He was a German. Wasn't he was meant to be better than this?

He focused on the house instead, as Joe led him along the worn wooden hall. He caught a glimpse of a living room through an open door, a faded rag rug on the floor. An old sofa was covered by a knitted blanket, an armchair sitting companionably close.

They arrived in the kitchen, led there by the enticing smell of onions and meat. It was a good size, with clean floors and a scrubbed wooden table in the middle, surrounded by three chairs. Sun shone through the south-facing window, casting shadows of leaves and branches on the floor, rippling like water as the wind moved them. The room was warm, no doubt from the iron stove in the corner, and in the middle of the table was a pot of what smelled and looked like chicken soup, with freshly made bread steaming to one side.

Daisy broke the bread between the three of them, giving her father a much larger piece than she gave herself. He didn't seem to notice. Erich tried to work out if she was younger or older than him. She looked nervous. "I'm afraid it's probably not as nice as you get at the camp."

Joe maneuvered himself into a chair with a grunt and propped the crutch up next to it. "We hear you get absolute feasts in there." He gave a sniff. "While the rest of us have to get by best we can."

Erich didn't understand all the words, but he got the sentiment.

"The food look delicious," he said in his best English, careful to keep his eyes on the soup, not the girl. She seemed to be doing her best to fade into the background anyway.

"You're recovering yourself, I hear," Joe said. "Leg injury."

"I am sorry. I am weak." He wanted to say "weaker than usual," but didn't have the words. "Getting better."

"You're doing fine, lad," Joe said.

A small knot of warmth formed in Erich's stomach.

There was no butter to go with the bread. Erich took a spoonful of his soup. The broth was weak and under-seasoned, with a few overcooked vegetables floating in it. No wonder Daisy was so thin. Erich felt awkward about the plenty back in the camp.

"Lovely," he said with a smile.

"Shall I put on the radio?" Daisy asked. Without waiting for a reply, she hurried over to a small box on the side and fiddled with the dial. A serious voice came through the crackling static. Erich wondered if he should be listening. In the camp, the only news allowed was from the official German announcements picked up by their illicit radios, although that didn't stop rumors spreading.

Erich didn't try to hear, but he couldn't help but catch a few words. The announcer spoke fast, but in a clear, clipped English. Something about Allied troops advancing on Caen from Cherbourg. He knew those were both cities in France, but where?

It didn't matter. It was propaganda. The Allies could not be advancing in France. That was what Meyer had said, and Meyer was a communist and a liar.

"Perhaps we should put on something else?" Joe said. He was staring at Erich with a look of concern. Erich realized he had paused with his soup spoon halfway to his mouth.

Daisy quickly adjusted the dial, looking pleased. "That was Daddy's program anyway. It's boring, and we're just in time for *The Happy Gang*."

Joe rolled his eyes at Erich, who hadn't followed at all and wasn't sure how to respond.

Polka music came on, then there was the sound of a knock at the door.

"*Who's there?*" called out the voice from the radio.

"*It's The Happy Gang from Toronto*," came the answer.

Erich was baffled, but Daisy beamed at the radio, enthralled. Erich noticed the pinkish hue in her pale cheeks. Her whole face had lit up.

He turned back to his soup quickly.

When George came to pick Erich up, he and Joe stepped to one side and talked too quietly for Erich to follow. But once they'd finished, and the ever-present paperwork was done, they both smiled at Erich.

"See you tomorrow," Joe said as George led him back to the truck.

Erich grinned and waved, glad he'd passed the test of the first day.

It was only once they were bumping along the dirt road again that Erich realized he hadn't worried about his mother for hours. He leaned back against the tattered seat. It had been a good day, even if his whole body felt soft, limp, and aching. It had been a new day in a life that had been without variety for a very long time.

And maybe, once he got back to the camp, there would be a letter waiting for him, letting him know that his mother was fine.

CHAPTER SIXTEEN

I ran into Asha in our shared kitchen on the morning of the first day back. I was surprised to see her there in a long, orange-and-yellow tie-dye dress, fingers weaved around a mug of steaming coffee. She'd obviously been waiting for me instead of heading straight to work, like she had before our break. I wondered if she'd got her hair touched up in the week at home, as no roots showed in her rainbow.

"I've decided how you can atone."

"What?" For a moment, I thought she was talking about Ruth's death. I couldn't imagine how I could possibly make that right.

"For going to the Hoppers' party."

I stared at her for a long few seconds, still waking up and astonished that after everything that had happened since, she'd come back to that.

"Oh. What did you decide?" I had visions of her demanding I call them fascists to their faces or throw red paint over something.

"You didn't like what they said about the library, right?"

"Yeah?"

"So prove it. The Drag Queen Story Time is this weekend. There's a group of people who'll be there to help out. You'll join us, right?"

Volunteering at the library actually sounded great. I could even put it on my resume. I couldn't believe she was letting me off so easily.

"Okay. Sure, absolutely."

Asha treated me to a dazzling smile. "It's this Saturday at eleven a.m. We'll go together."

I wasn't sure if I was being punished or getting a new friend.

Back at the museum, it was hard to concentrate. Sarah let us know that curfew had been moved to nine-thirty and demanded we all account for our movements whenever we weren't with her. None of us argued.

The office was quieter. Not from the loss of Ruth, who had hardly been there at all, but because Max wasn't his old self, clattering up and down the stairs and generally being sarcastic at people. He sat at an empty desk, staring into space, only waking into life when Sarah called for him. There were dark circles under his eyes. I wondered if he was having trouble sleeping too.

Randall didn't bother to acknowledge that we'd been away or that we'd returned. And if Ephram felt bad, it was impossible to tell, since he quietly went on with work as usual.

There was a comfort in slipping back into the old routine, in spite of Ruth being gone. I could slide into the scanned documents on the computer and, through them, into the rhythms of the camp. For the POWs: roll calls and work calls, meals, lessons, and lights out. For the guards: deliveries and shift changes, work duty transport, and daily reports.

Each day in the afternoon, the mail appeared on the front desk in reception. I always found an excuse to look through it, but there was nothing for Ruth. I wasn't even sure if she'd have gotten the DNA results sent here or to her home.

Once everyone had settled in again, I went to look for Sarah. I found her in the brightness of the pristine, cream-walled education room off the main gallery, elbow-deep in boxes filled with tissue paper. Modern plastic chairs were stacked to one side, along with a few folding tables. She barely looked up when I came in.

"Oh, hi Keira. Do you need something?"

"What were you and Ruth fighting about on the day before she died?"

She paused, the crinkling of the paper falling silent. She gave a sad kind of laugh. "Can't you guess?"

I shook my head.

"She wasn't doing her work. She hadn't turned in a single report about her meetings with Bertie."

I felt nauseated. "I haven't turned in a report either."

Sarah waved a hand. "But I know you're working hard. I've seen you up there in the office every day, reading. You've asked me how to find things, where to save your notes, you've requested access to the shared drives. Ruth did none of those things, she was never here, and there was no evidence of her work. That's why I asked her for a report, or at least her notes from her meetings. Repeatedly."

That didn't make me feel any better. I'd still got precisely nowhere in my investigation, in spite of that work.

"What did she mean when she said it wasn't 'up to you'?"

Sarah rolled her eyes. "I warned her that I'd have to terminate her place in the program if I didn't get something from her in the next week. I think she was planning to go over my head."

"To Peter Hopper?"

"He's the chair of the museum board. I get to hire and fire the museum staff, including students, but the board gets to hire and fire the curator, so I guess she thought he could overrule me."

That made total sense if she thought they were family. The next question was more awkward. "Umm … Ruth said that you had a secret. And if the Hoppers knew they wouldn't let you keep your job."

Sarah froze. "I … have no idea what that would be about. I don't have any secrets like that. I'm quite boring." She shook her head. "Anyway, you're not the only one who needs some answers around here. Where did Ruth get the drugs?"

It was my turn to feel uncomfortable. "I don't know."

That sounded odd now I said it out loud.

Sarah put her hands on her hips. "I packed up her things, so I know there were no drugs in her room, so it's not like she brought a stash from home. Nothing on her body either, apparently."

"Perhaps she didn't have much. Perhaps she took everything she had that night?"

"Or perhaps she got them from someone at the party you were all at." She fixed me with a glare like she was trying to see right through me.

"She could have, I guess. I don't know."

The floor creaked as she paced. "The board are asking questions." She stopped, staring at me again. "If you do hear anything, you had better let me know."

"I will." I started to head toward the door back to the main gallery.

"Oh, by the way, I got a phone call from a man in Kitchener. His father was a prisoner at the camp. He offered us a few items his dad left. I thought it might also be worth setting up a call and seeing if he knew anything about his dad's time here. He might not, but if you'd like to do the initial contact, I'll give you his email."

"That sounds great." At least I could write a report on that.

My mind turned back to Sarah's question as I made my way back up to the stuffy office in the attic. Where had Ruth got the drugs? When I thought it was weed, it was obvious; there had been people smoking by the fire, but LSD was something else altogether. No one else at the party seemed to be on that. Although, what did I know?

The thought continued to distract me as the morning crawled along, marked by the movement of the patch of sunlight from the attic window across the broadloom. Its oppressive heat approaching my desk, inch by inch. I tried to focus on the incident reports and hospital admission documents for the camp. There were fights, work refusals, and prisoners hiding for roll call, people admitted for pneumonia, cancer, and ongoing issues with war wounds.

My mind slid off the words. The sentences sunk into meaninglessness. I reread a paragraph three or four times, whispering it under my breath, but the feeling of flow I'd had before had evaporated. The information wouldn't go in, wouldn't form itself into coherent thought.

"Trouble concentrating?"

I glanced up. Max smiled at me, but it was just a shadow of his usual sly grin.

"You've been staring at that same document forever."

I sighed. "It's just hard, you know?"

"Lunch at Sal's? My treat. I could use a break too."

I rubbed my forehead. My eyes felt dry, and the sharp square of sunlight had reached the corner of my desk.

"That sounds good. Thanks."

The road from the museum into town lacked sidewalks most of the way. Although there weren't many cars, the ones that passed went fast, kicking up dust and grit. Max and I sometimes had to step so close on the dry grass of the narrow verge that our shoulders or arms brushed. I was acutely aware of the touch of his skin on my bare arm, but he made no attempt to avoid it. Neither did I.

Sal's was a tiny, red-and-white tiled take-out place on Westonville's main street that looked like it wanted to be a diner when it grew up. It was boiling inside; if they even had A/C, it was totally overpowered by the grill and the boiling vats of fat.

It wasn't much better outside. There was no breeze to blunt the heat. I pressed the cool of my Coke can against my forehead as we wandered along the road, burgers clutched in checkered, greaseproof paper. The buns were soggy but the patties were dry, so it kind of balanced out. I tried not to drip the bright orange "special" sauce onto my white T-shirt, with limited success. Max pointed out houses and shops, telling me stories about the local oddballs, like the store owner who was so afraid of shoplifting teens that she insisted on serving all under-eighteens from the doorway, blocking the way in with her body as if they were about to try to rush past and ransack the place.

"That," he pointed out a Money Mart, "was a taco place for a while. They added ketchup to all their burritos unless you specifically asked them not to." He shuddered. "It must be great living in Toronto."

I tried not to think about my mother leaving, about losing the apartment that didn't even feel like home. "It's pretty good."

"I can't wait to get out of this town."

"Is that the plan? What about your grandfather?"

He kicked at a pebble. "I might have to put off university for a few years and stay here to look after him. I . . ." He was quiet for a bit, staring ahead of us, down the street. "I don't like to think about it, but he can't live forever. I just want to make sure his last years are okay. I don't want Peter and Jules to dump him in a home and claim he's lost it."

"You care about him a lot."

Max forced a smile. "He's, like, my only real family. I never had a dad and my mom wasn't exactly attentive. Even before she bailed for Europe, it was always Granddad who was there for me." He took a deep breath, blinking hard. "Ruth's death has broken his heart. If he ended up in some home too, it'd kill him."

I looked away, not wanting to make him feel awkward, but I was touched by how much he cared for Bertie. We were walking past a small church, built of orangey-red stone. A stained-glass window was set into the wall above the door, and a gray steeple rose above that.

"Is that the church where Harry's memorial is?"

"Yes." Max seemed happy with the change of subject. "Want to see it?"

"I'd love to."

"Around here." Max led me through the gate and into the churchyard, bumpy with old burials. Scattered unevenly over the dry grass was a mixture of shiny, dark granite gravestones and older ones, crooked and blotchy with lichen. A few large memorials demanded attention, emblazoned with what were no doubt once powerful local names: FISHER, BROWN, and, of course, HOPPER.

Max led me toward the latter, a plain gray obelisk. Harold's first name was much smaller than his last, and his short life was etched out in stark dates: October 3, 1926–April 16, 1945.

"On April 30, Hitler blew his brains out," Max said.

I shook my head, imagining how that felt for poor little Bertie. He'd have heard about the Allied advances, the victories. Everyone knew the end of the war was coming. I took a deep breath, looking up at the trees. Not a leaf moved in the stifling stillness. The blue shimmer of a darting dragonfly caught my eye.

"When was the last time Bertie saw him? Did he get to come home on leave?"

Max's brow furrowed. "I think he had time off after he finished basic training, then he was sent directly to Halifax. So right before, probably."

I nodded. Ruth's grandmother had to have been conceived in March or April 1945, so that worked out.

"Must have been so hard for him."

"Hello!" An old man in a blue shirt was striding over the graves toward us, sleeves neatly rolled up and one hand raised in greeting.

Max waved as he approached. "Reverend Campos, this is Keira, one of the students at the museum."

The reverend's smile moved up a notch. He had a big, brown mole on the corner of his mouth. I thought it was food stuck there for a moment. I tried not to stare at it.

"Ah, another one. Lovely to meet you, Keira. I see Maxwell is showing you the local sights."

Another one. I mentally filed that away. Ruth had clearly come here to see Harry's monument.

He reached us and put his hands on his hips. We all looked at the gray obelisk together, like we were waiting for it to do something. "Such a tragedy," the reverend said with a sigh.

"It's nice that the town put this up for him," I said.

"Harold Hopper was much loved around here, and long remembered. You know, when I first started here, there'd be flowers on this memorial every year on April 16. A big bunch of black-eyed Susans."

I wasn't sure what to say, so I went with general politeness. "That's nice. When did you start here?"

"In the eighties. Apparently, the flowers appeared every year, but no one knew who was leaving them."

"When did they stop?"

The reverend shrugged. "Mid-nineties, I guess."

Exactly when Ruth's great-grandmother had died.

"Rumor has it, they were from a local girl. I heard he was quite the ladies' man. A real pin-up." He nodded at Max and raised his eyebrows at me. "Runs in the family, don't you think?"

I wanted one of the graves to open up and swallow me right there and then. There was an uncomfortable silence where I knew I should say something. Absolutely nothing came to mind.

"Um, we should probably be getting back to work," Max said eventually.

The day felt unnaturally still, silence replacing the usual rustle and hiss of the trees and undergrowth as we walked back to the museum. The cars that broke the quiet felt brash, too loud on such a hushed day. One of those extra-loud motorcycles went by, where the rider might as well be shouting "Look at me! Look at me!" like a five-year-old desperate for attention.

"I should have taken away her wine earlier," Max said, when the silence returned.

"I should have insisted she come with us."

"I didn't know the lake could be so deadly." He shook his head. "But Granddad wasn't surprised. He says the lake has always been dangerous. Harry and George used to go there all the time, but George wouldn't let Granddad come because he wasn't a strong swimmer."

"I don't think any of us could have guessed what would happen."

We'd slowed as we talked. Our feet scuffed against the road. I reached out and put a hand on his shoulder. "You weren't to blame. You didn't know. And you weren't the only local there. Someone could have warned us that it was dangerous."

I felt awkward about touching him as soon as I'd done it, but Max reached up with his hand and touched my fingers briefly. "Thanks."

I let go, remembering Sarah's question. There were indeed lots of locals at the party. And every small town and suburb had someone to go to when you wanted to get high.

"Was there someone at the party who sold drugs?"

Max looked surprised by the question. "Um … probably. I can't say I'm exactly plugged in to that sort of thing. I used to smoke a bit of weed, but I could just order that online with Granddad's details and get it sent to the house. I quit about a year back."

I nodded.

"And if you were looking, I do have a medicine cabinet full of goodies prescribed to my granddad." He caught sight of my expression. "Joking! Obviously. Unless you have high blood pressure and pre-diabetes, then I've totally got you covered."

"Sarah was just asking where Ruth could have gotten the acid."

"Oh, yeah. That makes sense. Could she have brought it to Westonville?"

"Maybe. But there was nothing in her room."

The road ahead shimmered, mirages of puddles forming in the dips in the distance, silvered and shiny as a mirror. The sun beat down, and I felt a little lightheaded.

He shrugged. "Sorry I'm not much help. I don't even go to the school in town. I go to an independent school half an hour away. And I used to spend summers in Europe until Granddad got frail."

No wonder he didn't know the local dealer. He was barely a local himself.

"But I'm glad I got to spend this summer here, despite everything." He gave me a soft, almost nervous smile and bumped his shoulder gently against mine.

And, just like that, it wasn't the heat making me feel dizzy.

CHAPTER SEVENTEEN

July–August 1944

There was no letter waiting for Erich at camp.

Still, he slept well that night. Better than he had in a long time, physical exhaustion providing the unconsciousness that had eluded him. The next morning, his whole body screamed in protest as he rose, shoulders feeling like a solid bruise. He barely noticed the wound on his leg against the pulled muscles in his calves as he swung his legs over the side of the bed.

"Feeling better?" Lang asked him as they waited in line at roll call. In spite of all his aches, Erich grinned and nodded.

"See what I mean?" Neumann said as they lined up by the gate, clapping him hard on his sore back. Erich winced.

And so it went, with him juddering along the road to the wildness of the farm during the day and returning to the regimented barbed wire of the camp at night and for weekends. He grew familiar with Joe and Daisy arguing over the radio at lunch as they ate meatloaf, fried Spam, apple brown betty, and baked custard. Daisy always won. Erich suspected Joe gave in as much to protect him from bad news as to indulge his stepdaughter. He got to know *The Happy Gang* from Toronto, with their skits and songs. They talked fast, so the jokes were hard to follow, but the songs were easier, especially as they repeated phrases and choruses. He even found himself humming "There'll Always Be an England" when he was digging in the heavy, dark earth one day.

He stopped. It wouldn't do to be caught humming that in the camp. For a moment, he felt as if he were suspended over his old life, balanced on a tightrope. He shook his head and wiped the sweat on the dirty gray sleeve of his POW shirt. He remembered doing the same on his Afrika Korps uniform in the dry heat of the desert while clutching his useless rifle, jammed with sand.

He wasn't the same man he'd been then.

He leaned on his spade. Thinking like that was dangerous. He was still a German. He hummed "We March Against England," trying to get the traitorous verses from *The Happy Gang* out of his head.

Queedle, queedle, queedle, called a bird from the trees. In reply or competition, Erich couldn't tell.

Erich's English improved faster than it had in the camp. Before long, he understood Joe's jokes: usually puns and always told with a straight face. Slowly, Daisy joined in as well, and their lunches were filled with laughter. Her humor was cheekier than her father's, and she poked fun at his skinny frame and lack of muscles. Erich knew she was off-limits, but he came to look forward to her calling them in each day, to seeing her face over lunch and the challenge in her eyes.

One day, right at the end of July, he returned to what felt like a different camp. Usually, there were men sitting or lying back in the grass, often with a beer; men playing soccer; men walking together, gesturing and laughing. This afternoon, they clustered in tight, small groups, voices quiet.

Erich found Lang in their hut. "What's happening?"

Lang nodded at the door in answer. Erich followed him outside, but Lang didn't start talking until they reached the wire that marked the closest point the prisoners were allowed to the fence. Between the fences, a sparrow took a dirt bath, rustling and fluffing its wings until it was more ball than bird.

"Meyer's dead."

Erich remembered the vivid purple of the communist's face as he was brought into the hospital, his split lip bleeding down his chin.

"What happened?"

"Someone tried to murder Hitler; that's what happened."

Erich put out his hand to steady himself, but there was nothing to grab. He wobbled for a moment. "What? When? Is he okay?"

"He's fine. Apparently, it happened a while ago. News is just getting through now. A bomb went off in a room he was in. It was army officers who wanted to surrender, they say, and some quite high-up ones, too. They very nearly succeeded." Lang sounded distraught.

Erich wanted to sit down, but they kept walking. It seemed impossible that anyone would even get close to killing the Führer. He'd never really thought of him as a mortal man. It made the world feel unsteady, horribly unreliable.

He could feel the eyes on him from the nearest guard tower, and he realized he'd got too close to the warning wire. He turned his steps away from it, directing them more toward the hospital hut. He glanced up at the scaffold rising above. The sun was in his eyes, and he couldn't see the men within. The tower was a silhouette, a simple outline. He could almost pretend it was a child's treehouse looming above. But it was a treehouse with guns pointed at him.

"The Führer said that it's the duty of Germans to execute all traitors."

"Meyer," Erich said, as things fell into place.

Lang nodded.

"What happened to him?"

"An accident at the logging camp. That's the official word, anyway, and the Canadians seem to have bought it. But everyone here knows the truth."

Erich nodded. They kept walking. A moth fluttered ahead of him, wings grazing the grass. He stepped carefully, to avoid crushing its delicate body.

Lang's hands were pushed deep into his pockets, hunching his shoulders over. "You need to be careful." His voice was soft.

"What? Why?"

"Men who work closely with Canadians are seen as less trustworthy. Less loyal."

"I am loyal!" Hadn't he proved himself enough with his silence, his weeks in the hospital? But he remembered humming "There'll Always Be an England," and his cheeks heated.

"I know that. I'm just saying, be careful."

"What should I do?"

"Up to you. If you want them to know you're loyal, maybe you should join in a bit with some of the chants or songs."

The prisoners weren't allowed to call out "Heil Hitler" or sing Nazi songs. Being "political" was officially banned in the camp. But that didn't stop them, especially at roll call. The more militant men took pride in their time in the punishment hut for such petty acts of rebellion.

"You don't."

Lang shrugged. "And I'm under suspicion."

"You are?" Erich turned to look at his friend. Lang stared ahead, his chin dirty with stubble. There was a hint of darkness on his cheekbone, too. A bruise? When had that happened?

"Stein!" The call came from the hospital hut. Dr. Bauer was in the doorway. "Do you have a minute?"

Erich glanced at Lang, but he was already waving him away. "We'll talk later."

Erich nodded, feeling dizzy. He headed toward the hospital. The ground felt treacherous, laced with landmines that everyone but him could see.

The doctor stood in his white coat, and Erich remembered what Schmitt had said, back when he was injured — that he didn't trust Dr. Bauer. That made a kind of sense. Dr. Bauer got on well with the Red Cross representatives and the Swiss visitors. He worked closely with the Canadians, too.

"This way, Stein."

Dr. Bauer was all smiles as he led Erich past the hospital beds holding lounging or sleeping men. Bruises and bandages stood out on some. Others sweated, faces unnaturally pale. A few sat up under their neatly folded blankets, their ailments invisible. The room stank of disinfectant, barely covering the sickly sweet scent of flesh turning bad.

The doctor led Erich into his small office at the end of the ward. He asked him how the work at the farm was going and complimented him on the weight he had gained. He said he'd heard that Joe Novak was very happy with him and that he was a hard worker.

But once they sat down on the hard wooden chairs, his expression switched to concern.

“It’s been hard to get information from home lately, but we did manage to get news about your mother. I would have hesitated to break this to you a month or so ago. But I can see how much better you are doing.”

Erich leaned forward, unable to breathe. The room was tight around him. Dr. Bauer’s fingers skittered over the wood of the table before he brought them under control and pressed his palms together, like a prayer.

“I’m so sorry. Your home was bombed nearly three months ago. Your mother is dead.”

CHAPTER EIGHTEEN

I wasn't sure how to approach Ephram. Honestly, I was intimidated by him. He was more composed than anyone else my age, like a professor in the body of a teenager.

My nervousness made it hard for me to concentrate. He sat there, back so straight a Victorian would envy his posture. I'd barely talked to him, other than the briefest of polite but inconsequential conversations when we were both in the common room and Ruth wasn't there.

I tried to work as I waited for my opportunity. I re-read passages from the camp's war diary several times, trying to make the words go in. George Wright's name came up again as he was off on a long sick leave in spring 1945, coming back a month before he found Erich's body. Was that relevant? I couldn't focus enough to think clearly about it.

Just after one p.m., Randall left to do whatever Randall did around lunchtime. He was never gone for long enough to eat a proper meal, and given his bony frame and deathly pale skin, I suspected he quickly drained the blood of a sheep. Ephram had taken his normal-human-length lunch at twelve, so he was back to tap-tapping away productively as usual.

I stood, glad to leave my sun-drenched desk for the relative shade of the rest of the office, and wandered over, as casually as I could. I felt like I was approaching a teacher to explain why my homework was late.

I went with "Hi." Classic opening.

Ephram paused in his typing and looked up. "Hi?" he said, as if trying out this "small talk" thing for the first time.

"I don't think I ever asked you what your project was on."

He leaned back and let his hands drop into his lap. "DeNazification."

Obviously prompted by my baffled expression, he continued. "The Allies took a number of different approaches to try to change the minds of the most committed Nazis in the camps. They worried that sending them back to Germany with such extreme views would just lead to more wars."

I had only asked as an opener, but this genuinely sounded interesting and alarmingly relevant these days. I could see what Peter Hopper had meant about it being university-level.

"Did it work?"

Ephram tipped a hand side to side. "Kind of. Propaganda failed completely. No one likes having someone else's opinion shoved down their throats. What did work was just letting them see a different way of being. Those that were open-minded enough saw a prosperous country that wasn't geared toward total war and purging their own people of everyone who didn't fit the narrow Nazi mold. It was far from perfect, of course. Stolen land, residential schools, Canadian-Japanese internment camps, and so on. But I don't think former Nazis were that bothered about that."

Or anti-2SLGBTQ+ sentiment, of course.

"So that's why the camp had, like, nice food and all that? To win them over?"

"That was mostly because they hoped that if we treated their POWs well, they'd treat our POWs well too. And we did treat them well. Better than we treated Japanese-Canadians. But the fact that many enjoyed their time here definitely helped with reducing extremism. Lots didn't want to go back. Six thousand applied to stay."

"Wow. How many were accepted?"

"None. They were all sent home. But many emigrated in the fifties."

Like the father of the man I'd be interviewing. I really needed to draft some questions for that call. And to get to the point with Ephram. I decided to just go for it.

"Um … You had an argument with Ruth on the first night we were here. I kind of overheard a bit of it, although I didn't mean to. What was it about?"

Ephram exhaled and pushed up his glasses. "Well, I suppose it probably doesn't matter now. But Ruth was a fraud."

"A fraud? In what way?"

"Her awards, her references: all faked."

I think I blinked. "What?"

"She claimed to have won the Toronto Big Brothers Big Sisters' Big Sister of the Year award last year, which I knew was impossible. My girlfriend won that." There was a touch of pride in his words. "I went to the gala and Ruth definitely wasn't there. I was able to check a couple of her other prizes online. She didn't win those, either. When I confronted her, she admitted that her references were from fake email addresses she'd set up."

I tried to digest the new information, tried to restructure my brain around it. Ruth wasn't the overachieving genius I thought she was.

"That's why you said she didn't belong here."

"I promised I wouldn't tell Sarah, and I didn't. I still haven't." He rubbed at his temple. "But it's good to be able to tell someone, not that it makes any difference now."

"I don't suppose you know where she got the drugs?"

He gave a little snort. "She wasn't exactly going to share information like that with me."

The stairs up to the office creaked. Randall had probably finished with his sheep. We both glanced over.

"Thanks. I appreciate you telling me," I said, shuffling back to my desk as Randall re-entered.

Ephram gave me a small smile as I settled back down, then returned to his usual speed-typing. Clouds clustered above the skylight, softening the sharp square of the sun on my desk. I wondered if I was imagining it, or if there was a touch less tension in the stuffy room, in spite of the return of Randall's glower.

Of course, there was still no way I could concentrate on my work. If Ruth wasn't an award-winning brainiac, who was she? A girl who thought she might be a member of a rich and powerful family, clearly. A girl who was so determined to come to Westonville to prove it that she lied and faked references. She'd wasted no time making friends with Bertie and sucking up to Peter and Julia. She might only have been weeks away from getting the proof she needed.

But she said she'd fought with Julia. Over what? And why had she wanted to get high on acid on her own? That was weird, wasn't it?

Sarah was right. We needed to know where she got the drugs. I needed to speak to Asha. It was her party, and she'd been the one to invite the locals.

I muttered something about the bathroom under my breath and headed down the stairs. On my way through the museum's reception, I spotted the usual pile of mail balanced on the corner of the desk. It was mostly flyers, but the corner of a brown envelope peeked out between the colorful sheets.

I flipped through. The brown envelope was addressed to Sarah, but there was a white letter below it. Ruth's name was printed neatly on the front, and the logo of the DNA lab was in the corner.

The reception was empty. Everyone was hard at work. I could try to sneak the envelope to my room and read it in private, but my current skirt and sauce-stained white shirt combo lacked pockets. But if I could open it, scan through it quickly, and return it to the pile, no one would ever know.

I flipped it over, and opened it carefully along the flap, checking around me. All was still, empty frosted glass desks waiting for the opening at the end of the summer. I took my time, easing the envelope open without tearing it. The glue was weak, and I pulled out the letter from the un-ripped envelope triumphantly.

There were several pages. I glimpsed charts and graphs in color, but I focused on the first page. The re: line said *Results of Kinship Autosomal DNA Testing*. Bingo.

I glanced around. A flash of rainbow hair moved past the wide windows at the side of the building, heading toward the entrance. I doubted she was coming in, but still, I tried to decipher the letter as fast as I could. The whole thing was pretty technical. A couple of phrases stood out in the information about ranges and probabilities.

0 CM match between two samples; Statistically unlikely.

Did that mean Ruth wasn't related to Bertie?

I folded the letter hastily and shoved it back in the envelope. The automatic doors hummed open, bringing a brief blast of heat into the air-conditioned foyer. I was holding the letter in one hand, pressing down on the flap, trying to stick it back down as Asha approached. I tried to look casual, leaning on the glass desk. I don't think it worked, which made sense. Who leans like that innocently?

"What are you doing?"

"Just checking to see if I got any mail."

She pushed some hair behind her ear. "Are you expecting something?"

"Nothing in particular."

"What's that?" She pointed at the white letter in my hand.

I gave the flap a last squeeze and held it out to her, hoping the seal would hold. "It's for Ruth. I was going to give it to Sarah to send on to her family."

She turned it over, reading the front. "Did you open it?"

I shook my head, pressing my lips together. "Nope. It came like that."

"DNA testing. That's really private." She gave me a searching look. It was time to change the subject.

"Do you know where Ruth got the drugs from? That night, I mean."

Asha kept looking down at the letter.

"There must be someone people go to in Westonville, right? And it seems like you know everyone around here."

"What does it matter where she got them from?"

It was a good question. I went with the honest answer. "Sarah asked me, and the question's been bugging me. Something seems off. Like it's not what it seems, you know?"

Asha sighed. "I'm sorry. I know she was your friend for some reason. But I don't think there's some big puzzle here. She probably just bought a tab from Colt."

"Colt?"

Asha flinched, as if she hadn't meant to say his name. "An asshole from the trailer park. He was at the party. I didn't invite him."

"What does he look like?"

She held the letter back up again. The flap was loose at the edges. "Are you sure you didn't open this?"

"I'm sure."

Asha put it back on the pile. "I'll take these up to Sarah. And Keira, don't do this to yourself. Accidents happen."

Again, the long stare. I tried to look innocent, then realized I wasn't the one who needed to look innocent.

Asha hated Ruth and the Hoppers. Asha apparently knew who the drug dealer was. Asha was meant to be taking care of Ruth. But then again, so was Ephram and he hated Ruth too. But did either of them hate her enough to kill her?

That didn't feel right. If they'd been involved with her death, wouldn't they at least try to hide their disdain for her?

There was a more likely suspect, after all. One who had access to the drugs that might have killed Ruth, who was right there at the party when she died.

Thanks to Asha, I had a name and a place to start looking for him.

CHAPTER NINETEEN

August–October 1944

Erich barely heard the rest of what Dr. Bauer said. His mother was dead. She'd been dead for months.

Erich stumbled back to his hut, climbed into his bed without talking to anyone, and turned to face the wall. Rain thrummed on the tin ceiling of the hut. He hadn't noticed when it started, hadn't noticed getting soaked on the way back. It drowned out the conversations and clatter of the other men, leaving him cocooned in his own distress, clammy in his wet clothes.

The next morning, he missed breakfast but lined up for roll call, and then at the gate, jerking through the motions like an automaton. Stand here, wait. Sign here, walk here, wait. Get in the truck, wait.

Erich stared at the fields lurching nauseatingly past the window, at the splash of mud on the glass. George asked what was wrong. Erich shook his head. He was afraid that if he opened his mouth, he'd start crying and wouldn't be able to stop. He couldn't bear to do that, not in front of a Canadian guard. Not in front of anyone.

He was signed over at the farm, and heard George speaking quietly to Joe, who nodded and glanced his way. Erich wasn't sure if it was concern or suspicion in his gaze. He got on with his work in silence. Joe made his usual jokes, and Erich tried to smile in the right places, feeling as if he wasn't really there at all. Joe asked him if he was okay, several times. Erich nodded every time.

Later, he found himself staring at his own hand as he steadied a block, ready to cut it in half. If he swung at his wrist, rather than the wood, would it hurt? Would he feel it at all, or would his hand just fall into the pile, like yet another chopped branch?

Joe went inside while Erich was pulling up some weeds, and it took Erich a while to notice he was alone. Joe never left him alone. Erich straightened up, the breeze on his face.

This was the freest he had been in years. He could run now, if he wanted.

It would be madness, of course. He'd be caught in no time, or would die in the boggy land around. And he also gave his word, as a German soldier, that he wouldn't try to escape while he was at the farm. That was important. Or, at least, it had felt that way, once.

Nothing felt important now. A long, piercing birdcall came from the damp trees on the near horizon. He could run into them right now, but then what? Did it even matter?

A soft voice made him turn. Daisy's voice. He thought she was calling him in for lunch, but she sat down on the old wooden bench on the front deck of the house. She patted the empty space next to her.

Erich waved at the house. "Joe?"

"He said I should talk to you, as you won't talk to him."

Erich thought he'd have been surprised on any other day, but nothing could surprise him now. He dropped the wet weeds into the wheelbarrow. He pulled off the work gloves and slumped up the muddy field toward the deck.

No doubt Joe was in the living room. Close enough to hear if Daisy cried out, but far enough to give him a little privacy. Joe was no fool, especially when it came to his stepdaughter.

"You aren't okay, are you?"

Erich wasn't sure if he wanted to pretend or explain. But all he could do was sit next to her. The wooden bench creaked under him. Daisy looked as if she was going to reach for his hand, but instead, she curled her fingers around the air a few inches away.

A chicken squawked, the strangled sound half-swallowed by the hushed hiss of the trees around the small farm. Footsteps half full of rainwater glistened in the morning sun, like still pools of silver. The deck smelled of drying wood.

"What's happened? News from home?"

He tried to hold his face still. He really did. But it was the effort of understanding, of going from "home" to *Heim*, to *Heimat*, and everything untranslatable that word held, everything that was gone or twisted, that undid him.

His face crumpled. He knew he must look like a child, but he couldn't stop the tears, even as the shame washed over him.

Daisy shuffled closer, put an arm around his shoulder, and that somehow made things worse, and he was sobbing so hard breath wouldn't come. She patted his arm, a little awkwardly.

"Who?"

He had to say something. He couldn't just make a fool of himself like this without an explanation.

"My … mother." Then sobs swallowed his words again. "Bombs."

She stared at him for a long few seconds. Tears gathered in her own eyes.

"I wish there was something I could say. But there isn't. I don't know what anyone could have said to me. I'm so sorry."

Erich remembered, belatedly, that she'd lost her own mother just three years ago.

"And you're so far from home. Oh, Erich. Oh, how awful."

He hadn't expected this. Joe and Daisy were kind, but their countries were at war. It was Allied bombs that had killed his mother. Bombs that could have been dropped by a Canadian, perhaps someone they knew. She wasn't meant to be sad about it.

It didn't seem to matter to Joe and Daisy that Erich and his mother were the enemy. And, oddly, it didn't seem to matter to him that it was their side that had killed her. Here, on the small farm in the middle of nowhere, the war felt pointless, a hallucination no more real than his mother on the parade ground.

It was something they were all caught up in, not something they were a part of.

Weakened by his loss, held in Daisy's arms, a fracture in Erich cracked open.

From that day on, his life split into two.

He spent his mornings, evenings, and nights at the camp. Standing in line for roll call was painful, sorrow burrowing into his bones as he waited to be counted and dismissed so he could lie down on his bunk, alone. It wasn't that his fellow soldiers were unsympathetic, but there was too much loss, too much anger. Bad news became a steady drumbeat, pounding regularly through the camp.

The week after Erich heard about his mother, Karl learned his beloved brother had been shot down and killed. He, like Erich, was submerged in grief, their sorrow separating them like dark water. They floundered in a sea of it, unable to keep themselves afloat, never mind each other.

Each morning, George drove Erich to the Novaks'. Erich guessed Joe had told George about his mother, as he treated Erich with a quiet kindness. It wasn't that George had been cruel before, but he left more space around him. He no longer expected him to climb out of the car the moment they pulled up. He let Erich sit in the passenger seat as he took care of the paperwork with Joe.

Erich's days on the farm now began in the kitchen with coffee with Joe and Daisy. They chatted about the day ahead, eager for Erich's opinion on the work. Each morning, Joe said Erich could rest, if he wanted, and each morning, Erich insisted he wanted to help.

He wasn't lying. At the camp, he had no desire for anything other than oblivion. He was a prisoner, a faceless and replaceable soldier in the massive, brutal system that had killed his mother and sent him halfway across the world. At the farm, he was a person again, and he was useful. He could fix leaks and weed the vegetable patch. He could replace the rotten wood in the chicken coop and patch up the pig trough. He could leave each day knowing he'd made Joe and Daisy's lives a little easier.

When he'd signed up, he'd believed in glory and grandeur, in setting the world to rights and cutting the corruption out of Germany. He'd believed in the Reich's thousand-year destiny and its role in leading the world. He wanted to be a hero. But the war had smashed the world to pieces and ripped his mother away. He couldn't fix any of that. It was all too broken.

But on the farm, he could make things better, even if it was something that would need fixing again soon, like a blocked gutter. Even if it was only in ways so small no one but he, Joe, and Daisy would notice.

That, he learned, was enough.

CHAPTER TWENTY

I barely slept on Friday night. I stayed up, hunched over my phone until my back ached, room lit only by the ghostly light of my screen. Shadows shifted around me as I googled DNA autosomal results and tried to make sense of the scraps I'd seen of Ruth's letter. The museum was quiet, and I was too aware of the creak of the box-spring mattress as I shifted to stay comfortable at the edge of the bed, cursing my short, slow charger that kept me chained to the opposite wall.

I hated how silent it was here. It felt like the whole world was listening. I hadn't dared look anything up at work, and Ephram had unexpectedly joined me in the common room after work, reading a book on the armchair. I watched a documentary on astrophysics, too embarrassed to put on a reality show in front of him. I wasn't sure if he was being unusually friendly, or if he, like Asha, suspected something. Still, I appreciated the company. It had been hard being alone in the evenings.

It took a while to figure out the DNA stuff. The sites were technical and confusing, and it was tough to find information on how much DNA there would be in common in distant relationships like great-granduncle to great-grandniece. But I did learn that CM stood for centimorgans, apparently a unit of genetic linkage.

The fact that Ruth and Bertie had zero in common spoke for itself. I guessed Ruth's family rumor was just that: a rumor. It seemed strange that she'd been so wrong. She'd seemed so confident at the party, so sure she just needed the evidence. It was so easy to bring her to mind: the way she flipped her hair and threw her head back when she laughed. She'd filled up the space around her.

Even in the silence in my room, Ruth was there.

A whisper of wind could have been her turning in the bed in the next room. She was at the edge of everything: in my mind's eye, in the corner of my vision. She wasn't in the office, but during the day it was easy to imagine she was simply out at Bertie's. It was difficult to remember her body was rotting in the dark ground, miles away. Or maybe she'd been cremated, and was already ash, thrown to the wind.

The LSD thing nagged at me, too. There was definitely a dealer there that night, but acid was a weird choice. Who decides to drop that at a party where everyone's mad at her? I was no expert, but some more online searching confirmed what my embarrassingly little knowledge had suggested: it was an obvious recipe for a bad trip.

I yawned and shifted again. My leg was cramping up. I stretched it out, gazing at the small, dirty window. The trees outside held their secrets tight. As a city girl, it was easy to forget that Canada was still mostly wilderness — wilds that had eaten Ruth whole.

Maybe Ruth's fight with Julia had been worse than she'd let on. Maybe she was scared she wouldn't be welcomed into the family as a long-lost cousin. Maybe she wanted to forget about it all and asked Colt for something fun. Maybe that was the only thing he had to sell, or maybe he got stuff mixed up?

There was only one person who could answer my questions, and finding him online was even harder than translating the technicalese on the DNA websites. All I had to go on was "Colt" in Westonville. It wasn't enough. There were plenty of Colts, but none I could tie to the town. I wasn't even sure if that was his real name or a nickname.

My search for trailer parks went much better. There was only one anywhere near town: Tall Pines Mobile Home Park. He had to be there. It was a forty-minute walk, and apparently, they'd never heard of buses in Westonville. But the next day was Saturday. I had plenty of time to walk to the trailer park and back.

I had no idea what I was going to say to this Colt guy, but I'd have plenty of time to think on the way over.

Loud banging on my bedroom door the next morning hauled me out of a confusing dream about Ruth and Erich Stein snorting cocaine together.

"Come on," Asha's voice came through the door. "Or we'll be late!"

I grabbed my phone, suddenly sure it was Friday and I'd got my days confused and was late for work. But the screen showed 9:52 a.m. on Saturday.

"Wha?" I managed.

"The Drag Queen Story Time! It's at eleven. You're not breaking your promise, are you?"

Crap. I'd totally forgotten about that.

“No, no. Of course not.” I rolled out of bed. “Just give me five minutes, okay?”

I really was only five minutes, but Asha was in a total mood as we left the house together.

She strode ahead of me, rainbow skirt floating behind her as she stomped along the road to town in her big black boots. I’d pulled on a short-sleeved, button-up shirt with some black jeans, hoping to look neat-ish for volunteering, but, of course, I was even more crumpled than usual. It was overcast, the sky the color of my coffee-deprived headache.

“I thought you said it was at eleven.”

She kept a step ahead of me, as if that half-second of extra speed would make a difference when we arrived. “Turning up when it starts is way too late.”

“Sorry.” I was a little out of breath trying to keep up. “What exactly are we doing at the library again?”

“Keeping right-wing nutjobs away.”

“What?”

“We’re making sure the families who attend aren’t bothered by the protestors.”

I’d imagined we’d be ticking names off a registration list or something. “There are going to be protestors? In Westonville? But it’s tiny!”

“This isn’t about Westonville. Ever since the Hoppers mentioned the event at their rally, it’s been picked up by Twitter and some nasty far-right discussion boards.”

“Oh.” I swallowed. A car swiped past, too close to the shoulder, kicking up gravel that pattered against my jeans. How did I keep getting caught up in political things?

Asha turned and smiled. "Don't worry. I've been to this kind of thing before. There'll probably just be a few protestors. Our job is to keep them at a distance from the library and play fun music to drown them out. That way they won't scare the children." She harrumphed. "For people who claim to care so much about kids, they sure like to scream and swear at them a lot."

I nodded, not sure what to say.

Asha slowed a little, and moved farther onto the shoulder, where she had to stomp on undergrowth in order to walk alongside me, the soft squeak of my sneakers matching the crunch of her boots on the dry plants.

"I have to admit, I wasn't sure if you'd come."

"You weren't?"

"I mean, you said you were horrified by their rally, but there's a big difference between thinking something is wrong and doing something about it. Especially with the Hoppers dangling a scholarship in front of you."

I was trying not to think about the Hoppers. Hoping they wouldn't be there, hoping I wouldn't be putting the scholarship in jeopardy.

"Yeah," I managed. "Of course."

"Most people claim they care about marginalized groups, but they'll happily throw them under the bus if it suits them. Promise you'll make the trains run on time or lower taxes or inflation a little, and people will cheerfully vote for someone who'll rip families apart and put other human beings in concentration camps. People choose their own self-interest over others all the time."

"Yeah," I said awkwardly.

"I know you need that money. But you're still coming. You are choosing the right thing over making your life easier. Not a lot of people would do that. Historically, not enough people have done that."

"Thanks." I didn't say that I was hoping that doing the right thing and going to university wouldn't be an either/or situation.

We reached the main road where the sidewalk started. It felt like the clouds trapped the heat, pushing it down on us. I wished I'd worn a skirt, like her.

"I'm glad you're coming today," Asha said.

"Me too," I said, even though it wasn't totally true.

We approached the library from the crossroad, cutting through the Beer Store parking lot. Murmurings and occasional raised voices came from just out of sight: the sounds of a crowd. One woman's voice dominated, angry to the point of almost shrieking. I couldn't make out what she was saying. Asha's brow furrowed.

We came around the corner of the brick building and into an actual mob bristling with signs.

KEEP GROOMERS AWAY FROM KIDS; WAKE UP! THIS IS CHILD ABUSE; PEDOPHILE STORY TIME.

Asha froze. "Oh my God."

A handful of police there tried to maintain some space between what I could now see were two groups of people filling the road: the anti-2SLGBTQ+ mass in front of us, and another group with rainbow flags and *LIBRARIANS ARE SUPERHEROES* and *LOVE NOT HATE* signs. The library was a one-storey, concrete-and-glass-fronted building behind them.

"Come on." Asha grabbed my wrist and dragged me quickly around the edge of the anti-2SLGBTQ+ crowd to the brightly colored group opposite, where we were welcomed with smiles. Asha was greeted by name. She steered us through until we almost ran into a guy in a Bowie shirt, ripped jeans, and black Converse shoes.

"Max," Asha said. "I didn't know you'd be here."

Neither did I. He was holding a *BIGOTS GO HOME* sign and moving restlessly from foot to foot.

"I didn't know you'd be here either." He directed the comment at me, with a big smile. "Crazy huh?"

"Let me check what the plan is with Tariq," Asha said, and she ducked into the crowd.

"What's going on?" I asked Max. "Why are there so many people?"

"Most of them came in cars, but I saw a coach pull up too. Seems really organized. There's a church group there." Max pointed to a cluster of mainly women, holding *HOMOSEXUALITY IS SIN*, *JESUS LOVES YOU*, and *REPENT* signs. The shrieking woman was part of that group. She was still going.

"But it's that lot I'm keeping an eye on," he pointed to a signless group of men in a patchwork of camo and black. "Not sure who they are. Could be Proud Boys."

"Proud boys?"

Asha reappeared at my side and sighed. "Hate group. Bunch of white supremacist jerks. I don't even know if that's who they are. Some guys just turn up to this sort of thing to fight, you know. Proves their masculinity or some crap like that. War cosplayers. Pathetic."

"They want to fight?"

"We're hoping to keep it peaceful," Asha said. "We're not starting anything or giving them any excuse." She seemed to address that to Max. "Tariq says we're to keep the sidewalk safe, see?" She traced her finger in front of the library. "We want to keep things fun for the families, and we need to drown out that lot. Tariq is just starting the ..."

She was interrupted by the opening bars of "YMCA" blaring

into the road, finishing her sentence for her. A cheer went up, rainbow flags waved, and people began to dance. Those with their hands free formed the letters of the chorus while others held up their signs, blocking the hateful placards behind them. It felt like a party, and the singing silenced the boos and shouts. Asha was grinning, arms in the air, and we bumped hips as we danced, laughing.

Families began to arrive as "YMCA" faded into "Born This Way." Some danced down the street as they pushed strollers or led children. A few glanced nervously at the mass to the left and hurried into the library. A couple with a baby strapped to the man stopped at the end of the road, freezing when they saw the chaos. They conferred quietly before heading back the way they'd come.

Just before eleven, the door to the library opened from the inside and out stepped the drag queen. Her hair was a magnificent blond bouffant, and she was clad in sparkling blue sequins from head to high heels. Even on the overcast day, she gleamed and glittered.

Someone, probably Tariq, turned down the music and handed her a mic, and for a moment, we could hear the boos and yells of the protestors and the click of heels magnified through the speakers.

"Oh my goodness, what a crowd. You're all here for li'l ol' me?" The drag queen blew the angry mob a kiss, and we all cheered. "Well, sorry to disappoint, but I've promised some children I'd read them a story."

There was a push from the crowd to the left, some shouting from the police, and swearing from the men in camo.

"Well," she said. "I can't keep them waiting, can I?" She turned to us. "Thank you so much for coming."

She handed back the mic, curtseyed, then sashayed back into the library as the boos resumed. Her poise was impressive. A policeman positioned himself in front of the door, and the music came back on: "I'm Coming Out," this time.

The noise of the protestors grew louder, an angry swell of voices audible even over the song. They seemed enraged that they had seen their target and been dismissed. They surged forward, some clearly jostled from behind, some shoving. The policemen spread their arms, trying to keep the groups apart, but people rushed and stumbled around them.

The girl in front of me tripped as she tried to step back from the oncoming protestors, and the edge of her plywood sign slammed into my face. I reeled back, blind with pain. I stumbled into someone behind me, who yelled in my ear.

My hands were over my face, my nose agony. I tried to back up, tried to get out of the crowd, but people swarmed all around me, a blur of shoulders, signs, and shouts.

A smash came from the direction of the library, then screaming. I managed to grope my way across the road. Broken glass ground beneath my sneakers, people banged into me as they ran toward or away from the chaos. I tripped over the sidewalk on the other side, and my knees screamed in pain as they crashed into the concrete. I'd got out of the crowd, at least. I stumbled to my feet to see what was happening.

The camo guys were at the center of what looked like a riot, wielding other people's placards and their own fists. Some of our side were fighting back, but most had retreated and stared in horror from the sidelines. I saw Max in there, throwing a punch before others blocked my view. Diana Ross was still singing. No one was dancing.

A few of the police had formed a line in front of the library's smashed window, while others grabbed at people on the outskirts of the fight, dragging them away, but they were hopelessly outnumbered. I recognized one officer from when we found Ruth's body and felt cold, even in the muggy heat. Through the broken glass, I could see the drag queen inside, along with someone I guessed was a librarian, ushering the families out of sight.

How could they smash the window with children inside? What the hell was wrong with them?

There was wet on my hand and my upper lip. My nose was bleeding, obviously. The blare of pain made it impossible to think, impossible to do anything other than stand there with my hand over my face, staring in horror.

That's what I was doing when Max stumbled out of the melee. He straightened his shoulders, about to dive back in, when he caught sight of me.

"Keira?" He ran over. "You're bleeding!"

"Yeah. No duh," I said, but it sounded all wrong because of my nose, and then I was crying like an idiot, which only made everything hurt more. Plus, I was stupidly worried I looked my absolute worst in front of him: bleeding nose, red puffy eyes, the whole deal.

"Oh God, let's get you out of here."

"Where's Asha? We can't leave her."

We both scanned the crowd, but it was Max who spotted her. "There!"

She was with a group of people well back from the fight, in front of Sal's Burgers, on the other side of the chaos. Max waved at her. Her face crumpled with concern when she saw me. I couldn't imagine how bad I must have looked if she could tell from that distance. Max jerked a thumb over his shoulder to let her know we were leaving, and she nodded.

"She's safe. Come on. Let's sort you out."

Max led me across the Beer Store parking lot to the Coffee Time by the gas station. I stared at the grit and gray of the ground, and the faded white stripes that marked the parking spaces. I was unsteady on my feet and afraid of tripping. My knees ached with each step. Shouts and scuffling came from behind, and beneath that, "I'm Coming Out" was still playing. I couldn't believe things had changed so much in the space of one song.

Max opened the door of the Coffee Time. I stepped out of the stifling parking lot into fierce air conditioning, feeling the chill on my bloody knees. He steered me toward a plastic table. I eased myself into the hard chair, knees protesting as I bent them.

"Back in a sec." Max headed for the counter.

I checked my hand, and the whole side of my palm was smeared with blood. I touched the bridge of my nose, carefully. It wasn't hurting so much now. I peered down. My jeans were ripped, and I'd skinned my knees.

Max returned with some napkins and a bottle of water. He poured a little of the water onto the napkins and handed them to me.

"You can use this to clean yourself up, then hold this," he handed me the bottle, "against your nose. The cold will help with the swelling."

I wiped at my tears and the blood. I hoped I got it all off. My knees stung as I cleaned them, and I had to pick a couple of pieces of grit out of the cuts. The cool of the bottle definitely helped. But my thoughts were still tangled and bruised.

"Did you see which of those guys hit you? I bet there's footage. Lots of people were filming. We can identify them and press charges."

I shook my head, still holding the bottle against my nose. "I got hit by one of our own signs. It was an accident."

"Oh." Max looked disappointed.

"Were you fighting?"

One side of Max's mouth went up. "A little."

"Why? Weren't we meant to be peaceful?"

"We tried, right? You saw what happened. They attacked us. Proud Boys and their ilk are Nazis. You can't reason with people like that. The only good Nazi is a dead Nazi, right?"

I wasn't sure if I agreed. While we'd been at war, it was self-defence. But they weren't all the same. The Germans murdered their own in the POW camps for not being extreme enough and five thousand were executed on Hitler's orders after his own people literally tried to kill him. Out of those that joined the Nazi party, how many did so just to stay alive? When did survival become complicity? And when did complicity deserve a death sentence?

I really didn't know.

But that was beside the point. I was thinking about the camp. Max was talking about people now. If they were brainwashed by media, it was media they chose to consume, even if algorithms pushed them there. They'd not been subjected to an inescapable state-sponsored propaganda system. No one was going to kill them if they didn't become Nazis, and 2SLGBTQ+ people were certainly no threat to them.

"Why did they come here? Asha said it was going to be a few people with signs. What happened?" I moved the bottle up a little. The water was warming already.

"My uncle is what happened."

"I didn't see him." I peered out of the window in case he was there. The last of the crowd was clearing, some being led away by the police. Discarded signs littered the street. A rainbow *HATE IS A DRAG* sign had dark boot prints on it.

Max gave a humorless laugh. "Oh, he was there in spirit. He sent his goons."

I leaned back, feeling stupid. "They were working for him? The Proud Boys, or whoever they were. The ones in camo?"

He flicked his dark hair back. "Nothing that obvious. He points the way. His followers do the rest. Hitler did something similar, sent his militias to attack his targets. But my uncle is smart enough to allow for plausible deniability."

I put the bottle back down on the table and touched my nose gingerly again. It definitely hurt a little less. "I don't know if that's fair. I mean, we didn't know what would happen, so how could he?"

"He's been studying the right wing in the US. They won, so he figures he can too. Most of his advisors came straight from campaigns there. This is how it works." Max leaned across the table. "They give the rabid pack the scent of their target, then pretend to be surprised when they attack. Later, they hold the whole mess up as an example of why drag events are 'divisive' and should be banned."

Max and I waited out the chaos together. He bought me a coffee, which helped with my headache. His hand was close to mine on the table. I wanted to reach for it but didn't.

By the time we left the Coffee Time, the street was clear. Max walked me back to the museum. He tried to insist on coming in, but I was a mess. I just wanted to clean up properly.

As I opened the door, I was greeted with a waft of garlic and spice. I checked myself in the mirror in my room. My nose definitely wasn't broken, but a dark purple stain was spreading over one side, like ink seeping through paper. I changed out of my clothes, glad I'd worn black jeans that wouldn't show the bloodstains, at least.

I followed the scent into the kitchen and found Asha lifting an immersion blender out of a large pot of lentil soup. She dropped the blender in the sink with a clatter when she saw me, rushed over, and gave me a careful hug, a waft of pink hair getting in my mouth. She pulled back and examined my face, wincing in sympathy.

"I'm so glad you're home. I wasn't sure how badly you were hurt. Max said it was your nose, and I thought maybe you'd like something comforting and soft to eat."

I wasn't a fan of soup in the summer, and it wasn't like I'd lost any teeth. But I appreciated the thought, and I'd never seen Asha so solicitous. I'd had no idea she could cook or that we had an immersion blender. She even pulled out a chair for me.

"I'm really okay," I said as I sat.

She gave me a smile that suggested she thought I was being brave as she spooned out some soup into a bowl and put it in front of me.

"What happened to the people in the library?" I asked.

"They got the families out the back safely. A few people were hurt in the fighting. Leo's in the hospital with a fractured eye socket."

"Ouch." That sounded insanely painful.

"And a couple from our lot got arrested." She shook her head as she grabbed some crusty bread and started spreading butter on it. My real butter, I noticed, not her vegan "butter," and I appreciated it. "Typical cops. As if it wasn't obvious which side was causing the problems."

I took a sip of the soup. It was spicy and thick, with a nice hint of coriander. I was deeply impressed. It was way tastier than my pathetic ready-made food, and I was absolutely starving, which made sense, since I'd been rushed out of the house before I'd had a chance for breakfast.

Asha plonked herself down in the seat next to me, rainbow skirt pooling around her. "I'm sorry. I didn't know you'd get hurt. I didn't expect a riot."

I shrugged. "I'm okay."

Asha's phone buzzed, and she peered at it. Her jaw set.

"What is it?"

"The Hoppers are on TV," she said. "Making things worse, of course."

I pulled out my laptop and found a news site with them on it, speaking live.

"Do we have to look at them?" Asha said.

"I just want to see what they say."

"Notice they were all ready for this?" Asha jabbed a finger at the screen. "They knew this would happen, and they couldn't wait to get on TV to talk about it."

She was right. They didn't look like they'd pulled this together at the last minute. Peter Hopper sat at a table in a neat, blue shirt with pictures of his two beautiful daughters turned toward the camera. Jules sat next to him, make-up perfect, hair styled in soft waves. Who was that camera-ready on a random Saturday?

"... of course condemn, in no uncertain terms, the violence that was seen today, from both sides. Such shameful scenes have no place in our society, and our libraries should be places of peace where families can come to learn in safety."

"Both sides!" Asha yelled. "Seriously?"

"Maybe they didn't know who started it?"

She raised an eyebrow.

Peter continued, "Libraries should not be used as a front line in a culture war. We have said from the start that bringing this event to our town would cause nothing but trouble. There are those who seek to divide our society with violence and those who do so with pornographic books for children and extremist gender ideology. Both should be opposed in no uncertain terms."

Jules nodded solemnly next to him.

Asha slammed my laptop shut. "I think I'm going to throw up. There are no pornographic books for children in the library! To them, the very fact that queer people exist is obscene, so any books about us must be porn." She swore.

Even after the rally, I'd wanted to believe they weren't all that bad. Why? Because there were "two sides to everything," like Ruth said, or because of the scholarship? Max had been totally right about them. He'd even predicted what they'd say.

I stared at my bowl. I still really needed that scholarship. But could I take money from them if they offered it to me?

The orangish liquid looked like sludge. I let go of my spoon, letting it slide into the wide bowl, and watched as the soup folded over it.

CHAPTER TWENTY-ONE
Winter 1944–1945

The cold crept in early that year. Snow hid the perilous edges of the road, and the muddy ruts on the familiar route turned to frictionless ice. Farming season was over, and the working men returned to the camp full-time.

Erich thought he'd got used to the heart-stopping cold of the Canadian winters, but the brutality of that season caught him by surprise. A ruthless December snowstorm cut the camp off for days. Snowdrifts sealed them in their huts, shivering in their bunks and fighting over who would brave the pitiless cold to bring in more firewood.

Trapped within the confines of the wire, bad news metastasized through the camp from letters, whispers, and rumors: the Americans were advancing in the west and the Soviets clawed away at the east.

There was less talk of victory. Men avoided speaking of the future or used uncertain terms, like "when we get back." Erich tried to imagine a happy homecoming. But he had no home and no mother. And if the rumors were true, it would be to a shattered country.

Erich missed Joe, missed Daisy, missed the warm clutter of their kitchen and the satisfying ache of his arms after a hard day's work. The cheerful polka music of *The Happy Gang* was never heard in the camp. Even the official broadcasts picked up from Germany were turned down low. All other news was propaganda, the men were reminded. The Ardennes Offensive would change everything. They were days away from a breakthrough. Anything that suggested otherwise was a sign of Allied desperation, the flailing of a failing alliance.

Fights flared in the camp. Beatings were routine, bruises blossoming on cheeks like the purple crocuses that finally fought their way through the mud. Loyalty frayed as the men counted the cost of the war they'd been led into, and true believers lashed out desperately at the rest of them. Everyone knew such beatings were delivered by the *Heiliger Geist* — the Holy Ghost — as, miraculously, there were never any witnesses.

Men clustered in groups, voices low, glancing over each other's shoulders. Rooms went silent when others entered, air stinking with secrets. Rumors scuttled through the camp about who was informing on their hut-mates or who was disloyal to the Reich. Some even questioned the Lagerführer, whispering that he was a collaborator: too close to the Canadians, to the Red Cross, to the Swiss.

Even the escape attempts felt half-hearted. A man hid in the laundry but was found before he'd even made it out of the prisoner compound. Another clung to the bottom of a truck, but a lump of ice in the road knocked him off and sent him to the hospital hut with a cracked skull.

It was early March when word spread of Dr. Bauer's suicide.

Erich wondered if he'd received bad news from home, or if imprisonment had become too much for him. But there were darker whispers, about the doctor getting what was coming to him. Karl Lang grew paranoid that week and for several days, insisted that Erich not leave him alone.

The spring was slow to start, snow lingering in dirt-gray heaps. The chill clung to the men, cut through the thick wool of their uniforms. They shivered and stamped during roll call and huddled around the heaters in the education hut and the barracks. The skits in the theater hut stopped. Few of them felt like laughing.

Finally, the roads cleared enough to get to the Novaks' farm, and Erich was the first to find himself back at work.

"They put in a special request for you to come as soon as you could," George explained as they bumped along the rutted road together in the beaten-up truck.

Erich took in each scrap of the familiar scenery along the route, gazing at the bare trees and half-frozen swamps as if they were treasured haunts from his childhood. As they approached the farm, he could barely keep still in his seat. He leaned forward, the better to catch sight of it through the splattered glass of the windscreen.

Finally, they turned off the muddy smear of the main road and onto the Novaks' land. The truck juddered furiously as they made their way up to the house. Winter had all but destroyed the Novaks' driveway. The wheels spun in the slushy dirt with a furious roar for a moment, but the truck lurched out of the dip and toward the cottage.

Erich spotted Daisy's slim figure on the porch. She waved then disappeared into the house. Erich was out of his door before George had time to turn the engine off. He found himself suddenly shy as he approached, like on his first day.

By the time he'd reached the steps, no one had come back out. Erich glanced at George, but he was gazing down at his clipboard, getting the papers in order. Erich turned back to the house, noticing the new gaps in the shingles, the loose guttering at the side. It felt like a painfully long time waiting in the chilly morning before the front door rattled open, squealing on its hinges.

Joe stepped out, leaning hard on his cane, Daisy protectively close behind him. He'd lost weight. His once barrel-like chest seemed concave now, and his head hung forward a little, as if it was too heavy to hold up properly. He reminded Erich of the bent-double snowdrops clustering around the edge of the road.

Joe lifted his chin to show a wide smile and bright eyes. He held his hand out, and Erich hurried up onto the porch to seize it. Joe's grip was just as tight, just as warm as before.

"Good to have you back," Joe said, but his jovial tone sounded forced.

Daisy peered at Erich from over her stepfather's shoulder, the strain showing in the set of her jaw and the new tightness of her skin over her collarbone. She grinned as wide as a lost sailor sighting land. Erich could see the winter had been every bit as long for them as it had been for him.

It would be okay now. They were back together. The war couldn't touch them there.

CHAPTER TWENTY-TWO

By Sunday, the idea of going to Tall Pines Mobile Home Park to search for a drug dealer seemed like a fever dream, especially in the stifling warmth of the kitchen. I'd tried opening the windows, despite the rain cascading straight down outside. With no breeze to bring the cooler air in, it just made the room damp as well as hot.

The space was filled with the friendly murmur of a late breakfast eaten with Asha and Ephram with little excuse-mes and laughter as we maneuvered around each other in the tiny galley kitchen and the scrape of cutlery and clatter of plates as we ate our toast and cereal at the shared table. I'd been surprised Ephram had spent the weekend with us, rather than off with his family, but apparently his parents were at some conference, so he'd decided to stay.

Outside was wet and nasty. The trailer park was far, the quest uncertain. And in the kitchen, there was coffee and company. Ironically, I probably wouldn't have ended up going at all if we hadn't all been getting on so well.

“That lentil soup you made yesterday smelled good,” Ephram said.

“I should have offered you some! I’m so sorry. There’s leftovers in the fridge,” Asha said.

Ephram put his hands up defensively. “I wasn’t angling for your food, I promise. But I was thinking. My mom makes a great vegan domoda, if neither of you are allergic to nuts. I could ask her to cook enough for all of us for me to bring back next weekend, if you want.”

“That sounds amazing,” Asha said.

“It does,” I added, making a mental note to google “domoda” later. There was something comforting about the fact that Ephram obviously couldn’t cook. He seemed to be such a genius at the museum that it was reassuring that even my pathetic noodle-and-pasta culinary repertoire had him outclassed. I’d never even seen him make toast. His limit seemed to be adding milk to cereal and heating things up in the microwave.

But then I thought of the fridge, of his passive-aggressively labeled meals before Ruth’s death. I’d been assuming our shared loss had helped to overcome our differences, but in that moment, talking about meals together, I realized how wrong I was.

Ephram had complained about Ruth “accidentally” eating his food more than once, and after that, his notes had started appearing in the fridge. No doubt he’d felt uncomfortable around her because of her faked awards and references, and angry at the disdain with which she treated the program and his lunches.

Asha had rolled her eyes and walked out any time Ruth had mentioned any member of the Hopper family long before she started spending her evenings in town. I’d put it down to her looking down on us, or on “politics,” but it was painfully obvious now. Asha was queer and the Hoppers were actively attacking the 2SLGBTQ+ community. Of course she didn't want to hang around to hear Ruth drooling over them.

It wasn't our collective grief that had brought us together. It was the absence of Ruth.

She'd been a source of constant tension. She'd made the two of us a pair on that first night and driven a wedge between us and Ephram and Asha. Without her, the common room was a relaxed, comfortable place. Perhaps it would have been the whole time if she hadn't faked her way into the summer program.

I pushed away the rest of my cereal. It was growing soggy anyway. Ephram's and Asha's smiles made me feel suddenly alone. True, Ruth wasn't the person I'd thought she was, but I'd enjoyed her company each evening, loved the sound of her laughing too hard at dumb reality TV with me. Was I really the only one who mourned her? The only one who missed her and wondered what had really happened that night?

That's why I found myself trudging along the main road in the pouring rain half an hour later, on my way to Tall Pines Mobile Home Park.

It wasn't muddy, at least. The earth was too dry to absorb it right away, and it ran off the verge, forming deep puddles at the side of the road. There was no sidewalk here either, and cars sped by, occasionally getting close enough to splatter dirty water up my leg and onto my skirt.

I swore at every single one of them.

My hair plastered itself against my face and neck as my mind drifted back to the Hoppers on television the night before and, inevitably, to the scholarship.

I couldn't pretend that Saturday hadn't happened. What would I even say if I saw them? I knew I should stand up to them, challenge them, but that would torpedo any chance I had of affording university. If I refused the scholarship in some big noble gesture, how would that help anyone?

Not that I could expect to get it, of course. Asha would clearly turn it down if they even offered it to her, which I couldn't see them doing anyway. But was it brave and noble if you didn't need it? It was more like turning down seconds when you were already stuffed.

I hurried past a hydrofield. The electrical towers looked like giant alien invaders striding across the soaked landscape.

Ephram didn't need the money either, but he was intimidatingly smart. I wondered why I was even thinking about the Hopper Scholarship with him around. I wasn't even in the race. I could kiss Dad's dream of U of T goodbye.

The rain eased, then stopped. Shafts of sunlight cracked their way out of the clouds, but it was way too late. My clothes were soaked through. I was so separated from the real world that the sign at the edge of the road caught me by surprise. *Tall Pines Mobile Home Park*, it read, green letters on white. *A welcoming, year-round community.* On either side of the words were the basic outlines of pine trees.

I turned down the driveway as I tried, a little belatedly, to come up with a plan. I'd completely forgotten to think about what I was going to say, or how I was going to find Colt. The driveway opened out into a flat site with mobile homes spaced out on patches of lawn that seemed unnaturally green after the yellow of the verge I'd been trudging along. Trees dotted around the site, including a few pines, but none were tall enough to warrant the site name, or provide much shade.

It was nicer than I'd expected. Some of the mobile homes had flower beds sprouting dahlias and hostas, or barbeques set up. Most of them didn't even look like mobile homes, just small, single-storey houses that, if they were in Toronto, would be called "tiny homes" and sell for an obscene amount of money. Each of them had short, paved paths leading to the door.

Ahead, the road split into a grid that held more homes. To one side of the main driveway was a squat building with a sign that said *Office*. I headed there, but my feet slowed the closer I got. How exactly would it look if I asked which mobile home belonged to a known drug dealer, especially since I didn't even know his last name?

I steered myself away from the office, cutting across the grass and hoping no one saw me from the window. None of the people on the neat streets gave me a second glance, and I realized I didn't stand out. Everyone else wore normal clothes, too: clean T-shirts, shorts, sundresses, and jeans. I wondered why I'd been surprised at that.

Then it hit me.

I'd been expecting a run-down mess of a place populated by white trash in stained tank tops, empty beer cans piled in front of mold-blackened homes. I'd been a total snob. I'd thought that Mom and I, in our miniscule city apartment, were so much better than people here.

Idiot.

I stumbled along, feeling more nauseated with every step. What was I meant to do? Go up to one of those nice people and ask where Colt, a drug dealer, lived? Who would I pick? The sweet-looking woman wiping the rain off her toddler-sized slide? The old couple walking hand-in-hand down the road?

I rounded a corner, and a different trailer came into view, much more in line with what I'd been expecting. The lawn around it was patchy, and one of the windows was filled with a Confederate flag. Gross. It looked like an older design of home than most of the others, with brown accents on a cream-colored building. I was trying not to jump to assumptions, but the inhabitant of that trailer was making it hard. Parked in front was a shiny, red Camaro, way newer than my uncle's car and much cleaner. It seemed out of place outside the run-down home.

Okay, it might not have been Colt's home, but I wouldn't feel too weird asking whoever lived there about him. I took a deep breath, and before I could talk myself out of it, I strode up to the door of the trailer.

Wires protruded from the wall where the doorbell should have been, so I knocked on the glass panel of the door.

Nothing happened. I knocked again. Silence. I cupped my hands and peered through the window. The flag blocked the daylight and made the trailer gloomy. It took my eyes a few seconds to adjust.

The front door opened right into a small living room, with orangey walls and a built-in, brown couch. Someone slumped in a chair, head tilted back. He looked asleep. The table in front of him was a cluttered mess: an empty beer and vodka bottle, baggies, an overflowing ashtray, and a glass pipe. I could only see part of his face, and the side of his brown hair, but I recognized him. He'd been talking to Ruth at the party. He had to be Colt.

A creeping feeling stole up on me, and for a moment, I wanted to run away, back to the safety of the museum.

Instead, I forced myself to bang again. "Colt!"

I was definitely loud enough to wake him up. I was getting worried about drawing other people's attention and his lack of response.

"Colt?"

Still no sound. I cupped my hands around my eyes. He hadn't moved at all. And now that I looked at him, the angle of his head seemed wrong. Surely he'd be uncomfortable slumped like that. A chill cut through me, even in the heat of the day.

I tried the door handle. It opened and I stumbled in. I hadn't expected it to be unlocked.

The place stank of smoke and old sweat, but under that was something else. It wasn't strong, but it was bad: like rotting meat and cheap perfume. I'd never smelled it before, but somehow, I knew what it was. I wanted to be sick. I wanted to be anywhere else. Still, I approached the slumped figure, saw the blue lips, touched the pale arm.

His skin was the same temperature as the dim, stuffy room.

I ran back outside, gasping for air. As soon as I could breathe again, I called 911.

While I was waiting, I summoned the courage to go back in and took a couple of pictures of the scene. I felt weird about that, but if this was anything to do with Ruth's death, I needed all the information I could get.

The police arrived quicker than the ambulance. They took in the pipe, booze, and plastic baggies on the table and shook their heads. This didn't seem like a surprise for them.

"Did you touch anything?"

"Just the door and his arm. I didn't want to mess up any fingerprints or anything."

One of the officers gave me a sad smile. "It's not prints I'm worried about. It's fentanyl. If you touched some of it and ended up ingesting it," he nodded at the corpse.

"Oh," I said.

He took me to the trailer park office so I could wash my

hands properly there, just in case. In the little cubicle, I scrubbed at my trembling arms all the way up to the elbow, lathering them with the cucumber and mint-scented soap. I splashed water on my face and stared at my own wide eyes in the mirror, framed by my hair, curling slightly as it dried. My damp clothes still clung to me, and cold shivered through my body in spite of the stuffy heat of the trailer.

I'd seen three dead bodies in the last year: my father's, Ruth's, and Colt's. Two of them from unnatural and drug-related deaths. No wonder I was feeling so messed up.

Once I was cleaned up, the officers and I went through the inevitable questions.

Since it was obvious Colt had been dead for hours, I let them know they could check with Sarah, Max, Asha, and Ephram that I'd been with at least one of them all the time for the last couple of days. When I told them that I suspected he'd sold LSD to Ruth, I still thought that they'd insist I come down to the station, tell me to call my mother or a lawyer. But they just took notes and my contact details like last time and said they'd call if they had any follow-up questions. From their resigned faces, I had a horrible feeling that they found a lot of dead people this way.

One of the officers asked if I wanted a lift back to the museum, but I needed time and space to think, and I didn't want to show up back there in a police car.

I wandered back along the main road. Another wave of panic slammed through me, and my heart thudded way too fast. I tried to breathe slowly. Tried to focus on my surroundings. But I'd found a dead body. A dead drug dealer, who had been talking to Ruth the night she died.

Was that just a coincidence?

I pulled up the pictures on my phone. Was it illegal to take pictures of a possible crime scene? I tried to ignore the guilt. It wasn't like I was going to show them to anyone.

There was Colt, slumped on the sofa, head tilted back. It definitely looked like what the police had called "drug paraphernalia" on the table. Glass pipe, lighter, vodka bottle, ashtray, bottle opener, empty Doritos package, Molson bottle, plastic baggies, some kind of white powder, and two beer bottle tops.

I froze and zoomed in on the picture. There were definitely two beer bottle caps on the table, but only one bottle. And if there were two bottle caps, it meant that there had been two bottles.

If he'd drunk two bottles of beer himself, the other one would still be on the table, wouldn't it? The missing bottle suggested someone else had been there and taken their beer with them. Perhaps it was innocent enough. A visitor who hadn't finished their beer, so carried it home to another trailer. Or perhaps it was someone who, like me, had been worried about their fingerprints being at a crime scene.

That was a job for the police, though. They had access to the scene, and they'd know if the bottle was important or not. If so, they could run that second bottle lid for prints or interview witnesses who might have seen someone come to visit him. I wasn't going to tell them how to investigate. If I did that, perhaps they'd decide to investigate the girl who had been there when two bodies were discovered.

It was probably lucky I had solid alibis for both deaths.

Without the police's resources, I could only go by what I knew, and that wasn't much. Ruth and Colt had been hanging out together at the party. I knew that for sure now. I could see it. Ruth swigging from a bottle of wine. Ruth laughing as Colt talked to her.

Had she bought drugs from him? And even if it was that simple, how had she ended up in the lake, and how had she ended up drowning? A few people had been splashing about or swimming in the water. It had seemed shallow enough there, harmless.

But Bertie had told Max the lake was dangerous.

My memories were fuzzy and disconnected. I'd only seen the lake at night, I hadn't been close to the water, and I'd been rattled by the Hoppers' rally at the time. I didn't have any photos of the lake that I could look over.

I had to go back there. I had to see the scene again.

I was definitely missing something.

CHAPTER TWENTY-THREE

April 16, 1945

Erich could tell something was wrong as soon as he saw Daisy by the front door. The truck jerked and jarred along the rugged drive, and the image of her rose and fell as if he was at sea. She twisted her hands together in the way she did when she was worried. She stayed in that spot as they approached, not hurrying inside to fetch her father as usual.

As George and Erich approached, she took a step forward.

"Dad's got a bit of a cold," she said. "He's resting up, but I'll take the papers inside to sign, and Dad can supervise Erich from the window. Look."

She pointed to the upper window on the left, and Erich could see, through the streaked glass, a fuzzy figure reclining in bed. Joe raised a hand in a small wave, and this seemed to satisfy George, who handed over the papers.

George and Erich waited awkwardly for her to return. It was warm for April. The sun was out, drying the muddy ruts of the yard into a frozen sea. An oversized North American robin tilted its head to watch them from its perch on the chicken coop.

Daisy returned with the papers, and Erich waited until the rumble of the truck's engine had faded out, replaced by the hiss of the wind in the trees, and the squabbling squawks of the chickens, hungry for their morning feed.

"How is your father?"

Daisy slumped onto the bench at the front of the house. "He says he's okay, but he can barely get out of bed and he's really breathless."

Erich sat next to her, cocking his head. The language barrier had slammed down between them again.

Daisy explained, "He's breathing like this." She made her breath rattle, slow and labored, the sound painful to hear coming from her slender throat, even knowing she was pretending.

"The doctor?" Erich asked.

Daisy shook her head. "Dad says he's fine, and it's not worth the money."

Erich thought of how well he'd been looked after by the late Dr. Bauer. There had been no question of cost. How could they have better medical care than Joe did?

They sat in silence for a while, staring out at the farm. There was more life here than inside the barbed wire. Although they had a few pets around the site — a couple of adopted stray dogs, cats, and a raccoon that Obergrenadier Walter had managed to semi-tame — here there was the snuffling of pigs, the indignant fluster of chickens, and the heave and sigh of the wind in the nearby trees.

The trees were cut back around the camp, and nothing grew on the barren mud of the sports field in this season. Too many pairs of booted feet had packed the snow down to a hard ice during the winter and stomped out any growing life since. But here, grass and weeds sprouted around the well-trodden routes the Novaks took each day between the barns and the house, outlining the brown paths in vibrant green.

"Can I go in, see him?"

Another shake of her hanging head. "He wouldn't want you to see him like this. He's too proud."

Erich wasn't sure what proud meant, but the rest of what she'd said was clear enough to guess. Joe wasn't the kind of man who wanted others to see his weaknesses.

"I am sorry," he said and, without thinking, reached for her hand. She let him take it, and he marveled at the smallness of her fingers in his. Her skin was not soft; it was almost as rough as his. She was not the strong and pure German woman of the posters back home. She was not curvy like the drawings in the American *Esquire* magazine. But she was beautiful all the same, and he felt the weight of the world pressing down on her. Her mother was gone. He had no idea what had happened to her real father, but he clearly wasn't around. Her reddened eyes and the purple moons beneath showed her fear for her stepfather.

She leaned in, and her lips were on his. He hadn't expected it, hadn't been ready for the softness and warmth of her mouth in the cool air of the morning. He almost pulled away in shock. Instead, he leaned in, put his arm around her, and they kissed for what felt like a long time, until Erich became awkwardly aware of her father upstairs, no doubt wondering when they would come out from under the overhang that hid them and get to work.

He broke away, and they both smiled shyly. Erich looked up, pointing with his eyes, as if Joe could hear if he spoke his thoughts aloud.

Daisy nodded. "You'd better get on. And I should check in on him."

There was a new bounce in her step as she hurried back into the house.

Erich grabbed the chicken feed and trudged over the mud to the coop. His legs were spongy, his head light. The morning seemed dazzling, in spite of the gray clouds above.

He'd never dared to wonder if she could like him. It was unthinkable. He tripped and almost dropped the heavy burlap sack. He struggled with the latch on the run as the chickens clattered out to greet him. He stared at the trees, at the sky, at the wonderful morning as they scrabbled and scratched around him.

He was working in the barn when she approached him again, just before midday. He'd taken down a door that had been sticking and was planing a quarter inch off the bottom. The shavings smelled like spring, ringlets of wood scattering on the floor, and the hiss of the plane hiding the soft sound of her footsteps as she entered.

He only noticed her when she was close enough for him to catch her scent, soapy and sweet.

"My father is sleeping," she said as he looked up. "I think he sounds a little better."

Then they were kissing again. She stumbled as their lips connected, pulling him toward the hay at the back of the barn, and they collapsed into its prickly embrace.

There was a sureness to her movements that he lacked. She steered him gently into the right places. It was easy to forget, with her being so small and her stepfather so protective, that she was no child. She'd lived for twenty-four years compared to his twenty-one. He'd spent the last two years in captivity and had no experience to speak of before that. But if he did anything wrong, she didn't show it.

Afterwards, he felt dizzy at the audacity of it all, at how quickly the day had changed and the world with it. She left him with another quick kiss on his cheek.

"I'd better get lunch ready," she said. "And see if Dad is well enough to eat with us."

He apparently was, although Daisy had been right about his breathing. He struggled with each breath, as if he had to think about it, to fight his body to get the air in and out. He should have stayed in bed.

"Definitely getting better now," he said between wheezes. Erich wondered if that was true. If so, he hated to imagine how bad he'd been before.

It was all Erich could do to keep his eyes on his food, on Joe, on anything but Daisy, who was grinning so much that Joe must have noticed, even if her smile faltered each time he coughed or struggled with a breath. She sang along to *The Happy Gang*, and even the notes she didn't quite hit sounded perfect to him.

Joe insisted on sitting outside for the afternoon, cocooned, at Daisy's insistence, in so many blankets that he looked like a man-sized worm on the bench where Erich and Daisy had kissed. Whether he sat there because he really felt better or because he suspected something, Erich didn't know. But Erich and Daisy avoided each other that afternoon — Daisy busying herself in the house and Erich up a ladder in full view, fixing some rotting patches on the barn roof, trying very hard not to look over to see if she would appear through the door.

He was almost glad when he heard the growl and splutter of the old truck approaching as the sun began to sink. He'd been terrified he'd give them away with an unthinking gesture or word.

He grinned, ready to greet George, but the face that jerked behind the wheel as the truck bumped over the ruts was unfamiliar. Erich straightened his gray uniform. You never knew how new guards were going to treat you.

"Where is George?"

"Off sick," the new soldier said brusquely. "Stand there. Don't move."

Erich did as he was told, reminded of his first days at the farm when the Novaks were strangers. The new soldier took his time with the paperwork, pointing out where Joe needed to sign as if he didn't know.

Eventually, things seemed to be resolved, and the soldier jabbed a thumb at the back of the truck. Erich got in and settled as comfortably as he could against the side of the hard truck bed. He focused on the back of the new guard's head in the cab as they jolted toward the main road.

It took all his willpower not to turn to see if Daisy was watching him leave.

CHAPTER TWENTY-FOUR

Finally, I found something at work.

I'd been struggling to concentrate, to latch my scattered mind onto the documents instead of the image of Colt's body that was seared in my head. But as I was scrolling through endless incident reports, a name jumped out at me: Rainer Schmitt. He was the man who was found dead on the same day as Erich Stein. I grabbed onto the words. The report was on a suicide. Dr. Emil Bauer had apparently killed himself in January 1945, and the witness for his "distressed" state of mind was Rainer Schmitt, who claimed he'd confided in him about his despair just the day before.

The death happened overnight in the hospital hut where Dr. Bauer worked. The report noted that Rainer Schmitt had slept in his hut that night with dozens of other men. I couldn't help thinking of the Nazi order to execute "traitors" and make it look like suicide. Why had the Canadians made a note of where Schmitt slept that night? Had he been under suspicion?

Schmitt's name came up in another death report, too. The

dead man, Otto Meyer, had apparently been cutting down a tree in a remote part of a logging camp when the saw slipped and sliced deeply into his leg. He bled out before his two comrades could get help.

Once again, Schmitt wasn't there. But he was the one who requested the two witnesses be released from their work duties and allowed to return to the main camp to grieve.

The request was denied.

I probably wouldn't have thought much of the reports earlier, especially given that one happened far from the camp, but since reading the accounts of the deaths at Medicine Hat, I wondered if the two men were more than just witnesses. Perhaps the deaths had been ordered by Schmitt himself. He was a feldwebel, which was like a sergeant-major, and was in charge of his hut, so he had some power in the camp.

I was going through the reports in my mind as I set out to check out the lake at lunchtime. The bodies were piling up, both in the forties and now: Dr. Emil Bauer, Otto Meyer, Rainer Schmitt, Erich Stein, Ruth, and Colt. But were any of them more than they seemed?

The sun felt low, violently close. The trees were miserly with their shade, keeping shadows tight around them, and I wished for the rain of the day before. I struggled my way along the road from the museum, sipping from my lukewarm water bottle and regretting not waiting until the cool of evening.

A part of me just wanted to go back to our museum wing, to curl up in my bed there. Or to call my mom and ask if she could come and get me and take me home. Way too much bad had happened, and I wanted to run away, to hide from it all. I could totally do it, too. No one would blame me.

But I owed Ruth more than that.

I turned over the evidence for the recent deaths in my head. Who would have killed Ruth, and how? She'd argued with Asha and Ephram, but I couldn't imagine either of them drowning her. And wouldn't they have been wet? I supposed the walk home might have been enough to dry them off, but it still seemed unlikely.

She'd fought with Julia. That was interesting. Perhaps Ruth had told her about her possible connection to Harry, and Julia had been afraid of Ruth claiming the Hoppers' property as her inheritance, and she'd sent a goon after Ruth.

Nope. That was ridiculous. No one actually had goons, and inheritance laws didn't work that way, did they? It was more likely that Max would be afraid that her sucking up to Bertie would get him cut out of his inheritance. But he was with me when she'd drowned. He'd tried to convince her to come home with us. He'd asked Ephram and Asha to make sure she was okay. He couldn't have known that none of that would work, unless Ephram and Asha were in on it too, and that didn't seem likely. It was hard enough to imagine one of them as a murderer, never mind all three.

Birdcall came from the wood beside me. I had no idea what kind of bird it was, but it made a peeping sound as it darted between the branches.

Colt could have killed Ruth. Maybe he fancied her, she rejected him, and they fought by the lake and he drowned her, then killed himself later, overcome with guilt. Or he could have killed her but still died of an accidental overdose. Those happened all the time with fentanyl, as I'd found out when I googled it. About 170 people died from fentanyl every single day in North America, which was absolutely horrifying. Basically, the entire population of Westonville was found each week, cold and slumped on floors, beds, or couches like Colt. No wonder the police seemed unsurprised. Finding bodies must be routine for them.

If Colt were murdered, there was no shortage of motives. If he sold LSD to Ruth and someone saw, they might have wanted revenge for her death. But it didn't need a connection with Ruth for someone to want to bump off a drug dealer. He could have owed money, could have been involved in a dispute with other dealers. It wouldn't have been hard for someone to slip some of his own merchandise into a bottle of beer and hand it to him then leave with the bottle and any telltale residue after he was dead.

Of course, Ruth could have been deliberately drugged, too. But if someone had wanted to kill her, they'd have given her fentanyl as well. Clearly, Colt had access, so it wouldn't have been hard to get. They wouldn't have given her LSD, hoping she'd happen to stumble into the lake and somehow drown while everyone was momentarily distracted. That was too risky.

Either someone had held her under and the LSD was irrelevant, or it really was just an accident.

By the time I saw the track to the lake, my head felt swollen, pulse pounding against the tightness of my skull, and I was considering googling the symptoms of heatstroke. Instead, I dove gratefully into the shade of the path. Of course, the bugs wanted to escape the sun as badly as I did, and they crowded around me, so many little ones getting stuck in my sweat. I wiped them off my arms in dark smears.

The lake shone silver through the trees, so different from the oily black of the party. The fractured sun dazzled on the ripples. The trees petered out ahead, giving way to smooth lumps of granite that rolled down to the water. I was reluctant to leave the shade and brought my aura of bugs with me out into the glare.

Right. What was I looking for? It was tough to superimpose the dark of that evening over the blinding heat of the day, especially with a headache building. But there were clues. Charcoal and scorch marks stained the stone, showing where the fire had burned that night, and a few pieces of green glass glittered in the crack of a rock, clearly the remnants of a broken bottle.

Ruth had stood here, talking to Colt. I could see her now, frozen in time, head tilted back, laughing at something he'd said. He'd been grinning, face dark with stubble, clutching a tallboy, unlike everyone else with their stolen Hopper wine.

It seemed impossible that both of them were dead now.

Was this the only time they'd met? They'd seemed at ease with each other, but Ruth had been pretty drunk. Did money change hands, or did he just give her the acid, caught in that same magnetism that had drawn me to her?

I had to keep moving. Standing still attracted the bugs, and there were more here, no doubt due to the swampy ground at the side of the lake. Blackflies buzzed in my hair, and I swatted around my face to get them out, get them away.

A crowd of geese honked aggressively at each other, or the world in general, on a small island some way out. I remembered a meme I'd seen online. It claimed that Canadians put all their nastiness in their geese and that's why they were so nice. People who said things like that had obviously not been at the library riot.

Canadians could be every bit as nasty as anyone else.

I paced around where the fire had been, checking the moss and lichen that punctuated the swells of granite like old gum. The blackflies kept coming, and the sharp flare of a bite on my neck drew a loud, frustrated swear. I flapped my hands around my head like an uncontrollable tic, glad there was no one to see.

I checked in the trees that surrounded the clearing, feeling like I was looking for Ruth all over again. There was nothing except undergrowth, an empty bottle, a couple of cans, and yet more bugs. What had I expected? I swore again, louder.

I tried to ignore the cloud of insects as I went down to the water, but I inhaled one of the little ones and started coughing. I spat out on the ground a load of times, and as I raised my head, something yellow caught my eye.

It wasn't far, just along the lake edge but separated from the main shore by a small stand of trees. I hurried over and into the tangle of the branches. It was only a few meters deep, but there was no helpful path here, like the one I'd followed from the road. Blinded by bugs, scratched by branches, and tripped by roots, I stumbled through, longing for stronger swear words.

I came out at a little indentation in the shore. Here the granite formed a kind of uneven mini-cliff that dropped into the lake, rather than the soft descent of stone into water where the fire was. Just beyond that bloomed the bright yellow flowers with black centers that I'd spotted from the fireside: black-eyed Susans. Just like those brought to Harry's grave each year. Hundreds grew in the marshy earth, swaying in the slight breeze, yellow heads rocking.

A blackfly flew right in my ear.

I yelped and hit myself in the side of the face. The deafening buzz continued, the vibration of the creature deep in my ear canal. My foot slipped on the edge of the lopsided rock, shattering my delicate balance. I fell backward, arms flailing as the world tilted and the sharp, bright sky filled my vision.

I was underwater, suddenly, impossibly. I screamed, swallowing the cloudy lake. I struggled, and my head broke the surface. I coughed and slipped under again, feet fumbling for solid ground, but there was nothing but reedy mush that gave way beneath my sneakers. I thrashed upward, desperate for breath and the shore, and one wild, bruising swing of my arm connected with stone. I grabbed onto it, pulling myself to safety.

I leaned both elbows on the rock, choking up lake water, retching and spitting. I waited until I could breathe properly again before dragging myself up onto solid ground, and lay there, half-curled on my side.

I shook, in spite of the heat. My lungs felt scoured out and sore. I was soaked, of course, and my thoughts briefly went to the phone in my pocket. Ruined, no doubt.

There were fewer bugs now, at least. The lake water had rinsed off the sweat that had attracted them, and the stupid blackfly responsible for the whole thing seemed to have been washed out of my ear. As soon as I was able to sit, I examined the shore where I sat. The lake was shockingly deep here, the slippery granite dropping at least a couple of meters straight down to a reedy lakebed that gave way underfoot. I shouldn't have been surprised. Bertie had said the lake was so dangerous George wouldn't let him come with him and Harry.

I could see why.

Is this what had happened to Ruth? Had she simply stumbled into the water out of sight of the party? If she'd seen the black-eyed Susans, she'd have been attracted to them too, remembering the posies left on Harry's memorial, wondering if her great-grandmother had come here each year to gather the flowers she left in memory of her lover. They could have been visible that night. They were just close enough to be caught in the firelight or by the sweep of a phone flashlight from the main shore.

Pine needles and small twigs clustered on the water's surface, and as I watched, the wind or the current rocked them gently toward the shallower water in front of the bonfire where we'd found Ruth's body. No wonder she washed up there.

It had only taken a headache and a well-targeted blackfly to make me lose my footing. Ruth had been wearing heels and was drunk and high when she drowned. The rocks here were uneven and treacherous. Was there no mystery at all, just a simple accident?

I ran my hand through my wet hair, squeezing out the ends so water splattered onto the stone, staining it with blotches of dark gray.

Ruth's great-grandmother couldn't have gotten the flowers here. Black-eyed Susans bloomed now, in the heat of summer. They'd have to be grown in a greenhouse to be put on Harry's grave in April, when only daffodils and crocuses were budding. And Harry probably wasn't the father of Margaret's child, if the DNA test was to be believed. So why would she be leaving flowers for him?

I coughed again, hard, as what should have been obvious hit me.

I'd assumed Margaret Wright left the flowers because the posies stopped when she passed away. But she wasn't the only person who died in 1995.

I was an idiot. I'd let the norms of the 1940s hide what should have been clear from the start. Whoever put the black-eyed Susans on Harry's grave went to a lot of trouble to get them out of season. They might have had to grow them indoors or in a greenhouse. They must have had a meaning. And this lake was where George and Harry came together, alone.

George had taken a month off right around the time of Harry's death. I'd assumed he'd had one of those lingering 1940s diseases like tuberculosis or polio. But perhaps he'd been grieving. I had no idea if Harry had felt the same way. He might not have. But I guessed that, at least for George, this was their special place: this lake where the black-eyed Susans thrived. George was the one who told young Bertie he couldn't come with him and Harry, using the lake's hazards as an excuse to allow them to be alone.

I started to cry, weeping and retching. Partly from delayed shock after almost drowning. But partly for George, unable to share his sorrow, leaving his lonely flowers for his love each year.

It took a few minutes to get myself back under control, slowing my sobs until they convulsed into hiccups. The lousy blackflies were back again, with no regard for the pain of the past.

I stood up, shirt and shorts dripping, and began the long walk back to the museum, shoes sloshing with each step.

CHAPTER TWENTY-FIVE
April–May 1945

As soon as Erich stepped back through the gates to the outer camp and the Canadian offices, he felt the change in the air, as if it weighed more heavily on everyone. As he was signed back in, he was struck by the grim silence, the lack of banter and jokes as he was passed from the custody of his new guard to another. He caught sight of a secretary hurrying between the offices, dabbing at her eyes with a tissue.

Had there been some change in the German fortunes? Perhaps Schmitt had been right and they'd been on the cusp of victory after all. Excitement shot through him as he imagined going home finally, to celebrations and triumph. But the joy evaporated as his old fantasy collapsed. His mother couldn't welcome him home anymore. His house was rubble. Daisy wasn't there.

Did he want to go home? Where was home?

His confusion deepened as he entered the main camp and was greeted by the same surrendered expressions on his comrades, the same listlessness he'd left that morning.

He found Karl in his bunk.

"What's going on?"

Karl rolled over and faced him. "Commandant's son bought it. Watch your step, guards are taking it out on everyone."

Erich nodded, finding vague memories of a gangly boy he'd seen at the offices once or twice. "But he's so young. What happened?"

Karl shook his head. "Other one. He was in the navy. Just joined up."

"Oh." Feelings flickered over him before settling on Daisy's face, on the promise of continuing his work at the farm.

Karl frowned at Erich, pushed himself to a sitting position, feet hanging off the side of his bunk. "You seem … I mean, I'm not expecting you to be cut up at the chap's death, but it's not like you to smile over it."

Erich hadn't realized he had been. He tried to rearrange his features to something more neutral. There was an effervescent excitement in him, a restless joy, and it pushed up the corners of his mouth. He struggled not to giggle.

"What is going on with you, Stein?"

He wanted to deny it, but her name was right there on his lips, surprising as her kiss.

"Daisy."

Karl smiled. "Oh, the farm girl, right? You're sweet on her?"

The room was mostly empty, other than Weber's grinding snores from the opposite end of the hut. Erich lowered his voice anyway.

"And … she likes me."

"Something happened between you?"

Erich nodded.

His friend took a deep breath and checked around carefully.

"That's not a good idea. I'm sorry, but it would cause all kinds of trouble for you here. And it's not good for her, either."

Erich felt as if the bubble inside him had popped. "But …"

"How do you think German girls would be dealt with if they got involved with the enemy?"

Erich swallowed. He'd heard about a woman down their street who'd had her head shaved after the last war and was treated like a whore.

But that was Germany. Canada was different, right?

"We have to go back eventually, whether it's in triumph or shame. You have no future with this girl. If you care for her at all, you'll leave well alone."

A thought floated into his mind then. A thought so wrong, so treacherous he closed his mouth tightly around it, before it could slip out.

What if he didn't go home when the war was over? What if he could stay here?

Lang's warning couldn't stop Erich's excitement on heading back to the farm the next day. The stone-faced expression of the new guard had told him there was no question of asking if he could sit in the front, in spite of the fact that it was drizzling and no other prisoners shared their ride this early in the year. The guard drove faster than George and hit every pit and rut in the road with a precision that seemed deliberate. By the time they'd reached the Novaks' farm, Erich was shivering, wet, and bruised.

Joe seemed a little better, at least well enough to sign the papers on his arrival, but when he retreated to his bed, Daisy found Erich in the barn again.

Afterwards, the rain thrummed on the newly patched roof above them as Erich tried to explain his conversation with Lang. Daisy shook her head.

"So why don't you stay? There are lots of German immigrants in Canada. Many of them came over after the last war to work on the railways."

It wasn't treason for her to say it, for her to reject the Fatherland. After all, what was the Fatherland to her? A distant country, at war with her home. But to hear his thoughts on her lips made it more real. Hope unfolded in him. Could he have a future here? Would he be accepted? He wondered how it would reflect on Daisy, having a German husband. Not that she'd said she wanted to marry him.

He didn't know if he even had the right to ask.

His days grew polarized. The death of the commandant's son reminded the Canadians that they were at war. No more smiles and nods as he was signed from one side of the camp to the other and then out to the farm. He missed George's cheery chatter on the drive over.

"What is wrong with George?" he asked once.

"None of your business," was the predictable reply.

Joe's daytime naps stopped, but he no longer helped Erich on the farm, even as the last of winter's grip slipped and the spring jobs began in earnest. Erich missed his workmanlike companionship and the solid thud of his hammer.

The camp was clutched by rumors. Some said the Soviets were approaching Berlin and the Allies had crossed the Rhine. As May began, word spread that Hitler had fallen fighting the Bolsheviks. Some said that was yet more propaganda, and even if it were true, Germany was more than just one man. Germany would never give up.

One morning, the Commandant himself came to roll call for the first time since the loss of his son. It was early May, and the blush of summer was in the morning air. He wore his full dress uniform, but his face sagged in a way it hadn't a month earlier. He held a sheet of paper and strode toward the group, chin high. The mud was dry, the sky blue.

"The German forces on land, sea, and in the air have been utterly defeated, and Germany has surrendered unconditionally," he read.

Gasps, mutterings among the men who understood English. Eyes turned to the Lagerführer. He nodded silently.

Erich held his hands tightly behind him. The warm wind was soft on his fingers and the back of his neck. It ruffled the hair of the soldier in front of him, gentle as a mother.

The Commandant continued reading. The Allies had supreme authority over Germany. They were in control now. The Commandant did not sound triumphant. Victory had come too late for him. When he'd finished, the same message was read in German by one of the camp translators.

Erich's heart thudded in his chest. Whispers moved through the men like the wind. An unseen bird called out as if in protest: a crow-like caw. Erich felt like he was falling backwards, away from the gentle spring day, into the chaos of his own bomb-blasted country. Someone behind him wept.

"It's not true!" Schmitt shouted.

The Commandant ignored him. "I am sure you are all wondering when you will be able to go home, but much work must be done to ensure the demilitarization of Germany. You are likely to remain here for a good while longer."

Erich exhaled, steady again, feet placed firmly on Canadian soil.

The Lagerführer spoke next, ordering the discontinuation of the Nazi salute and the resumption of the older German military salute. Indignant murmurs spread through the men. They returned to their huts to chew over the news, air thick with debate, denial, and the smoke from their Canadian-issued cigarettes.

Once it got dark, fireworks burst over Westonville, bright even from the camp. Lines of light shot across the sky like tracer fire, booming like mortars.

Obergrenadier Walter shook and sobbed all night, keeping the hut awake long after the distant celebrations had faded. Erich didn't know if it was from the news or the noise.

Defeat was a strange thing. It touched each of the men differently. For some, it was liberating, and they leaned back, beers in hand, sitting on the steps of their huts, enjoying the summer sun. Some turned to religion, clutching bibles and attending services. For some, it was torture. They roamed the camp like spirits trapped in an earthly hell, heads and backs bowed, struggling against a wind the others couldn't feel. There were those who denied it altogether, insisting it was misinformation, or a temporary stratagem on the German side to unmask the communists, Jews, and saboteurs in their ranks so they could be purged. They dealt brutally with those who disagreed. After Klaus Huber spoke of his excitement in going home, in seeing his young family again, he limped for a week.

On the other side of the wire, things grew lax. Erich wasn't sure if it was because of the end of the war or the collapse of the grieving Commandant's careful discipline. The guards from outside Westonville talked about having done their duty, about wanting to go home. The Germans had never been welcome, but now they were no longer a threat, just a burden.

The old man on gate duty seemed to have given up on his job altogether. He kept asking Erich when he and his "friends" were leaving, and on more than one occasion, didn't bother to check the papers George's standoffish replacement carried when he came to collect him, simply waving them both through.

"Maybe I can stay," Erich said to Lang, one mild evening, as they shared a cigarette on a walk around the perimeter, away from the wrong ears. Surely it wasn't treason to say it out loud since Germany had fallen?

The scent of the kitchen hut wafted their way, promising beef and *bratkartoffeln*. The cooks made the potatoes perfectly, laced with bacon and onions, the edges crisp, the centers soft.

Karl shook his head. "You know Becker, over in hut B? Guy with the —" he mimed at the side of his face, and Erich nodded. He'd seen him around, his ear and upper neck mottled and half-melted from a fire in his plane before he was able to bail.

"He's been working at a farm, and apparently, his boss there spoke to the Commandant about him staying. They said we're all going back, no exceptions."

Erich exhaled. Lang always knew more than him about what was going on.

"We're all going home, and there's nothing any of us can do about it." He took one last, long drag of the cigarette, swearing as the embers touched his fingers. He dropped it, pausing their walk to grind it out with his foot. "And it's our duty, too. We have a country to put right."

But that country was thousands of kilometers away, and the Canadians seemed in no great hurry to send any of them back. They'd said they'd be staying for months.

Things could still change, couldn't they?

A week later they did.

Daisy came running out of the house, screaming Erich's name in the late afternoon. For one frozen moment, he remembered a comrade screaming like that in the desert as he fell to his knees, remembered the red blooming impossibly fast through his khaki uniform. As soon as Erich was able to move, he ran to her, looking her over for blood, for an injury, but she was perfect as ever.

Her cheeks glistened with tears, and when she took his hands in hers, they were wet. "It's Joe. Please, come quickly."

They hurried to the house together. She led him into the short hallway behind the kitchen, where he'd never been allowed before, and up the stairs. At the top, a door stood a little ajar, revealing the corner of a patchy fur rug on the wooden floor. She pushed it open.

Her father lay on the small bed, covered with a faded, home-stitched quilt.

"I can't wake him!"

Erich ran over and touched his arm. Joe was warm, and Erich shifted his grip down to Joe's wrist, fumbling until he found a pulse.

"Alive," he said, then leaned over his mouth. For a moment, he couldn't catch the sound of Joe's breath, and when he did, it was so soft he thought for a moment he only imagined it, and he waited for another whispered inhale before he was sure. "Breathing is bad. We need help."

They looked at each other.

"Our truck isn't reliable," Daisy said. She glanced at her father and back at Erich, before realizing he hadn't understood. She mimed a steering wheel. "Kaputt a lot. And I can't drive."

"I drive," Erich said. He wasn't at all sure he'd be able to do much if the truck broke down, but he could see in the way Daisy fluttered around her stepfather, reaching for him then pulling back, that she wanted to stay by his bedside.

"They'll think you're trying to escape. They'll shoot you."

Erich shrugged. "I drive to camp. No one escape to camp. There are doctors there." He felt like an idiot with his broken English, drowning in the distance between them and all he wanted to say.

Daisy's movements stilled. She nodded. "Please be careful."

"I will."

She clasped his hands, leaned in, and kissed him hard.

A wheeze came from the bed. They both turned. Joe's eyes were open, but they fluttered and closed once more.

"Did he see us?" Daisy whispered.

Erich shrugged. He wasn't sure if there was any consciousness behind that momentary gaze, and while the prospect of Joe catching them filled Erich with terror, it didn't change what had to be done.

"Keys," he said, and she ran to get them.

It wasn't easy to get the old truck going. Erich had seen Joe do it a few times when they'd had rocks or wood to move, and he was sure there was a trick to it. He banged on the wheel and kicked at it before the engine finally turned over with a juddering roar.

Daisy's face was pale at the window as Erich put the truck into gear and it lurched and shuddered down the dirt road. The truck was hard to steer, sticking in the ruts of the road as he leaned his whole weight on the worn wheel. It was slower than the camp truck he rode in on, and the delay was agonizing.

A couple of kilometers out from the farm, the old engine gave a whine and shook itself into silence, other than the ticking of the metal as it cooled.

Erich tried to restart it, but it was completely dead. He swore at it, jumped out, and lifted the hood. The engine steamed, and Erich squinted at the mess of gray metal, realizing his basic mechanical training was too rudimentary to get the truck to restart. It might need parts, and he had none, but the farm they'd dropped the other two men at couldn't be many kilometers farther. They might even have a phone. It had to be faster than trying to fix the engine. Erich abandoned the truck and jogged on.

It was harder going than he expected. The road was in a state after the long winter, the ruts deep and criss-crossing, and he turned his ankle more than once when it landed on a ridge of dry mud or a stone. His run became a fast limp. He wished he'd kept up his exercises, kept up the soccer and running. He coughed, struggling to catch his breath. His lungs felt scratched and sore. Beside the road, white webs hammocked between branches, caterpillars clustering darkly within. He'd destroyed many moths' nests like these on the farm, and he itched to rip down these ones, frustration at his uselessness now, when it most mattered, filling him with anger.

For the first time, Erich cursed Canada, cursed the vastness of the country, the isolation of the Novaks' farm.

The shadows were lengthening. It had been too long since he'd left the house. He tried not to think of Daisy back there, impatient for help.

When Erich heard the roar of a truck, he mouthed thanks to God. He waved his hands as it came along the road toward him, jolting in the ruts. He recognized the vehicle, the man behind the wheel.

It was the camp truck, the surly new guard. Was it that late, already?

The truck clattered to a halt. The guard leapt out, rifle in hand. "Hands up!"

Erich complied. "Help! Joe need help."

"Quiet!" There was triumph in the man's eyes.

"Please!" Erich cried. "Joe, at the farm. Sick!"

The guard gave a harsh bark of a laugh. "You must take me for an idiot."

He leveled the barrel at Erich's chest. "Down on the ground. One more word and I'll shoot."

CHAPTER TWENTY-SIX

Being wet made the walk home easier, in spite of my pounding headache. The sun mostly dried my hair and clothes, but my sneakers were still soaking. When I was back at the museum, I kicked off my shoes under the desk. I caught the damp reek of my wet socks and was revolted. I shoved my feet back into my sneakers, hoping no one else could smell them.

I just stared at my screen for a while. The idea of working seemed absurd. In the last two days, I'd found a body and almost drowned, and I couldn't even talk to anyone about it.

Once I'd calmed down a bit, I noticed an email had come in from the man in Kitchener whose father had been at the camp, and I robotically set up a Zoom meeting for the next day. After that, I went back to the camp war diary, and re-read the simple entry that started George's long leave. *George Wright left at 3 p.m. He reports he is unwell and unable to attend to his duties.* I double checked the dates. It was the day Harry died. The ship had sunk in the very early morning. Word could have reached the camp by telegram by three p.m.

There was so much unspoken within those two lines. Would people at the camp have known how George felt? Even if they did, in the repressive 1940s, perhaps they thought it would be better if they stayed silent, if they didn't mention what he'd lost, who he'd loved.

My feet were still wet. I could feel the shriveled skin on my toes and thought of trench foot, even though that was a different war. There was water trapped in my ear, producing a scrunching, staticky noise when I moved my head. I felt too gross, too damp to be sitting in the neat office, to be putting my wet shoes on the perfect, cream broadloom. The heat from the square of sunlight didn't seem to help, just warming the water my body stewed in.

Randall glanced my way twice, which had to be the most he'd acknowledged my existence in the whole time I'd been there. I wondered if I smelled that bad, or if he could hear the crackling in my ear.

I really, really hoped Max wouldn't come in and see me in that stinking state.

Poor Margaret. Her fate was obvious, even if Harry wasn't the father of her child. She could have been knocked up by another dead soldier or just some local guy she shouldn't have trusted. Either way, she was clearly unmarried, pregnant, and out of options. I knew enough about the intolerant attitude then to realize George needed to hide who he was. Were they able to find a little happiness together, to make a happy home for Ruth's grandmother? I hoped so. Perhaps they found friendship, but if I was right, they wouldn't have found the love either of them wanted.

It seemed unbelievably cruel that this was the world the protestors at the library wanted back. The language at the trial in Medicine Hat, with its condemnation of "homosexualist natures" and "perverted minds," didn't feel any different from the placards I'd read at the library. Hate and slurs intended to make people feel unsafe, feel they had to hide who they are. How dare they try to get rid of 2SLGBTQ+ books? How dare they try to put more generations through that kind of torture and heartbreak?

But if Harry wasn't Ruth's great-grandfather, who could be?

I went back to the ancestry websites. I wasn't really expecting to find anything. I was barely focusing as I scrolled through the familiar information, when a name floated before my eyes.

Novak.

I paused and scrolled back down, looking for where I'd seen it. There was Margaret Wright, Ruth's great-grandmother. Her maiden name was Fortin, like Ruth had said. But right above her was her mother: Adelaide Novak.

It took me a moment to work out why they had different last names. Adelaide had been married twice, first to Arthur Fortin then to Joseph Novak. Margaret was from Adelaide's first marriage and had kept her father's last name. Margaret Fortin was Joseph Novak's stepdaughter.

I hadn't bothered looking at Margaret's parents before. But I knew exactly who Joseph Novak was. He owned the farm Erich Stein worked at. The farm Erich tried to escape from. There had even been a mention of a "Daisy" in the note about his attempted escape. I did some quick googling and found out "Daisy" was a common nickname for "Margaret."

I felt dizzy. Ruth's family knew Erich Stein. There was even — my breath caught as I thought of it — a chance Erich Stein himself was Ruth's great-grandfather. It would certainly explain why she'd married George Wright and moved away. She would have been just as desperate to keep the father of her baby secret as

George would have been to hide his sexuality. The social penalties for both were unthinkable. Margaret Fortin could even have been the one to start the "family rumor" about Harry, in case anyone suspected that George was gay. Harry couldn't very well deny it when he was dead.

Ruth obviously knew none of this. But did anyone else? Was it why Erich Stein was killed? And could what happened eighty years ago have had anything to do with Ruth's death now?

I slipped out of work early, using my headache as an excuse. Sarah seemed lost in her own thoughts, barely listening when I told her I was going home for a lie-down. I showered and left my shoes outside to dry in the sun. I lay down on my bed and promptly fell asleep.

I was still reeling as I woke and wandered into the kitchen to get food hours later. Ephram, Asha, and Max were there. Ephram sat on the sofa next to Max, who looked perfect as usual. I wished I'd styled my hair properly instead of falling asleep after my shower. Although, I was glad I didn't smell, at least. Asha perched on the edge of the worn armchair. They all watched me enter and wander toward the fridge.

"What's going on, Keira?" Max asked.

"What do you mean?" I opened the fridge and stared at the shelves, already forgetting what I'd been planning to eat.

"You came back to the museum with your hair a mess and wet shoes today. And yesterday, you disappeared for hours."

"I just went for a couple of walks. It was raining yesterday, and my shoes didn't dry out properly." I selected the milk, although I didn't want it. I shut the fridge door and pulled out a glass.

"You totally read that DNA letter to Ruth, didn't you?" Asha said.

"If you're looking into Ruth's death," Max said, dark hair in his eyes, "if you think it wasn't an accident, we should all know. We worked with her too."

"Ruth and I were close," I said, a little petulantly.

Asha folded her arms. "Yeah, right. You were just a bigger sucker than the rest of us."

That stung.

"Did she tell you about all the things she made up to get in the program? The faked awards?" Ephram asked.

My silence answered him. I stared at the cold, white glass in my hand, knowing I couldn't stomach a sip of it.

"She lied to you just as much as the rest of us," Asha said. "And if there's anything suspicious about her death, we all deserve to know. I've been feeling awful ever since that night."

"*You* have? What for?"

"I promised I'd walk her home, remember? Ephram and I said we'd make sure she got back safely. And she didn't."

Ephram nodded, gaze stuck to the table.

"But it wasn't your fault."

"Wasn't it?" Asha lowered her head, her rainbow hair falling over her face. "I should have been watching her. It was my party. Do you know how much I've wished I never threw the damn thing? If I hadn't, she wouldn't have been high and drunk near a lake. If there's another reason why she died, I would really, really like to know about it."

The fridge started beeping. I hadn't closed the door properly. I hit the door, and it shut up.

"I don't get any of it," Ephram said, pushing up his glasses. "I don't even know why she went to such lengths to fake her references. She never seemed interested in the program."

I rubbed at my forehead. The whole thing felt like an intervention. The worst thing was that they were right. I'd been treating Ruth like she'd been mine. But I'd barely known her.

All three of them watched me, waiting.

So I told them about the DNA test, about everything I'd found out about George, Harry, and Margaret. About how Ruth probably thought she was a Hopper, but wasn't. About how Erich Stein might even have been her great-grandfather, although there was no way of knowing.

Ephram leaned back, smiling. "Wow. That's some impressive research."

Coming from him, it felt like the most amazing compliment.

Asha nodded, throwing a leg over the side of the armchair, so she was sitting in it sideways. "And that's why she was sucking up to them so much. She was hoping she could join the family, be a special little rich girl."

"I overheard her saying she had something on Bertie, at the party. That's what she meant. The DNA." Max shook his head sadly.

"She was definitely talking about the DNA," I said. "But I got the impression she knew something else, too."

"Do you think Harry was gay?" Asha asked. "That would be funny. If the Hopper family golden boy was one of us."

I shrugged. "I don't know. I don't even know for sure if George was. It's still possible he was just, like, super sad about his best friend. And even if George was gay, his feelings could have been unrequited. People talk about Harry as if he was a bit of a ladies' man. Perhaps that's why Margaret let people think he might have been the father of her child."

Asha sighed. "Shame."

"But what would any of that have to do with Ruth's death?" Ephram asked.

"I don't know. But that's why I went to the lake today. I just wanted to try to work out how it happened."

"And?" Asha asked.

I shrugged. "I fell in, hence the wet shoes, when I was looking at the black-eyed Susans. It's entirely possible Ruth just slipped. It was deep there and tricky to get back out. In her state, she might not have been able to."

I didn't tell them how I'd struggled and panicked, even sober. That was too raw.

"So you think it was an accident after all?" Max said.

"Maybe, but ...," I paused, not wanting to admit to going to the trailer park, to finding a body. "You know that guy at the party? Colt — the one who dealt drugs? I saw him talking to Ruth. He was found dead yesterday. The police are looking into it."

"You think he murdered Ruth?" Max sounded horrified.

"He could have, but I don't think there's any way we could know. And the police think he died of an accidental fentanyl overdose, so it's totally possible it was all really bad luck. It's just ... There were two beer bottle tops in his trailer and only one bottle. Like someone was there, maybe around when he died, but they took their drink with them when they left."

"Wait." Ephram held up a hand. "How on earth do you know all that?"

I should have realized I couldn't get that past him. The three of them looked at me. I took a swallow of my drink, trying to think of some nice, innocent way I could have found out. Instead, I almost gagged on the thick coldness of the milk.

"I ... found his body."

"Oh my God," Asha said.

"You did what?" That was Max.

Ephram shook his head. "What were you doing there?"

"I wanted to ask him if he'd given Ruth the LSD."

"Holy crap," Asha said. "Keira, that's insane."

I leaned against the countertop. It dug into my hip.

"Does Sarah know about any of this?" Ephram asked.

"No one does," I said in a small voice. "Except you three and the police, obviously."

Max looked at me, concern in his eyes. "Keira, you should have spoken to us. That was crazy dangerous. I don't know who this Colt guy was, but going to see a drug dealer who possibly killed Ruth on your own … He could have … I don't know. He sounds like he was bad news."

"Yeah," I said, feeling warm at Max's worry for me. "I know it was stupid."

"So who do you think was there with him?" Asha asked.

"Not a clue. And it's probably nothing. But maybe the police will be able to check for prints and find out."

Ephram interlaced his fingers. "It sounds like you're overthinking this. Occam's razor. The most likely explanation is the obvious one. Ruth bought acid from Colt, fell in the water, and was too incapacitated to get out, and Colt died from an unrelated fentanyl overdose."

"Or this Colt guy felt guilty for selling her the stuff and killed himself," Max added.

I didn't know Colt, but I'd been thinking about that, and a dealer displaying a Confederate flag in Canada didn't seem like the kind of person who'd feel much shame. There was a "screw your feelings" vibe that didn't mesh with overwhelming guilt for a stranger's death. But I couldn't expect Max to know that.

"I'm not sure if the Hoppers would have cared about Ruth being a distant cousin, even if she had been," Asha said. "It's not like she would have been entitled to inherit, right?"

She directed that comment at Max, who shrugged. "I guess not. But it could still be a threat to them. They hate anything that could be bad publicity."

"Well, in that case, they have much bigger problems now," Asha said.

"What?" I asked.

There was a certain glee in her reply. "Haven't you seen the news?" She leapt out of her seat, picked up her phone from the table. She brought up an article and handed it over.

PETER HOPPER EMPLOYEE ALLEGES AFFAIR, PRESSURE TO ABORT, the headline screamed.

The picture underneath was Peter at an event, zoomed in and cropped so it showed him and the woman standing behind him, her sleek black bob pushed behind her ears. It was the woman who'd been at the house when I interviewed Bertie. I scanned the article. She claimed they'd had an affair and she'd had an abortion at his insistence. Peter was denying everything and planning to sue.

"We heard them arguing," I said. "Max, Ruth, and I, on the day he fired her. She was pretty upset."

"You heard him fire her?" Asha asked eagerly. "Did he say anything about the affair?"

Max shrugged.

"I'm not sure," I said, trying to remember. "I was focusing on what Bertie said. But I was recording it. I might have caught something in the background."

Asha grabbed my wrist. "You recorded it? Oh my God, Keira! You could have caught him admitting to everything!"

"He did ask if we'd overheard, remember?" I asked Max. "He seemed worried, too. Maybe he said something incriminating."

Max sat forward, animated. "That's right. He was totally surprised we were there. Maybe that's why he invited you to their party, to change the subject and distract us all."

"Maybe Ruth heard and confronted him," Asha said. "That's a motive."

"She did say she'd argued with Julia," I added.

"We should listen to the recording before everyone gets too excited," Ephram said. "He might not have said anything."

They all leaned in, and I pulled up the file on my phone. I put the phone on the table between us and hit "play." There was an odd crackling.

"What's wrong with it?"

I slumped back. "I fell in the lake, remember? It was in my pocket."

Asha's face crinkled in disappointment. "Is the file destroyed, or just the phone speaker? Did you make a backup?"

"I was going to upload it at work and transcribe it. But then came the party and everything. I forgot all about it. I can try to send it to one of you and see if it works on your phones."

But when I tried, I couldn't connect to the Wi-Fi, either.

Ephram took my phone and looked it over. "The water might have damaged the internal antenna or the speaker or both. It might just need to dry off some more."

"Put it in rice," Asha suggested.

Ephram shook his head. "That's actually bad for phones. Just put it somewhere warm and dry for a day. If it doesn't work tomorrow, we can hook it up to my portable speaker. If the file's okay, and it turns out there's something on there, we can upload it to a computer using a cable."

He handed the phone back, and I stared at the useless brick in my hand, silently praying that it would work when it dried out properly.

CHAPTER TWENTY-SEVEN

May–June 1945

Erich's hands were handcuffed behind him at gunpoint, his legs shackled. The guard threw him in the back of the truck. The metal of the truck bed bumped and bruised him as the guard drove toward the camp, faster than they had ever gone before, the vehicle leaping as it hit pits and holes in the roads, Erich landing hard on his hip, his shoulder, and his face.

Still, Erich tried to sit up, to kneel up, to get close enough to the cab to shout, to yell about Joe needing help, to beg and to plead in his bad English that was further broken by the bumps in the road.

It was clear from the guard's face in the rearview mirror he didn't believe a word of it.

At the camp, Erich was bundled out and onto his knees at gunpoint, surrounded by yet more guards. Still, he begged for them to send help. He was dragged through the gates and thrown into the solitary hut.

The first evening was the longest.

His body felt like tenderized meat. His shoulders, elbows, knees, and hips had all taken their turns being battered on the rough drive back, and the only distraction from the pain was the fear for Joe's life and his deeper, queasier fear that Joe had seen their kiss. If Joe had, he'd never be allowed back to the farm. And if Joe died, he'd never be allowed back to the Novaks' farm. They'd never let a POW work for a lone woman, unsupervised.

Would he ever see Daisy again?

He waited for someone to come to tell him what had happened, but the hours passed and the hut grew dark with no news. He barely slept, the flare of pain waking him whenever his body twitched or rolled in the night. Dawn brought breakfast from a guard who ignored his pleas. Time rolled on, marked only by meals delivered by silent guards and the change in the colors of his bruises from red to purplish black, to green, to yellow. Finally, they faded completely. Time stretched out. The hut was comfortable enough, but each moment without news was agony.

Twenty-eight days. That was how long prisoners were locked up for escape attempts. And there would be no cheers, no congratulations in the camp when he was released. Escaping while on work duty was not okay. He'd given his word, as a German, that he wouldn't.

As the days passed, he stopped pacing the small room, sweating in the tight space. He stopped begging the guards for news. Stopped hoping George would come and tell him what was happening. He hunched up on the bed and stared at the walls until his gaze blurred.

He was sure it was far longer than twenty-eight days when

the door finally opened. He was sure he'd been imprisoned forever when the guard gestured at him to come out. He stepped out into the sun, blinking. The guard led him back to the main camp wordlessly.

Erich found Karl outside their hut, smoking.

Karl hurried over as soon as he caught sight of him. He hugged him, then clutched at his arm. "What happened?"

Karl gave him not just one, but two cigarettes as he explained. Erich paced, kicking up dust from the dry earth with each emphatic step. When he was done, Karl exhaled.

"So, you weren't trying to escape. I'll let our lot know, or you'll be up before a court of honor for breaking your word. Don't worry. The Lagerführer will listen to me."

Erich struggled to take this in. He hadn't even thought about punishment from his own side. It didn't seem important.

"But no one will tell me anything about Joe, about Daisy! I have to find out." He turned, intending to head for the fence, for the guards there, to demand answers. But Karl caught his wrist.

"Stay back." He glanced around. "You don't want to be seen cozying up with the guards. Things haven't been great here the last few days. Schmitt and his lot are making things hard. Demanding everyone demonstrates total loyalty to the Reich."

Erich stared. "But … it's over."

Karl bit his lip. "Don't say that. They won't accept it. They insist it's just a ploy to get the POWs home as reinforcements, or to flush out the traitors, or to get the Allies to let down their guard. Or they say they've been betrayed by Jews and Bolsheviks, and once we get back, we'll purge the state and put things right."

Erich shook his head. "They can't believe that."

"They seem pretty convinced. And they've been threatening people's families."

Erich thought of his mother and, for a moment as he remembered, felt as if he were falling. But they couldn't hurt her anymore, at least. And they had no way of reaching Daisy or Joe.

"And there's something happening here later. Some kind of a film they're showing."

Erich brightened slightly. He could use a distraction. "A movie?"

"Yeah, but I don't think it's a good one."

Karl was right. They were filed into the main hall, filled with chairs. At the front hung the usual white screen they put up for movies. But there was a solemn kind of anger among the guards that squashed any remaining hope of entertainment.

It was a newsreel in German, showing camps being freed by Allied soldiers. Erich thought they were prisoner-of-war camps for a moment, but there were children in there too. And the people were too thin, impossibly so. He wondered that they were still alive with so little flesh on their skeletons. Many of them wore the Star of David on their striped outfits, marking them out as Jews. The camera lingered on heaps of things he didn't recognize for too long, until the horrifying understanding of what they were settled on him.

Bodies. Mounds and mounds of bodies. Children, women, men, a nightmarish collection of dead, naked, tangled limbs. Erich felt dizzy. They'd all been murdered by Germans. Slaughtered by the Reich. Uncountable numbers.

Laughter came from behind him. He craned around in his

seat and caught Schmitt's gaze. "Fake. Hollywood propaganda," he said with a wave of his hand. "Ignore it."

The man next to Schmitt joined in, their dismissive chuckles sounding forced.

Erich turned back to the screen and to the emaciated faces of children through barbed wire. It didn't look fake. The snickers from behind continued, and he felt sick. In spite of their dismissal, the film rang true. It connected with too much that he'd tried to ignore.

He'd read the newspapers. He'd witnessed the anger at the Jews, the "degenerates," the communists. He'd heard the claims that the German people and their way of life were under attack and had to be defended, that the corruption in their state had to be cut out. He'd seen furious protests, smashed storefronts, and people spitting on others in the street.

They'd been discouraged from shopping at Jewish stores, then the stores closed and the people who ran them were gone. He'd been told that to be sympathetic to them was to be feminine: sentimental and weak-minded. There had been talk of expelling the Jews from the Reich, of resettling them elsewhere. But there had been darker talk too, and songs about Jewish blood being spilled.

Erich had been a part of it. A stupid, ignorant part. He should have known. They all should have known. He'd told himself that was metaphorical. He'd told himself anything to avoid the truth. He'd focused on the bright future he'd thought they deserved, the restored and glorious Thousand-year Reich, their fixed country, and ignored the rest.

Daisy's face floated into his mind, and he retched. How could he have thought he deserved someone like her? How could he stain a girl like that, link her with this?

He stumbled out of the screening into the bright afternoon light, Karl beside him.

"We have to do something," Karl said, glancing at Schmitt.

The days lurched by. Karl was as good as his word, and things were smoothed out with the Lagerführer. But Erich wasn't called for work duty again. No news came on Joe and Daisy, and Erich no longer sought it out. He didn't deserve to know. He didn't deserve the happiness he'd found at the little farm. He didn't deserve her.

He spent his days walking listlessly around the edge of the camp or lying in his bunk, facing the rough splinters of the wooden wall, like he had after his mother died. But this time there was no Dr. Bauer to pull him out of his depression.

He'd looked the other way then, too. He'd suspected Bauer's "suicide" was no such thing, and he'd done nothing, in spite of everything Dr. Bauer had done for him.

Karl, on the other hand, seemed to have found new energy. He met with others, whispering together in clusters, many of them bearing the bruises that suggested a run-in with Schmitt's boys. There was a new tension in the camp, electricity building like the air before a storm.

Erich was on one of his endless walks, feet dragging as he stared at the ground ahead of him, when a familiar voice called out.

"Erich!"

George stood in a guard tower above. "Wait there!"

Erich froze, paralyzed by hope, as George scrambled down the ladder, glancing around.

"George! You're back!"

But any hope Erich had dissolved at George's grim expression.

"Joe?"

George shook his head. "Not good. He was in the hospital for a while, but there's nothing they can do for him. He insisted on going home for the last of it."

Erich stumbled, almost tripping over the warning wire.

"Get back," George said. "I shouldn't let you this near anyway." He glanced around.

Erich took a step back. "Daisy?"

George's face tightened. "She's pregnant."

"What?" Erich didn't know the word.

"She's having a baby, Erich." He mimed the swell of a stomach. "Yours, I presume?"

Erich stumbled and sat on the hard, dry ground. "Baby?"

George nodded, and Erich tried to sort out his thoughts, joy and horrific shame fighting for dominance.

"My baby?"

George looked at the ground. "You know you've put her in an awful situation?"

"Joe, he knows?"

George shook his head. "Not about the baby. But he knows something. He was so angry when I mentioned your name. He doesn't want you back at the farm."

He had seen them kiss. Erich swallowed, feeling the pain of that. He'd betrayed Joe's trust. He'd got Daisy pregnant. He'd messed up everything.

George looked awkward. "I've proposed marriage. She and Joe have agreed."

"What?"

George took another breath, tried again, pointing to himself. "I will marry Daisy. She will be my wife. My frau."

"Ehefrau? You?"

"It'll make Joe happy for the little time he has left. We'll move away after he … Get a fresh start, leave the talk behind."

"No! I …" Erich tailed off. Of course he couldn't marry her.

George sighed. "Look, maybe once this is all over, you can come back to Canada. Maybe we can sort a quiet divorce in the city and put things to rights."

Erich didn't understand. Couldn't have understood, even if he knew the words. It was too much. Joe was dying, hating him. Erich was going to be a father, but Daisy was marrying George. Erich had no right to her, no claim to the future that George was taking from him.

But still.

"Look, I've got to go back before I'm seen." He pointed back up at the tower.

"Tell Daisy," Erich paused. There was so much he wanted to tell her. "I love her. I'm sorry. I …"

"I'm sorry too," George said. "But you know this is best for everyone, right?" He reached for the ladder.

Erich couldn't reply to that. He stayed sitting on the ground. George climbed back up to his post. For a long while, they just looked at each other, George from his post, Erich from his place trapped inside the rusting barbed wire.

When Erich could finally move, he went in search of Karl. They found a spot by the hut, and Erich told him everything.

Karl lit a cigarette for each of them. They smoked in silence for a while, looking out at the other men, exercising, walking, or talking in laughing or solemn clusters.

"You know it's for the best."

"He's stealing my girl."

Karl laughed at that. "Your girl is safe with him."

"What do you mean?"

He spat out the stray ends of tobacco from his cigarette. "Let's just say he doesn't want her for himself, but it'll make things easier for him. Moving away is smart. Too much gossip here."

"But …"

"You know everyone would put it together if he didn't marry her, right? The German soldier and the lonely farm girl?"

Again, the gut-deep nauseating shame. They fell silent as the hut door opened. Two other soldiers thudded down the stairs, giving them a quick nod as they passed.

"But what am I meant to do? Just go home, and leave her?"

Karl turned on him, a sudden intensity in his expression. "You're meant to try to make things right. What kind of country are we going back to?"

Erich shook his head.

"We pretended we didn't see, all of us. But we see now, don't we? So we have to stop what's left of it. You know there are people here who won't accept that we lost."

Erich got it now. The meetings, the whisperings. "You're planning … What?"

Karl stared at him for a long time, as if deciding. Eventually he nodded. "It's not my plan. It's Schmitt and his lot. I found a noose in my bed."

Erich put a hand over his mouth.

"On Thursday next week, they're coming. They've passed a death sentence on me because of what I've been saying. But Schmitt's boys aren't as loyal as he thinks, and I got wind of it."

"What have you been saying?"

"Exactly what I've been saying to you. That when we get home, we need to purge every last one of the Nazi Party from their positions. We need to flush the poison out of Germany."

Erich froze. "You need to go to the Canadians and ask for protective custody."

Karl shook his head. "This is about more than me. The Lagerführer disagrees with Schmitt and has ordered him not to carry out the attack."

"Schmitt's disobeying the Lagerführer?"

"It's a deliberate challenge. If Schmitt succeeds, it'll show that the Lagerführer has lost his authority. He'll have no choice but to resign."

Erich snapped his head up. "What? But …"

"The Lagerführer knows the war is over. Schmitt is still fighting it. He sees the surrender as a setback, not a defeat. He thinks that once we get home, we can restore National Socialism and restart the war. This is where we decide who we are. This is where we fight back. We're going to be waiting for them."

Erich kicked at the dry mud by the hut steps, thinking of the bodies, of the emaciated faces, of Dr. Bauer's "suicide," of everything he'd been a part of, everything he should have been paying attention to instead of his relationship with Daisy, his betrayal of Joe's trust.

"Me too," Erich said.

Karl frowned. "I need all the help I can get. But it's going to be dangerous. People will die."

Erich took a deep breath. The wind paused, trees beyond the wire silent for a moment, as if waiting for what he was about to say. But there was only one real option.

"Let's make sure you're not one of them."

CHAPTER TWENTY-EIGHT

My phone still wouldn't connect to Wi-Fi the following morning. I only tried once and turned it off after that as the battery was super low. I wasn't sure if plugging it in would short it out completely if there was still water inside, and I didn't want to risk it. It still had just about enough power to try it out with Ephram's speaker later, and I could charge it after that, if it worked. I shoved the charging cable into the mess of my bag.

At breakfast, Asha passed me the milk for my cereal without me even asking, and Ephram asked if I wanted some of his French press coffee instead of the drip stuff I usually made. I guessed this was what it felt like to have housemates who were your friends. I held the feeling gently and felt it brighten me.

Was this what it would be like at university?

Even Sarah joined us just before we left for work, hastily making a cup of tea and carrying it into the main museum with her. She was quieter than usual, her whole body tense.

Randall looked up as we entered the upstairs office that

morning. He glanced at his watch, pointedly, even though we were only three minutes late.

"Sarah," he said. "The Chairman of the Board and I need to have a meeting with you at nine-thirty."

Sarah paused. "That's very short notice. I have a busy day ahead and …"

"I'm sure you'll manage to fit us in. It is very important."

"I suppose so." The frown lines etched themselves deeper into Sarah's forehead.

"Excellent. We'll talk then. I've booked the education room. That reminds me, I need to set up a few things there." Randall headed downstairs.

"Right," Sarah said, so quietly I almost missed it. "Right." She pressed her lips together, waited until Randall's footsteps had faded, and headed to the gallery.

Not long after she'd left, more footsteps came up the stairs, and Max strode in. "Just passed Sarah. She looked upset. Did I miss anything?"

"Not yet," Asha said. "But the coast's clear. Let's get to work then, shall we?"

The three of us went to Ephram's desk, which was in the opposite corner from Randall. I turned my phone back on and plugged it into his little speaker. I brought up the sound file and hit play.

"*This is Harry.*" It was Ruth's voice. I shouldn't have been surprised, but it still came as a shock, hearing her. "*The whole of Westonville adored him. There's a memorial to him in the churchyard.*"

Asha gasped. Max's gray eyes met mine. Ephram shook his head sadly. Ruth could have been in the office with us. She felt so close.

I turned it up.

"*So, Harry was best friends with George Wright?*" I said.

"*George would have done anything for Harry, from what Bertie's told me,*" Ruth replied.

I swallowed. The numbers at the bottom ticked off the first few seconds into the recording, a tiny ball crawling along a line. I wasn't sure I could hold it together.

Asha pointed at the battery symbol in the corner, keeping her voice soft. "That might not last the whole thing. When during the interview do you think ...?"

"Not sure," I said, trying to keep my voice steady. "Probably about halfway." I moved the ball to the midway point.

As Bertie's voice cut back in, the sound of footsteps came from the stairs, and Randall re-entered the room.

"*... was a ... hero. He died fighting ... the worst evil our world has seen.*" Bertie coughed.

We all froze. I paused it.

"What are you listening to?" Randall demanded as he entered the room. "Shouldn't you be working?"

"It's an interview with my granddad about the camp," Max said.

"Oh," Randall seemed disappointed that he couldn't be angry at us. "Well, I suppose you have to carry on then."

We all glanced at each other.

"We don't have to do it now if it'll disturb you," Asha said.

"Oh no, you're not getting off work that easily. This has to be less disruptive than your usual teenage chatter. Get back to it."

That was totally unfair, since we were usually all quiet in the office. But now we couldn't turn the interview off without looking really suspicious. I put my finger over the play button, and Ephram nodded.

I turned it down, and we carried on listening, all of us leaning right in toward the speaker, Max's face too close to mine. Out of the corner of my eye, I could see his lips just inches away.

"*He sounds amazing,*" Ruth said, bringing my attention back to the interview, to her still alive and breathing, preserved on my phone.

"*… best if you just go. We can sort out the details later.*" A male voice in the background.

"There," I whispered.

"*After all I've done, I can't believe …,*" A female voice this time, barely audible.

I clicked the circular backward arrow and the recording replayed the last few seconds. We all looked at each other as it came through.

"*After all I've done, I can't believe you're ending things like this.*"

My voice came back, ridiculously loud compared to Peter and his assistant's. "*Do you have any theories on how Erich Stein escaped?*"

I cringed.

"I thought I heard someone that sounded like Peter Hopper," Randall said. I was kind of impressed. I could barely hear him myself.

"Did you? Oh, that's probably just background noise during the interview. Maybe the radio was on or something."

Randall's face creased in disapproval, but he gave a small nod, out of reasons to object. He was the one who'd insisted we keep playing it, after all.

I turned the volume down again slightly, and we leaned in even farther as I hit play.

"*Not much of an escape … was it? He only made it a few … meters.*" Bertie was loud and clear.

"*Any idea how he was killed?*" I hated my own voice by this point.

"*No idea. But he and that other one got ... what was coming to them. Do you know how many Canadians were ... killed in the war?*"

Peter's voice again, softer than his father's. "*Look, I'm sorry. But with the leadership run, there's more scrutiny and ...*"

"*Forty-four thousand. Forty-four thousand ... good men like Harry.*"

The voices continued as Bertie coughed. I leaned right in, ear tilted toward the speaker.

"*But I did everything you wanted. I even went through with ... you know, got rid of our ...*"

We all leaned forward, as she trailed off.

"*Maybe we should stop.*" Me again. I willed my past self to shut up.

"*I'm fine. I wanted ... to sign up too. But I was just a child.*"

It felt almost sacrilegious to ignore Bertie's words and his obvious pain, but Peter was talking now.

"*That's not a bad thing, is it? You wouldn't have been able to raise a baby on your own. But you're still young. You can find someone else, start a real family —*"

We all exchanged excited looks. I glanced at Randall. He was staring at his computer and hadn't reacted. He was probably too far to have heard and didn't look like he was paying attention.

A loud sigh from Bertie. "*I ... don't want to tell Sarah how to do her job, but ... maybe you should focus more on the Canadians, and less on the ... Jerries.*"

The speaker suddenly fell silent.

Three pair of eyes turned to me. I peered down at the blank screen of my phone.

"Crap. Battery died."

"Well, perhaps we should get back to work while it charges and listen to the rest of the interview later," Asha said, too loudly.

More footsteps came up the stairs. I turned, expecting Sarah, but Peter Hopper himself walked in. I snatched the phone off the table and slid it into my lap, as if he'd be able to tell what was on it just from looking.

"Great to see you, Peter," Randall stood, and the two of them shook hands.

"Ephram, Asha, Keira, I hope the projects are all going well," Peter said. We all nodded, Max grinning like the Cheshire Cat.

Randall glanced back at us. "We have an important meeting now, so perhaps you could all finally keep things down?"

"Yessir," Max said, glee spilling out of him as Randall and Peter headed downstairs together. The four of us exchanged looks.

"It's there," Asha whispered as soon as their footsteps faded. Her voice vibrated with excitement. "Proof. He made her get an abortion."

"We've got him," Max whispered. "She said she 'got rid of' something, and he said she couldn't raise a baby on her own. There's no way he can deny it now."

"We need to get this online," Asha said.

Ephram looked at me. "Only if Keira is okay with that. It'll be clear who released it. The interview with Bertie and the fact that you spoke to him outside right after he had the conversation will make it obvious."

I swallowed, my future collapsing beneath me. "This is more important than the scholarship."

"No, I'll say it was me," Max jumped in. "I was there too, and he's not going to know who recorded it, is he?"

"I ... guess not." I'd been thrown a life preserver, and I grabbed it desperately. "I mean, only if you're sure."

"Honestly, nothing could give me more pleasure than him thinking it was me."

Ephram nodded while Max and Asha looked like they'd won the lottery, and we all headed back to our desks.

I plugged the phone in, scrambling under my desk to reach the socket. We could upload the recording with Ephram's cable and make copies as soon as it had enough power.

I had forgotten all about the Zoom call with the POW's son until a calendar reminder popped up on the screen. I swore under my breath. After falling in the lake and everything that had happened since, I hadn't prepared any questions.

Oh well. I'd have to wing it and hope it wasn't too obvious.

I joined the call at the exact right time, and he was already there: Ben Lang. He was an older man, probably well into his sixties. He had gray hair at his temples, a wispy mustache, and a wide smile. I guessed he had his laptop actually in his lap, as I could see right up his nose, which was impressively hairy. I introduced myself, but my brain was so stuck in everything that had just happened, I was on mute, and I gabbled on for a bit before I realized.

I tried to focus on him. My phone felt like a bomb under my desk, which it was, in a way. If things went well, it would cause a precision explosion that would destroy Peter's political career but might just leave my scholarship, my future intact.

Once I'd unmuted myself, I introduced myself again, let Ben Lang know I was recording, and we launched right into it. His dad, Karl Lang, had been at the camp from 1943 until 1946. He'd then spent a while as a prisoner of war in England before returning to Germany. He emigrated to Canada in the fifties and lived there until his death in 2001.

"He said he couldn't stand the denial in Germany," Ben said with a sniff of those nose hairs. "By the time he got back, virtually no one would admit to having been a Nazi. Everyone knew the war had been bad, but no one really thought it was their fault. They just wanted to move on, to put it behind them."

The screen blurred, and I was looking at the ceiling for a moment before Ben straightened it. I guessed he'd shifted in his seat.

"My dad was a wonderful man: kind, open-minded, loving. It was hard to reconcile that with the fact that he fought for the Nazis. He always said he was glad he'd been captured before he'd had a chance to fire a shot as he wasn't sure if he could have lived with himself if he'd helped Hitler."

I nodded, watching the little image of myself in the corner of the screen doing the same. My hair was a total mess.

"Did he tell you much about his time in Westonville?"

"He said the Canadians treated them much better than they deserved. He said he was lucky to be here because as soon as he arrived, it was obvious how much of what he believed, what they all believed, was a lie."

I thought of Ephram's research and made a mental note to suggest he interview Ben Lang too.

"Did he speak at all about the deaths in the camp? Of Rainer Schmitt and Erich Stein?"

The screen bumped again. I caught a momentary glimpse of Ben Lang's chin and realized he was nodding emphatically.

"He did?"

"I asked him about it. He was … a bit vague. He clearly hated

Schmitt. Said he was an awful man and deserved what he got, but when I asked him if he knew how he died, he clammed right up. I couldn't get anything else out of him, but he definitely knew something."

Interesting. That didn't make it sound like an accident. I leaned forward. "And Erich Stein?"

Ben tilted his head and breathed out through the corner of his mouth. "Dad obviously liked Stein, although he said he was really immature and naive. I think Dad felt sorry for him. He missed his mother badly, apparently. Always carried a Glücksschwein — a German good luck charm — she gave him, everywhere he went. Was devastated when she was killed."

I felt my heart beat faster. "Did he know anything about Erich Stein and his relationships at the farm he worked on? Did he know what happened to him?"

Ben shook his head. "I don't think he mentioned the farm to me at all. And I got the impression that Erich Stein's death was a mystery to Dad too. He seemed pretty sad about it."

I saw myself frowning in the corner of the screen. "So, it sounds like the deaths might not have been connected if your dad knew something about one but not the other?"

Ben Lang shrugged. "Honestly, I have no idea."

Sarah hurried upstairs, hands over her face. She grabbed her bag and ran back downstairs again.

"What happened?" I mouthed at Asha.

She shrugged.

"Um, can I call you back?" I asked Ben Lang. "Sorry, something urgent has come up at the office."

"Of course," Ben said. I felt bad, ending the meeting. But I could prepare better for a follow-up call and get Ephram on it too.

"I'll email you, okay?"

He nodded, and I closed my computer. Asha and I stood at the same time and hurried downstairs.

Sarah paced in the main gallery. She glanced up as we came in. Her expression was utterly lost.

"What's going on?" Asha asked.

"I …," she paused, and we all glanced at the stairs as footsteps followed, but it was Ephram who entered, Max close behind.

Sarah kept up her pacing. "Um … I …" She swore. "You know what, they didn't tell me I couldn't tell you, so I'm going to. I was just fired."

I froze, thinking of the phone under my desk and wondering if it was our fault somehow.

"Why? What did they say?"

She stopped and put her hands on her hips. "It's because I'm gay, okay?"

Asha's hand went over her mouth.

"But … they can't do that," I said. "That's got to be illegal."

Ephram nodded next to me. "It is."

"Yeah, and they're not that stupid. I knew being gay would be an issue with Peter Hopper on the board. When I got the job, I told them my wife was my roommate and marked my status as single on HR stuff, which they are claiming is fraud. They're firing me for that and because they said I should have checked Ruth's references more carefully and supervised you all better."

I gaped as things fell into place. That's what Ruth meant about Sarah, why she said the Hoppers wouldn't let her keep her job if they knew. Nausea swirled in my gut, both at the idea that Ruth would consider using that against her and that the Hoppers had.

"That sounds like my uncle," Max said. "How did he find out?"

Sarah gave a sad little laugh. "I came out to them in an email last night. After the library thing on the weekend, I didn't want to hide who I was. Interesting how everything with Ruth wasn't an issue until after that email, eh?"

She looked at us properly for the first time. "I'm sorry though. I should have told you all."

We stood there in silence for a bit. Ephram shook his head.

"That's so awful," I said.

"But you're fine," Sarah added quickly, raking a hand through her short hair. "I'm here for another two weeks until the summer program ends and the museum opens, so this won't affect you."

"You should quit right away," Asha said. "Let them try to cope without you."

Sarah gave a slightly twisted smile. "They are letting me 'resign,' and it was made clear that my job performance right up until my final day, rather than my 'deception,' as they called it, would form the basis for my references."

Max's jaw clenched. "They always find some way to get you. Some way to make you do what they want you to."

"Well, they got me good. Do you know how hard it is to get a museum job? Without a good reference, I have no chance."

Asha glanced at Max, Ephram, and me. "Maybe we can get them good, too."

Sarah tilted her head. "What do you mean?"

"Watch this space," Asha said.

The door to the education room creaked open, and we all automatically took a step back, as if to hide our conspiracy with a little distance. Peter and Randall entered and stopped as they saw us.

Peter put his hand behind his back. "I assume Sarah has let you know she will be leaving her position at the end of the summer."

"You're firing her!" Asha said. "For being gay!"

"That's not even slightly accurate. Our HR discussions are private and will not affect the summer program. It is an unfortunate situation, but we need to have full trust in our curator. As a board, we have an obligation to do our due diligence and to reassess when we learn new information. Sarah agreed that seeking a new position would be the best thing for everyone under these circumstances and is resigning."

It felt like a carefully rehearsed speech. Randall nodded along.

"But I do think Sarah should reflect on the impact that spreading untruths about the circumstances of her leaving the museum will have on our final assessment of her job performance."

"It's not because I'm gay," Sarah said to Asha, in a small voice.

Asha looked like she wanted to punch something, but she nodded.

Peter straightened up, inhaling through his nose. "I'm glad we've cleared that up. I'm sure Sarah will ensure that the rest of your program will be rewarding and that everything here is tied up nicely before the end of her contract period."

"I will," Sarah said, looking defeated.

"I look forward to seeing your final projects." There was a distinctly triumphant tone to Peter's voice. He gave us a little parting nod and turned and headed for the door. Randall headed back up to the office.

"I'm going to take a minute, if that's okay," Sarah said. "Just to walk around the site. You can come and find me if you need me."

We all nodded. We watched her back as she went out of the side door. The label was sticking up at the back of her shirt, and that one tiny, vulnerable detail made me want to cry.

Asha waited until the door had closed again behind her, then practically growled, "Let's get that recording uploaded now."

"It might not be charged enough to turn back on," I said. "It's an old phone, but I'll check."

We bundled back upstairs together and hurried over to my desk. I crouched down and pulled out the charging cord.

My phone was not attached to the other end.

I wondered if I'd knocked it off the charger, perhaps kicked it during my call to Ben Lang, or when I hurried down to see what was the matter with Sarah. I knelt under my desk, sweeping my hand over the broadloom, reaching right into the corners, but my fingertips found nothing.

"I can't find my phone," I said.

Max stiffened behind me. "Did you unplug it once it was charged? Maybe you put it in your bag?"

"I don't think so." I checked anyway, reaching right into the bottom where old receipts clustered. My phone wasn't in my bag.

Asha got down on her knees too and fumbled around under my desk.

Ephram paced on the other side. "Are you sure it was there?"

"Yes. I definitely plugged it in here." I held up the charging cord and waggled the empty end. "See, the charger's here, still plugged into the socket."

"Randall," Max said, straightening up. "Have you seen Keira's phone?"

Randall didn't even look up from his computer. "It's not my job to watch you or your personal possessions."

We all looked at each other. Max raised a dark eyebrow.

"Let's head down to the gallery," Ephram suggested with a look.

Back in the gallery, it was Asha's turn to pace. "Who could have taken it? Randall? Why?"

Max nodded back to the stairs, keeping his voice low. "Do you think he heard the recording? He's extremely loyal to my uncle."

"He definitely heard part of it," I pointed out. "Including Peter's voice. But it was super quiet. I could barely hear."

"The two of them were in the room together after their meeting," Max said. "If Randall heard the recording, he had more than enough time to tell Peter and then go upstairs and take the phone. My uncle did look particularly smug, don't you think?"

"What do we do?" I asked. "I mean, even apart from the recording, I need that phone!"

Ephram shook his head. "We shouldn't have left it up there."

"Sorry. I wasn't really thinking. I just followed Sarah downstairs."

He held his hands out, placating. "It wasn't an accusation."

But Asha was looking at me, suspicion in her expression. "I guess you definitely won't be losing your scholarship now."

"You think I took it? I was the one who told you about the recording in the first place!"

That shut her up for all of a second. "Well, can't we just tell everyone what we heard. We're all witnesses, right?"

"They'll sue the hell out of us," Max said, throwing his arms up. "They'll paint us all as politically motivated, which, to be fair, we totally are. We're also right, but without any proof and against expensive lawyers, we won't convince a single person who wasn't already against them." He glanced at me. "You wouldn't just lose your scholarship, you'd owe them money for the rest of your life."

I opened my mouth and closed it again.

Ephram rubbed at his forehead. "Do you have a 'Find My Phone' app?"

A bubble of hope rose in me before bursting painfully. "The phone was dead, remember? And it wasn't connecting. But if whoever took it turns it on, there's a chance it'll register."

"Well, we can check that now and keep an eye on it in case it does get turned on," Ephram said. "That's something, at least."

So we all trooped back upstairs, and I checked on my work laptop. As expected, the last ping on the app had come through just before I fell in the lake. Nothing since then.

I glanced up to see three expectant faces peering at me over the tops of their computers and shook my head sadly. Randall continued his single-fingered typing, head down. It was impossible to tell if he was avoiding my gaze because of guilt or just being his usual self.

I waited until the office grew quieter, until Ephram was at lunch and Max had popped out. I wandered over to Randall's desk.

"Sorry to have disturbed you earlier."

He grunted.

"Did you hear much of that recording?"

"Couldn't avoid it, could I? You and that proto-alcoholic were practically yelling."

"Proto-alcoholic?"

"Ruth."

For a moment I was too shocked to speak. "Wha… why do you call her that?"

"Desperate little booze-hound, wasn't she? Jules was furious at her for sneaking wine at their party. Not really a surprise that a girl like that came to a bad end. She'd have been fired if she'd survived until Monday."

I had to walk away to avoid punching him. It took a long time for me to stop shaking and to feel another piece of the puzzle fall into place.

That's what Ruth and Julia had fought over.

No doubt Julia had indeed planned to have her fired. But Ruth's death changed that into a potential political bombshell. She drowned at least in part because she was drunk, so getting served underage at the Hoppers' party potentially contributed to her death. No doubt Randall wasn't meant to mention it, but his bitter streak triumphed over his discretion. He really was a deeply nasty man.

But what did that mean? Did it change anything? It strongly suggested the Hoppers weren't involved in her drowning, except indirectly. Angry as they would have been, her death had the potential to be very bad for them.

I barely noticed when Max returned until I realized he was standing by my desk, holding out a phone.

"Hmm? Sorry."

"I said it's for you. It's an old one of mine you can have. I've reset it. You'll have to get a new SIM card, but it's better than nothing."

An iPhone sat in his palm. It was only a couple of models out of date. I briefly wondered what it must be like to have something like that to spare.

"I can't take this. It's way better than my old phone."

Max shrugged. "Please do. I'm not using it, and I feel bad." He glanced over and lowered his voice. "We should have made an excuse to wait until Randall wasn't in the office. We should have talked quieter."

I stood and hugged him without thinking. I realized what I'd done as soon as my face was pressed against his chest. I let go, awkwardly, but he was beaming, eyes intent on mine.

I'd heard the term "butterflies in your stomach," but that wasn't quite right. It was more a sparkly feeling than a fluttery one, and it wasn't confined to my gut. The fizzy feeling was in my blood, in my head.

"Um … sorry. Thanks," I said.

"No need to be sorry. That was really nice."

I had absolutely no idea where to look or what to say.

CHAPTER TWENTY-NINE

June 20, 1945

The week passed in an agony of regret and listlessness, broken up only by whispered meetings and planning for the expected attack on Thursday. They mostly met outside, where the rustle of the wind and the distance kept their conversations private. The bugs were back, flying in their faces, interrupting and biting, and it felt like the whole world had set itself against them.

Erich's world contracted to the bleak boundaries of the camp. He missed the ramshackle farm, missed Daisy so much it was a constant ache, and when he thought of the baby she carried, he wanted to scream, to thrash against the fences that kept him in. He wanted to rip them down and run to her.

He wanted to apologize to Joe, to tell him his intentions had been honorable. But that was a lie. He'd been caught up in the moment. He'd pretended he was as free as the Canadians, as blameless as them.

Now the letters received from home were no longer silenced by the censors, the reports they received were bleak. Hunger and homelessness plagued their friends and families. There was no Germany anymore, just a fractured and occupied land of chaos and starvation. There was nothing for Erich there: a broken country that he didn't know how to start fixing.

A part of Erich was glad his mother hadn't lived to see it, hadn't lived to beg and struggle for survival. He wondered how much she'd known, how much she'd suspected about the concentration camps. She'd probably been like him and not thought too hard about it, knowing on some level that if she did, she'd learn something she couldn't unlearn. But surely that knowledge had been harder to avoid in the last few years, living right there, where it was happening?

The thought that she was complicit was as painful as a burn, but try as he might to avoid it, his mind kept swinging back to it.

The plans for Thursday didn't help. Erich had always suspected he was a coward, and their improvised weapons made it all worse. He could all-too-easily imagine the brutal pain of the blows from the stolen iron piping hidden under their beds. No doubt Schmitt's men had similar weapons ready for use on his body.

He'd known nothing of real pain when he'd signed up. He'd imagined combat at a distance with guns, death coming bravely and instantly. Since then, he'd learned what pain was, even if he'd been spared the worst of it. He'd seen mangled bodies, seen men screaming for hours before death took them in the Tunisian desert.

He still had nightmares of such things.

This would be face-to-face, hand-to-hand fighting against men who intended to kill. There would be seven on Karl Lang's side, but they had no idea how many of Schmitt's men would be coming.

On Thursday afternoon, dark clouds seeped across the sky, sinking the camp into an unnatural twilight. Lightning twitched in the distance long before the rain began. And when it came, it came with force, hammering on the ceilings of the huts, a constant drumroll adding to the painful anticipation.

No one heard the knock on the hut door over the din of the rain and the rumble of thunder. The Canadian scout opened it from the outside and leaned in.

"Erich Stein is to come to the gate."

Erich and Karl exchanged glances. There were still two hours before the attack was due. Karl nodded.

"I'll be back soon," Erich said.

The weather was violent. Rain roared on roofs and kicked up the puddles in clumps, like gunshots in mud. He was soaked through long before he reached the open gate.

George stood there, looking every bit as wet as him, but his guard's helmet kept the rain from his eyes, at least.

"I shouldn't be here," George said, shouting over the rain. Erich glanced around, but no one could hear them in the cacophony of the storm. The old gate guard had retreated into his shelter.

"I just thought you should know. Joe died."

Erich stood still for a long moment, not bothering to wipe the blinding rain from his face as it stung and blurred his vision.

"I'm sorry. It was a few days ago now, but we've been busy with …" He tailed off. No doubt with the funeral that he obviously hadn't been invited to. Why would he be?

"Today is my last day. Daisy's putting the farm up for sale. We're leaving for the city tomorrow. People will notice soon if we stay here. They might guess that it's yours."

"How is she?"

George shook his head sadly. "Heartbroken over her stepfather." He reached into his jacket and pulled out a piece of paper. At first, Erich thought it was something official, a pass for the gate, a chance to see her one last time. But as he took it, as the rain soaked the sheet, he saw it was a letter.

"I can't leave it with you," George said. "But she wanted you to read it."

Erich read quickly. The ink was already running, the rain washing away her words, but the letter was short.

Dear E,
I'm so sorry. But this is for the best for all of us. I hope you are able to go home soon. I hope you are able to forgive me for marrying someone else.
I miss you.
D

George took the soggy letter back when Erich looked up at him.

"Tell her … I love her. I miss her."

George gave him a sad smile. "Take care of yourself, Erich." He turned and walked back through the gate.

Jealousy twisted in Erich's gut. Why did George get everything, and all he got was a broken country, a dangerous fight? He wanted George's happy future. He wanted to be the one leaving the war behind, moving to an undamaged, prosperous city with Daisy and their baby.

Erich didn't mean to follow George. Didn't even think about it. His feet simply led him toward George, wanting the life he was walking into, not the storm that lay behind Erich in the camp.

He expected to be stopped as he passed between the fences, but George obviously did not hear the footsteps behind him above the hiss of the rain. The guard simply nodded from the shelter of his hut as they went by. Erich realized he thought he was with George, thought the letter melting in George's hand was the official papers he couldn't be bothered to check.

Erich stumbled on into the Canadian outer camp, half in a dream, but George turned to the right, heading for the main administrative hut, and with a crash like the thunder above, Erich realized what he'd done, where he was.

He ducked behind the bed of a nearby truck, trying to work out what to do. The gate to the main camp hadn't closed yet, the guard clearly reluctant to leave his hut in the downpour.

He could go back. The guard might challenge him, but if he explained that he'd simply forgotten himself for a moment, Erich doubted he'd be reported. It would raise questions about why the guard hadn't checked any papers, for starters. Plus, he'd have to trek across the camp with Erich to report him in the rain. No, it was a safe bet he'd be let back in without much fuss. No harm done, after all. And he should go back. He needed to defend Karl, to fight against the evil they'd all been part of.

But …

Joe was dead. That was awful, and it meant Daisy was at the farm all alone. He should be there to comfort her like she'd comforted him. He owed her that, surely? But how would he get out of the outer camp?

Even as he imagined it, wild thoughts blossomed in the madness of the storm. Why stop there? Why should it be George who took her to her new life? Couldn't he and Daisy find somewhere no one would ask questions? Buy another small farm far away with the money from selling hers?

The truck juddered to life in front of him. In a moment he would be exposed. But, he realized with a jolt, this was his way out. It was a sign, a gift. He scrambled underneath, remembering the man who'd tried to escape that way and hoping he had time before it moved and crushed him. There was no ice to crack his head on today, and he knew the truck well from the bumpy rides to and from the farm. He grabbed the metal struts and pipes, slipping his arms and legs into place just as the truck leapt into life.

It drove him straight out of the camp gate.

CHAPTER THIRTY

The dead ends continued as the last two weeks of the summer program went on. I checked several times a day, but my stolen phone was never turned on. I got Max's old phone working with a new SIM card and called the number the policeman had given me to use "if I remembered anything else" about Colt's death. I explained that I'd lost my phone and wanted to check in, in case he'd been trying to contact me.

He hadn't.

I let the others know. Max's shoulders drooped, as if the air had been let out of him. "That's that? But what about the bottle cap?"

"I guess they couldn't pull any prints," I said.

"Did they even try?" Asha asked. "Maybe they were told not to. Maybe they're in the Hoppers' pockets."

Ephram shook his head. "It's only on TV that the police do the full forensic thing all the time. In this case, it sounds like they found a known dealer alone in his home, dead of an overdose with evidence of his drug use right in front of him. In real life, the police aren't going to waste their limited resources when there's nothing to suggest it's anything other than exactly what it seems."

I'd hit nothing but dead ends in my search for Erich Stein's killer too. I could hardly share my suspicions about Ruth's great-grandfather being gay and her grandmother being Erich's child as part of my final report, and I certainly couldn't contact her family to ask more, not after they'd lost her in such shocking circumstances.

Without that, I had nothing new at all.

Asha's sculpture grew outside, hidden under tarps to protect it from wind and rain as she worked. The fierce tap of Ephram's fingers on the keyboard suggested he was having no problem with his report.

A tension permeated the office, as if all our breath was stifled. Sarah spent a lot of time on her own in the education room. Randall's slow typing was a constant reminder of his sullen surveillance on behalf of Peter Hopper. Max carried on working in the gallery, but whenever he came upstairs to pick something up, he always glanced over at me with a smile. His dark eyes tied my stomach in knots and made me lose my place in the documents every time.

On the Tuesday of the final week, I was glued to my computer, re-reading the same files I'd been over a hundred times, hoping I'd missed something. But the war diary and the accident reports were exactly as I remembered them: suggestive, but painfully light on detail. My interviews with Bertie and Karl Lang's father had added color and interest, and I'd added in what I'd learned about Rainer Schmitt and the deaths of Dr. Emil Bauer and Otto Meyer, but there was nothing I could put in my report that justified a full summer spent at the camp.

Thudding came up the stairs, a welcome interruption. Asha

appeared in the doorway. “Um, can I borrow Max and the other students, please? I need help lifting things.”

Sarah nodded. Randall didn’t even glance up, which was probably just as well — there was a spark of mischief in Asha’s eyes. We followed her down the stairs and out the side door.

Her sculpture was hidden under blue plastic sheets that strained and shuddered with the breeze, an unnaturally blue sea undulating over the yellow grass.

“I don’t need anyone to lift anything.” Asha’s rainbow hair streamed behind her as she approached the covered sculpture. The hollow flapping and snapping of the tarp almost drowned her out. “The museum board asked to see my sculpture tomorrow, as they want to ‘approve it’ before it’s open to the public.”

Her smile was sharp. “I might have lied just a little bit about what I planned to build, and they will definitely not approve of what I actually did. I need people to video me talking about this so I can put it online before they have a chance to take it down.”

My stomach tightened. I wasn’t sure if it was through apprehension or excitement. I exchanged a glance with Max, whose eyes were wide.

Asha hurried to the corner and pulled up the hook that stuck the tarp in the earth. Max mirrored her, pulling up the next corner, and I copied them both, yanking the nearest metal hook out of the dry earth. Asha pulled the untethered tarp toward her, gathering it up in her arms: a blue mass that almost hid her face. She chucked it to one side, not bothering to fold it. The breeze rolled it away for a few meters, like brightly colored tumbleweed.

Asha had revealed a rough recreation of the camp around four meters wide, set out much as we’d seen it in old photos, with the fence at knee-height. But instead of guard towers, there were a dozen signs hammered into the ground around the perimeter, with the barbed wire strung between them. Signs exactly like the ones we'd seen at the library, saying STAY AWAY FROM OUR KIDS; GOD HATES FAGS; GO HOME GROOMERS.

A small double gate stood at the front with a pink triangle over it.

Inside, instead of huts, were graves. I leaned over to read them: Eldorado Nightclub, Willem Arondeus, Henny Schermann, Damenklub Violetta, Institut für Sexualwissenschaft.

"What are these?" I asked.

"People and institutions destroyed by the Nazis. Film it," she commanded. "And film me too, so I can explain it."

Asha gave me her phone, and Ephram and Max pulled out theirs.

Asha cleared her throat and ran her hands over her purple shirt, smoothing it down. "Okay," she said, and we started filming.

"We used to lock up Nazis on this site," Asha said, walking around the sculpture. "We used to fight their evil. But now the board of this museum, led by Peter Hopper, is continuing their work: banning books, attacking queer and trans communities."

It sounded like a well-practiced speech. I kept Asha's camera focused on her as she walked around the edge of her creation.

"This piece is called *We Bury Nothing*. I wanted it to say two things. Firstly, we've always been here," she gestured at the graves in the middle. "Fascists have always tried to kill off queerness, but they can't. It's a natural part of being human. Nazis can close clubs and right-wing nutjobs can shoot them up, protestors can attack drag events, and politicians can cut off healthcare and persecute us. But we'll always build spaces where we can be ourselves. We always find each other.

"Secondly, bigotry never dies," she waved a hand at the signs that made up the fence. "We're under attack again. Book banning is back. At least the Nazis didn't bother pretending they were into freedom of speech while censoring everyone they disagreed with, like the right wing does now. And they're not just attacking anyone who isn't straight. I could have made this piece about practically any group the Nazis victimized: Jewish people and everyone who isn't white, cis-gendered, neurotypical, or able-bodied. Hate against all minorities is unmasked and on the rise, just as it was in the thirties in Germany. But I chose to make this piece about the group I know best. The group I'm a part of."

She stepped over to the gate and gestured at the pink triangle. "It's ..."

"What's happening?" Randall was striding over the grass, toward us.

Sarah followed in his wake, looking confused.

Randall stared at Asha's sculpture. "This isn't what you said you were building. And didn't we tell you that the board would need to approve it before it could be shown to the public? Why are you filming?"

He grabbed at the phone in Max's hand, but Max pulled it out of his reach.

"You don't have permission to film here."

Asha took her phone back from me. "This is my art," she said, turning the camera on Randall. "Are you saying I'm not allowed to show it to anyone?"

Randall picked up the discarded tarp and tried to drag it back over Asha's sculpture. "You signed a contract when you started. We paid for the materials. This is the museum's property, and all installations need approval from the board before being shared with the public." He covered up part of the fence and its screaming signs, but Max caught the edge of the tarp and tugged it right back off again.

"Sarah," Randall snapped. "Get your students in line."

"This has nothing to do with Sarah," Asha said. "I made this. She hasn't seen it."

Randall's neck snapped around, and he glared at Asha. "You are her direct reports. It is her job to make sure you follow the rules outlined in your contracts, and she should have been monitoring the development of this sculpture." The wind caught at his wispy hair. "Inadequate supervision reflects badly on her management skills."

"She's been checking in on me all the time!" Asha said. "But I only showed her the fence and the gates. She saw a sculpture developing exactly according to the approved plan. I hid the signs and didn't put names on the graves until today."

Randall shrugged. "With your attitude, she should have been prepared for something like this. And she's a witness to your unauthorized filming right now and is doing nothing. If videos are released that damage the museum's reputation, that's her fault."

Asha stopped, pain clear in her eyes. "That isn't fair. None of this is her fault."

Sarah's mouth was open, standing behind Randall. After a long moment, she closed it. She pushed her jaw out a little bit, and the lost expression in her eyes evaporated.

"Post it online," she said to Asha.

"What?"

Sarah turned to Randall. "I quit, effective immediately. I don't want a reference from you. When potential employers ask why I don't have one, I'm going to point to this video. I don't want any job that would consider a recommendation from this bigoted board a good thing."

She smiled at Asha. "Thank you for this sculpture. Thank you for reminding me of the price of not standing up."

She turned to the rest of us. "I'm sorry to walk out before you've finished your program. I know how much you all put into this, and I'm happy to give any of you a reference, for what that's worth. But I can't let those swine get away with blackmailing me, and I can't let them hide Asha's work."

And, just like that, it clicked. I knew exactly who killed Erich Stein.

It was as if I were at the top of a mountain, the air so clear I could see everything spread out before me, but so thin I was dizzy. Maybe it was the fact that I'd gone over the reports and interviews so much. Maybe it was just so obvious I should have seen it weeks ago.

But it was also Sarah's words.

"I … have to go," I said. I wanted to congratulate Sarah on quitting, to praise Asha for her amazing sculpture, but the picture in my head felt fragile. Details were missing. "I'll catch up with you all soon."

"What's happening?" Max asked.

I didn't answer, already turning my back.

"Where are you going, Keira?" Sarah asked.

"Sorry. I just need a moment."

"Keira?" Max said, but I ignored him, hurrying toward the museum exit and the main road beyond. No one followed, I noted with relief.

I practically sprinted down the dusty road, running through the pieces in my mind. The interviews with Bertie and Karl Lang's son, the length of the war, Ruth's "nuclear option." How hadn't I seen it before?

It was all just supposition, but if my suspicions were right, there was someone who was desperate to confirm everything.

CHAPTER THIRTY-ONE

June 20, 1945

Erich found it hard to keep hold of the bottom of the truck.

The rain had softened the ruts in the road, but the truck shook, vibrating through Erich, rattling him to his core. His hands slipped in the wet, and he heaved himself up, hooking his elbows in place, holding himself above the muck as the truck sped up.

He squeezed his eyes closed, a second too late as mud splashed into them. He almost let go as the pain screamed through his face, but he blinked and winced. He held on, trying to focus on Daisy's face.

He adjusted a few times, the wet of the road threatening his grip, lubricating the metal he clutched, rocking and swinging below the truck. The truck jumped and shuddered its way down the road. Erich prayed it was taking him to Daisy and he could hold on long enough to reach her.

Finally, the truck came to a halt. Erich held on for a long few seconds, trying to hear if it was safe to come out, but the barrage of rain on the metal above drowned out everything else, like shrapnel and sand after a bomb blast, and the truck continued to judder above him, engine running.

It lurched into life again, turning around in a loop and jolting back the way they'd come from.

He was returning to the camp.

Erich's grip weakened. Should he keep hold of the truck and be dragged back? Or should he let go and risk being crushed beneath the wheels?

His exhaustion and a bump in the road made up his mind for him. His hands slipped, his feet flew free, and he found himself flat on his back, winded.

He gasped for air for a moment, but it wouldn't go in. He wondered for a long second if his chest had been crushed. But he caught a breath and another.

He sat up. He was in the middle of the road, half-submerged in a deep puddle, surrounded by forest. He pushed himself to his feet and hurried into the trees.

Where was he?

Nowhere near Daisy's farm, that was for sure. He wasn't sure which way he'd gone out of the camp. Or where he needed to go. He lurched over the verge and into the woods. He should stay near the road so he didn't get lost in the wilderness, but wouldn't that make it more likely he'd be caught?

A light glimmered through the trees.

It was a sign, or at least something to head for, something away from the road. Erich stumbled that way, still feeling the vibrations of the truck in his bones. The rain cascaded down, washing the mud from his gray uniform and the red circle on his back.

He only got a few steps into the wood before he could see what the light was.

It was the prisoner-of-war camp itself.

Erich slumped down onto a fallen log among the trees, out of sight of the wire and the nearest tower. Clearly, the truck had followed a road that ran parallel to the fence. But at least Erich knew where he was. He could work out how to get to Daisy's. All he had to do was to follow the road back, get past the front of the camp without being seen, and go on to the farm from there.

But it would take hours. What time was it now? He'd be missed at evening roll call.

With a twist of his gut, Erich remembered that he'd be missed long before then. He was meant to be there to help Karl. The attack was expected an hour and a half before roll call.

Still, this was his only chance to see Daisy again.

But then what? Even if he made it to her without being caught, what was he asking of her? They'd be on the run together. He'd be a marked man. Who was he to ask her to do that, and while pregnant, too?

She had a respectable marriage with a good man ahead of her: a new start in a new city. And as he thought of that, he realized what she hadn't said in her letter.

She hadn't said she loved him.

Erich leaned back, looking up at the rain that washed the mud from his face and uniform. She'd said she missed him. She'd said she was sorry she was marrying another man. She never said she wanted to marry him instead.

He was such an idiot. He couldn't run away with Daisy. Erich had fallen in love with Daisy, Canada, and a fantasy of the future that had nothing to do with reality. In doing so, he'd forgotten what he owed to Karl, Germany, and the present.

He should be there defending his friend right now.

Erich peered up at the nearest guard tower, through the trees. The man in there looked like George. It was hard to be sure through the rain and with everyone in uniform, but his stance was the same as he limped around the small platform. It had to be him.

Maybe he could get George's attention. Maybe George could get him back into the camp unnoticed somehow. It had to be worth a try.

Or maybe George would arrest him, and he'd be thrown in solitary again. At least then he'd be on the right side of the fence. Erich stood. He'd been a stupid, selfish fool, but it was time to try to make things right.

A part of him knew he was too late, even as he strode toward the guard tower. A part of him knew he'd betrayed his friend and what was left of his country. A part of him knew he'd made the wrong decision when it mattered most, and he couldn't take it back.

Then his head split open with pain, and the world went dark.

CHAPTER THIRTY-TWO

Sweat soaked my shirt by the time I reached Bertie's and Max's house. I'd taken the long way around, using the road. It would have been too obvious where I was going if I'd cut through the museum grounds. But the extra distance left me sticky and gross.

I paused in the turning circle driveway to catch my breath and wipe my face on the bottom of my T-shirt. I straightened my shoulders and stepped up onto the veranda, hesitating at the front door, finger hovering over the bell.

I wasn't sure if Bertie would be able to make it downstairs to answer, and I didn't remember the door being locked when we'd visited, so I tried the handle instead. It turned. Silently thanking trusting rural types, I stepped into the front hall.

"Hello!" I called out loudly. "Bertie? It's Keira. One of the museum's students."

"Oh, lovely!" His voice was soft but just loud enough to be heard from upstairs. "More questions? Come on up."

I hurried up the stairs toward the second-floor lounge we'd

spoken in before. The door was open, and Bertie's face crinkled into a wide smile as I entered. He smoothed down his wispy hair.

"Keira, how lovely to see you. Max … talks about you all the time. If you ask me, he's sweet on you." He gave me a little wink.

I swallowed, trying to get the competing feelings that bloomed in me under control. I had to approach this carefully. I couldn't let myself get distracted. I checked the mantelpiece.

It was still there.

"You've been so helpful, and it's been so lovely to talk to you." I hoped I wasn't pouring it on too thickly, but I thought of Ruth and all her sucking up. If that approach worked with him before, it was probably the way to go. "I'm so sad our time at the museum is coming to an end. I've learned so much from you."

Bertie straightened his shirt proudly. It was loose on his thin frame. "I'm happy to help."

"And it was such a shame about Harry. A true Canadian hero. He was so handsome as well, wasn't he?"

His smile quivered. It was still raw to him, even now. "Yes, he was."

"You must have been so angry at the Nazis for all the terrible things they did."

Bertie nodded and a faraway look settled in his eyes.

"You were what, thirteen?" I'd done the math. Max said Bertie was seven during the war, but his memories of his brother and George seemed so vivid for such a young kid. It took a long time to realize that Bertie was probably seven when the war began. Max needed me to think of his grandfather as a small child. But the war had gone on for six long years.

"If I'd been a bit older, I'd have lied and … signed up anyway. I was so close. I was tall, big for my age. I was going to try in Toronto in a year or … two. No one knew me there."

"But the war ended and your brother was lost. You must have wanted revenge. You must have wanted to do your bit, to be a hero like your brother, to get out there and kill some Nazis yourself."

"I did what I could."

Bingo. I put on an innocent-but-fascinated face. "What do you mean?"

He gripped the arms of his chair. "I didn't want to let those Krauts get away with it."

"You didn't?" I opened my eyes wide. "And you were able to get some kind of revenge?"

He nodded, clearly eager to tell me. I just needed to push a little harder.

"Even though you were only a teenager? That's amazing. What did you do?"

Bertie glanced at the door, but there was no one in the house but us. "I can … trust you, right?"

I looked into his eyes. He couldn't trust me. He was a fool to tell a near-stranger, just as he'd been a fool to tell Ruth, to give her a "nuclear option." Was that bad decision born of age and the failing of his mind, or was it a desperate need to have his actions seen — his war triumph recognized?

"You can trust me," I lied.

"He was clinging on to the bottom of the truck my father sometimes … got driven home in. I didn't even notice at first. It was raining hard. The driver dropped my father off. I went to greet … him, but he went straight into his study and locked the door without even saying hello." Bertie swallowed. "Those were bad days. My mother and father … barely talked to me after Harry's death."

He didn't take as many breaths now. The momentum of the story carried him on.

"I slouched over to the window. I spotted the Kraut as ... the truck turned around. He gripped ... on to the metal frame, half-covered in mud. I didn't have time to grab my coat or get my father. I ran out the door into the rain, yelling and ... waving to try to get the truck driver's attention. He didn't see me."

Bertie coughed, and I glanced at the oxygen tank, wondering if I'd need to use it.

"I chased behind the truck as it turned ... back onto the road. The Nazi obviously realized it was taking him back. He let go and landed in a puddle. I hid in the trees before he noticed I was there, and I watched him. At first, I wondered if he was dead, if a wheel had gone over him. But ... as soon as the truck was out of sight, he jumped up and hurried into the forest."

"And you followed him," I prompted.

"Of course," Bertie said. He smiled, showing a dark filling in the back of his mouth.

I could see it now. Young Bertie, heartbroken and aching for revenge, yearning to be a part of the war. Young Bertie following Erich Stein into the wood.

"What happened?"

"He went a little way in and ... sat on a log."

"And?"

"He just sat there in the rain. Probably for about five minutes. I knew I had to do something. I wasn't sure what, but ... I started creeping toward him. But then he stood up and ..." He tailed off.

"He headed toward the camp," I prompted.

That's where he'd been found, after all. Not in the forest but in the clearing surrounding the fence. Everyone thought he'd almost made it to the wood, but the opposite was true. He'd come from the wood and, for whatever reason, he'd changed his mind and decided to go back.

He'd almost made it to the camp.

Bertie nodded, looking uncomfortable. "He was lost. He was trying to escape." He didn't sound like he quite believed it.

"What did you use?"

"A rock I stubbed my toe on as I … followed him. It was like it had been placed there. It was … meant to be. The noise of the rain hid my approach. He … got to the edge of the trees, and I had to do something."

"Or he would have turned himself in, and you would never have been able to get your revenge."

Bertie opened his mouth to deny it but shrugged instead. "They killed Harry," he said simply. "They killed millions." Unburdened, he slumped back in his chair.

"And you took a trophy, too."

I wandered over to the mantlepiece, with its smattering of children's crafts. Hidden among them sat a small, crudely carved, wooden pig: a Glücksschwein. I hadn't understood the word when Ben Lang said it, and he'd translated it just as a "good luck charm." But that wasn't exactly what it meant. It was when Sarah called the museum board "swine" that it clicked into place. German was so close to English in some ways. Glücksschwein — good luck *swine* — a pig. Erich's charm from his mother.

I picked it up. It was a simple thing, worn almost smooth. I ran my fingers over it, like Erich Stein no doubt had so many times. I'd seen it weeks ago. I'd looked right at it, but my gaze had drifted to the other crafts.

"It was in his pocket," Bertie said. "I was looking for … proof that he was escaping. Tickets and cash and forged documents."

"You didn't find any?"

He shook his head. "I should have just told someone … what I'd done. I was just a kid, and I stopped an enemy soldier! Did it matter that it … wasn't a great escape attempt? Did it matter that he might have changed his mind? He could have … changed it back again! I was … defending Canada."

It was clear it was an argument he'd been having with himself for years. Was he the heroic boy who stopped an escape and got revenge on Hitler for his brother's death? Or had he murdered a man who was trying to get back to the camp, who was trying to fix his own stupid mistake?

No wonder he wanted to tell someone.

"But you went home instead?"

Bertie nodded. "It started to get dark. The camp alarm … sounded. The truck passed me on the road as it came to get Dad again, but I hid in the trees as it went by. I left my muddy boots … by the door, but no one even noticed I'd been out. I'd been invisible since Harry died."

I nodded. After all, who would have suspected little Bertie had anything to do with the deaths at the camp?

"You told all this to Ruth?"

He smiled faintly. "She was sweet. She listened."

That's why she'd said her nuclear option would totally help out "some people," why she'd put such emphasis on those words. By "some people," she'd meant me. It would help me with my project.

"She understood. She always wanted to hear more about Harry. Such a … shame, her accident."

I thought about telling Bertie of my suspicions — that Ruth was the great-granddaughter of the man he'd killed that night.

"Thank you," I said instead. I sounded way more composed than I felt. I put the Glücksschwein back on the mantelpiece. "It's been really interesting talking to you."

I stumbled out onto the landing, wondering what to do about

any of this. I'd solved Erich Stein's murder. Yay me. But could I put it in my report?

An awful thought hit me way too late. I put one hand out to steady myself against the wall. Ruth knew Bertie was a killer. Did that have anything to do with her death?

I turned to the top of the staircase and ran right into Max.

CHAPTER THIRTY-THREE

I stepped back. Max's eyes were fierce. My traitor stomach flipped at the sight of him.

"He told you. I heard it."

There was no point in lying. "Well," I said, trying to keep my voice light. "At least I completed my project, right?"

It felt flat, even to me.

"Are you going to tell anyone?"

"I don't know." That was true, at least.

"He killed a Nazi! My granddad is a hero, like his brother."

"I'm not sure how much of a Nazi Erich Stein was. I think he might just have been someone who didn't know how to stand up to them."

"Same thing."

"Is it?" I honestly didn't know the answer. Did cowardice and ignorance deserve death? What if their consequences were as horrific as the Holocaust?

"Do you think everyone in Germany was fully committed to Hitler? Of course not. But they all enabled it. It was up to Germans to stop Hitler, and if they wouldn't, it was up to the world to stop Germany."

"And we did. The war was over. Hitler was dead. And surely in those conditions, everyone at least deserves a trial before execution."

Max shrugged. "Most Germans were let off too easily. Erich Stein was killed trying to escape. And my granddad was just a kid."

"He was. But Erich Stein was heading back to the camp. Even Bertie admits that."

"They killed his brother. He was fighting for his family. I'd have done the same."

I believed that. That's why I didn't want to say the next words. I didn't even want to think them. "You … overheard Ruth at the party telling me that she had a 'nuclear option' with Bertie, didn't you?"

She had been practically shouting, after all. And he'd mentioned it when I'd told them all about the DNA test.

Max's expression crumpled. "I didn't kill her. That was an accident."

"But you did drug her."

"Barely! I put two acid tabs — just two — in a bottle of wine. I didn't even give her the bottle. It was her decision to grab it from me."

"You knew she'd take it from you. She'd already taken mine."

The sides of his mouth wavered. "I panicked. I had to protect Granddad. I'd already bought the tabs off Colt for myself, for later. I just had this stupid idea that if she was the kind of person who acted weird and said crazy things, no one would believe her if she did try to tell anyone. It was a spur-of-the-moment thing. I didn't want her to get hurt, I promise."

"That's why you were talking about being worried about her

mental health and drug use when we walked home together. You wanted me to think she was unreliable."

"I asked Ephram and Asha to watch her!" He grabbed my wrist. "I tried to keep her safe! It was an accident. You believe me, right?"

I nodded, looking down at his fingers, the grip so tight they were white. We stood right at the top of the steep, wooden stairs. I'd misjudged things, badly.

Idiot.

I shouldn't have asked him about Ruth while we were alone. I should have pretended I was totally on board with the Bertie-killing-Nazis thing, at least until we were somewhere safer.

I plastered on a smile. "It was obviously an accident. There's no way you could have known that she'd go to look at the flowers and would slip and fall in the water. She was probably drunk enough to drown even without the acid."

"Yes, exactly." But he didn't let go. His gaze was intense as he searched my expression. "You've worked out the rest."

"The rest of what?" I didn't sound convincing.

"Colt knew Ruth had acid in her system when she died. I bought it from him. He knew I gave it to her. He blackmailed me."

The shiny new Camaro outside his trailer. I wondered when Max realized he could never pay enough, that there was only one way to be free of Colt.

"You don't need to tell me anything." I pulled lightly at my hand, trying to act like it was just a gesture, not an attempt to get away. His grip stayed firm.

"He was scum. I mean, I'm sure Ruth probably isn't the only person who died as a result of his drugs, you know? Total racist, too. I was doing the community a favor."

He looked like Bertie then, frantically justifying himself.

"It was a peaceful death. I promise. He was drunk anyway, so it was easy enough to slip his own drugs into a beer. He'd have overdosed sooner or later. I just sped things up." He shook his head, dark hair sliding over his eyes. "I took the bottle, but I didn't think about the cap. I didn't know if it had my prints on it or not. But the place was a mess. There had to be loads of people's prints there. I just needed an alibi."

His grip was starting to hurt, his fingers tight on my bone.

I hadn't made the final leap, but I made it now. "You took my phone! You threatened Peter with the recording unless he said you were with him that evening."

Max nodded. "But I didn't tell him it was your phone, or that you or the others had heard. I just told him I had a recording of it. You can still totally go for the scholarship."

That, more than anything, filled me with rage.

Ruth's death was an accident. It might not even have been Max's fault, given how drunk she was. And while Max clearly murdered Colt, he might believe his own justifications on why a drug dealer had to die.

But Max hated everything his uncle stood for. And the moment he had the opportunity to take him down, he decided to act in his own self-interest instead.

He continued as if he'd heard my thoughts. "There'll be another way to get him. I can work from the inside. He trusts me now." He was getting worked up. "And when there's political capital to be gained by being bigoted, someone's going to build their career on it. If it wasn't my uncle, it would be someone else. Better it's someone I can have some sway over, right?"

I wondered if I should call out, but even if Bertie came out in time, what would he do? Tackle his grandson? I was struggling to reconcile my new understanding of Max with the image of him

I'd had until just an hour earlier. A stupid part of me that was catching up way too slowly still admired his sharp cheekbones.

Max continued, "I'm going to be a lawyer. I'm going to support people who need it: charities and activists. I'll do tons of pro bono stuff. I'll be able to afford to, once I've inherited this place. What's done is done, and I can't take it back. But my going to prison would be a waste. It wouldn't help anyone."

The stairs loomed to my side: a cliff edge.

"And it's not right that someone like me should go to prison over Colt. He didn't contribute anything except poison and blackmail. The world is better off without him."

There it was: naked superiority. Max was rich and had a good life promised to him, so he had the right to get rid of anyone who got in the way of his glorious, imagined future. Ruth and Colt were just problems to be dealt with. The depth I'd imagined in his dark eyes evaporated, and they seemed shallow and selfish.

I wanted to pull my hand hard, wanted to twist it, to try to get free. But maybe I could still talk him down, still get away without a physical struggle.

I didn't like my odds against him if it came down to a fight.

"You're right," I said. "Colt was scum. I saw that Confederate flag in his window. I know you, Max. I know you're the good guy here. So let go of me." I tried to keep the panic from my voice.

"I ..." He looked almost apologetic. "You're going to tell everyone, aren't you?"

"No, not at all. You're right. It's better that you become a lawyer. You can do a ton more good that way."

"How can I believe that?"

"Apart from the fact you know I'm on your side, I don't have any evidence," I said desperately. "I'm not going to throw my life away making accusations I can't prove. I stayed silent about the recording of Peter, right? I've got the scholarship to think of."

I felt sick saying it, because it was the truth.

Was I all that different from Max? For a moment then, when we had the recording, I'd been willing to lose the scholarship. But once Max had taken the phone, he'd talked me into staying silent, to save myself from being sued, to have some hope of fulfilling my dad's dream.

He looked indecisive. Hadn't Bertie said he was sweet on me? I smiled, trying to look as if I still liked him.

"And I thought … maybe there was something between us?"

Max's eyes went wide, and, for a second, his grip loosened. Before I could yank my arm away, it tightened again, harder than before. He pressed his lips together.

I'd pushed it too far.

He dragged me closer to the top of the stairs, I pulled back with all my weight, but he was stronger, bigger.

"No! Wait, please!"

Those muscles I'd once admired stood out on his upper arm. The calculation had been made. I was a problem to be dealt with, too. Another "accident" was needed.

"No, please, don't!" I wrenched my arm as hard as I could. I wanted to kick at him, but I'd lose my balance. I swung with my free hand, and it connected with his face. He flinched. I'd felt the sting in my fingers from the force of it, but it wasn't enough.

"No! Max!"

He'd got me to the top step, and I teetered there. He let go of the wrist he clutched and pushed, right in my chest. I flailed, just managing to grab hold of his other arm.

He jolted forward, pulled down by my weight. He grabbed the banister.

We were suspended there for a moment, me desperately clutching his bare arm just below the elbow, my wrist at a weird angle, holding my whole weight.

I knew I'd lost.

I could feel the steep stairs behind me, the plunge I was to take, the painful ache in my twisted wrist. Max looked at my hand, my grip that was already slipping, and reached to loosen my fingers.

A crash came from below. The door had swung open and banged against the wall.

"Keira!" Asha's voice.

"Help!" I screamed. The pounding of footsteps came, running up the steps. I was still tipping, my hand still sliding off the sweat on Max's skin, the world terrifyingly horizontal.

Asha's interruption had bought me a second. I swung my other hand up and grabbed Max's wrist as it clawed at my fingers. He tried to shake me off, but he was distracted, staring over my shoulder. Then there were hands on my back, strong hands taking my weight, pushing me to safety.

I let go of Max. He retreated, horror in his expression.

My legs were boneless, my whole body quivering. I collapsed into a half-kneeling, half-sitting position, clutching the hard wood of the banister at the top of the stairs.

Ephram stepped between Max and me.

"Police. We need the police!" I heard Asha shout from downstairs. I turned and saw her staring up, phone pressed to her ear. Things had to be bad if Asha was calling the police. I had to smother an off-color giggle at the thought.

"Are you okay?" Ephram asked.

I nodded, feeling stupidly embarrassed, hoping he'd mistaken my laugh for a sob. Shock, I guessed. That didn't make it any less weird.

A door slammed. We turned. Max had vanished. My fractured brain took a moment to put it together. "Bertie's room."

I pulled myself to my wobbly feet and followed Ephram, who was already in pursuit. There was a creak from inside and Bertie's voice.

"What are you doing? Max!"

Ephram swung the door open. It thudded against the wall.

No Max.

For a stupid second, my mind ran through hide-and-seek locations: under the bed, behind the La-Z-Boy, in the wardrobe.

Bertie gaped at the wide-open window, lips trembling.

Ephram rushed over, pushed the fluttering curtains apart, and peered out. He closed his eyes for a long second.

Silence fell in the room, finally broken by Asha's footsteps on the stairs.

"Tell them we need an ambulance too," Ephram said as she entered, phone to her ear.

Bertie rose to his unsteady feet. Ephram moved quickly, placing himself between the old man and the window, hands outstretched.

"Please sit down, sir. You don't want to see." Ephram's voice was kind.

Bertie did as he was told, looking like a lost child.

CHAPTER THIRTY-FOUR

I kept my eyes on the shingle of the driveway as a too-familiar police officer led us away from the house, but out of the corner of my eye I saw the collapsed trellis Max had tried to climb down, saw the heap of black on the concrete side steps.

I really had liked Max for a while there, stupidly. I didn't want to see him dead. Didn't want to believe any of it had happened.

There were police statements and more police statements. Things were much more thorough this time. Our parents were called, and they took us home once the police were done. There was no talk of finishing our work at the museum. We didn't have a supervisor left anyway.

There was to be an inquest or something, but it felt irrelevant. We already knew the whole story. Asha filled me in on the bits I'd missed. It turned out that Ephram had been suspicious of Max ever since my phone went missing.

Ephram hadn't seen him take it, but he'd noticed Max had been slow to leave the office as the rest of us rushed downstairs to see what was happening with Sarah. Then he'd hurried to catch up with Ephram so they'd arrive in the gallery at the same time.

On the day I'd almost died, soon after I'd hurried off to confront Bertie, Max had made his own excuses and disappeared. Luckily, Ephram noticed and confided in Asha. They'd followed and saved my life.

I'd solved the mystery of Erich Stein's murder, but I couldn't see any of it going up on the neat information panels in the exhibition space.

I told the police who did it, of course. They told me they spoke to Bertie, attended by nurses and lawyers. The Hoppers said he found the wooden pig in the woods as a child. They said he was confused about the rest of it and had been having trouble telling the difference between reality and fantasy for a while.

I doubted there'd be a trial or even an arrest. But Bertie faced his own punishment. He'd lost Max, and the Hoppers had all the evidence of his infirmity they needed. They could imprison him in a long-term care home, and they'd get his house. They distanced themselves from Max, calling him misguided and constantly reminding their audiences that he'd tragically got himself mixed up with "Antifa," as if that had anything to do with it.

The irony was that Max hadn't needed to try to kill me. He and Bertie probably would have gotten away with it all, since there was no hard evidence for anything they'd done. Max hadn't needed to drug Ruth to discredit her. She'd lied her way into the program. Once that came out, no one would have believed a word she said anyway.

No one needed to die at all.

I wasn't sure how I felt. Max had accidentally killed himself in his panicked escape attempt, but was that justice? Was what happened to Bertie justice? Was Erich Stein's death justice?

What was "justice" meant to mean?

Asha's sculpture was allowed to remain up for a while. She'd posted the video online and it had gotten a load of views, especially because of the news coverage of Max's death. The board couldn't take it down without their agenda being obvious. Instead, they pushed back the opening of the museum to October, easily justifiable under the circumstances, perhaps even necessary. In the meantime, they left the tarps off the sculpture. A late summer storm destroyed most of it, although I suspected it had a little help from Randall.

Sarah and her wife moved out of Westonville, and she took an office job at an insurance brokerage through an agency. She hated it. She said she'd been applying for museum roles, but they were few and far between.

Wherever Max had hidden my phone, it obviously wasn't going to surface, so we couldn't prove what had happened between Peter and his assistant. He was voted party leader and continued to rise in the polls.

The Hoppers had won.

That's why I was so surprised when the letter came in early October.

Mom was sitting at our tiny kitchen table when I got back in from school. I chucked my bag on the floor and slumped into the other seat. A pot bubbled on the stove, steam fogging up the window that usually looked out onto the concrete wall of the next-door apartment building.

"I'm making soup. There's mail for you," Mom said. "And you left your dirty dishes in the sink this morning."

"Hmm," I said, inhaling the scent of overcooked broccoli and wishing Asha was there to make lentil soup. A large envelope lay on the table. I pulled it over, opened it, and tipped out the thick, paper-clipped wad onto the surface.

The first page read:

Dear Keira Martin,

We are delighted to inform you that you have been selected as a recipient of one of this year's Hopper Scholarships.

I almost dropped the thing in shock. I'd assumed I'd lost any chance of that on the day I accused Peter's father of murder and his nephew went out the window. I must have gasped, as Mom stood and edged her way around the table. She started reading over my shoulder.

"Oh! Keira! That's wonderful." She clutched at my shoulder.

I said nothing, scanning through the rest of the letter and the attached documents, which looked like some kind of a contract. I searched it for a non-disclosure agreement or something else dodgy, but it was entirely academic-focused. My scholarship depended on my attendance at university, keeping up good grades, and nothing else. I could only assume this was the same contract all Hopper Scholarship recipients received.

Where was the catch?

I picked up the empty envelope, about to put the papers back in, but it was heavier than I expected. I shook it, and a piece of thick, cream cardstock fell out. It was probably clipped to the rest but got stuck in the envelope. It was professionally printed, with words in elegant italics surrounded by gold-embossed vines.

You Are Cordially Invited to the Presentation of the Hopper Scholarships

Details followed: a time and place. At the bottom was a handwritten note in cursive.

Can't wait to see you there, Keira! — Jules

"Oooh," said my mother, snatching the card. "There's a ceremony and everything!"

That's when I got it.

They didn't know I disagreed with them and all they stood for. They'd seen me at their rally, after all, and probably hadn't noticed me leave amongst all the fuss over Ruth drinking. They weren't at the library and didn't know I'd been there with the counter protestors. I wasn't in Asha's video of her sculpture, and maybe Randall misinterpreted me running away when Sarah quit.

They wanted me on stage next to them. They wanted the world to know there were no hard feelings, no politically damaging resentments — that what had happened with Max had absolutely nothing to do with them. And, to be fair, it hadn't.

Look, they could say. *See this picture of us all smiling together? See her at our party? We're all friends.*

My mother was practically dancing. "Oh, Keira! This is it!"

I glanced up at her beaming face.

"You have the most wonderful future ahead of you. And you've worked so hard for it! You deserve this, even though it comes from that boy's family."

The pot bubbled over with a hiss, the flames erupting yellow up the sides. Mom hurried to deal with it as I stared at the envelope that had changed everything.

What could I do?

The ceremony took place in Toronto. They'd hired a "small" ballroom at the Royal York Hotel. I had to stifle a gasp as we stepped into the bright room, surrounded by the sound of classical music. The space was decorated with pink, white, and gold wallpaper; crown moldings; and a ceiling painted in the soft blue of a summer sky. I wasn't the only recipient, so there was a decent crowd — maybe a hundred, plus photographers, settling into soft seats under the delicate glitter of an elaborate crystal and gold chandelier.

There were even two television cameras, one set up on each side. I'd been expecting that. Having me there had to be at least a little newsworthy or they wouldn't have bothered doing it. But seeing them there, dark lenses focused on the crowd, brought back the Hoppers' party — the night Ruth died. My footsteps slowed. Could I do this?

"I'll try to bag us four spots together," Mom said, peering at the almost-full room as we approached a black-suited staff member at the door.

"Keira and Jane Martin," I said to the woman.

She didn't check her clipboard but smiled, recognition in her eyes. "There are seats reserved for you at the front." She led us over, removing the four "reserved" cards in the front row seats.

"Oooh!" said Mom. "We're VIPs!"

There were definitely eyes on us, and I didn't know where to look, so I sat down and stared at the lap of my dress while I waited. It was the black one I'd worn that first night at the camp, but Mom had ironed it, and it sat a lot better on me as a result.

I'd asked to bring three guests, and they'd agreed. I'd arrived with my mother, and Asha and Ephram arrived together a few minutes later. Asha wore her trademark, mismatched, vintage wear in blue and purple, and Ephram had yet another perfect suit. I hugged my friends tightly, wondering if they could feel me shaking. Asha returned my embrace fiercely, and Ephram gave me a gentle pat on the back, which was his equivalent.

Jules swooped in from the side of the stage as soon as we were done, arms wide. Given her timing, I wondered if she'd been waiting and watching until we were all there, perhaps hoping to be caught by the cameras.

"I didn't know you were bringing our other students! How wonderful!" She pressed each of us into an awkward hug.

"Thanks," I said lamely. The others stayed silent. The edge of Asha's mouth twitched. It was obviously an effort for her.

Jules nodded, apparently picking up on the frosty atmosphere. "Well, I should go and get everything ready for the presentation, shouldn't I?"

She bustled off, heading to her husband. Peter stood to one side, talking to two grinning parents, a tall, pale boy between them in an ill-fitting suit and a ridiculous teenage mustache clinging to his upper lip. No doubt another Hopper Scholarship recipient. Jules tapped Peter on the shoulder, and they both headed up onto the stage. The tasteful music was turned down, and the attention of the room turned on the Hoppers.

"Showtime," Asha said, and we took our seats. I arranged the skirt of my dress around me on the chair nervously.

The other recipients were called up first — winners of science fairs and math competitions sponsored by the Hoppers. Peter Hopper announced each one and explained how they earned their scholarship.

The boys and girls were each momentarily suspended in time, frozen as the flashes bleached out their faces. They beamed as Peter Hopper clutched them in his two-handed grip, cheered on by a luminous room full of family and strangers.

I tensed when my name was called. The applause seemed louder than it had with the others as I approached the stage, thundering in my ears. That made sense. Everyone knew at least some of our story.

It was hard to remember how to walk normally and I felt like a robot, too stiff as I jerked up the steps to the stage where Peter Hopper waited. I stood next to him, smoothed my skirt, and looked out into the crowd, into the golden room, into all the faces smiling up at me, into the future that the Hopper scholarship promised.

It was a wonderful future. It was the one I'd wanted so badly. The one Dad had dreamed of but had been out of reach since his death: a fully paid-for education at the university he had helped build. I tried not to look directly at the TV cameras, but I could see them, like crouching black insects at the periphery of my vision.

Mom was right. I'd earned this scholarship. I'd solved an eighty-year-old murder mystery and two modern, unnatural deaths.

But it would never be mine.

Questions about Erich Stein had tortured me ever since I'd left Camp 43. Had Max been right? Was the only good Nazi a dead Nazi? Was Erich really a Nazi? He was certainly a part of it, even if he was immature and naive, as Ben Lang had said. There was no sign he stood up against any of it. Was that enough to deserve what he got? It had taken me a long time to realize that none of those questions mattered.

The only thing that mattered was what I did, faced with my own choices.

I didn't even wait until Peter could get into why I'd been awarded the scholarship. His introduction would be a heavily edited version, and I didn't want to give him a chance to censor what we'd gone through.

I moved toward his mic. Peter was still clapping along with the audience.

My mouth was so dry it was hard to get the words out. "Can … can I get Asha and Ephram up on stage too, please?"

Asha leapt to her feet, while Ephram stood carefully, putting his hands on his knees as he straightened up. Asha had been the one to suggest they join me, but Ephram had quickly agreed. Asha bounced her way up the steps, the light shining on her rainbow hair. Ephram looked as stiff as I felt.

There was more applause, some of it coming from Peter. His smile was tighter, and his gaze focused on Asha, who he'd obviously pegged as a troublemaker after the sculpture stuff.

Asha took and squeezed my free hand. I leaned forward and spoke quickly but clearly into the mic before I had a chance to change my mind.

"I will be declining the scholarship."

Peter took a step toward the mic. I pulled it out of the stand and stepped back. He couldn't exactly snatch the mic from me, so he gave a confused shrug that was clearly meant to look bemused, but I could see the anger behind it.

I was glad I'd rehearsed what I was going to say, or I'd have totally blanked.

"When I was working at the museum, I interviewed Peter Hopper's father and recorded our conversation." My voice wavered a little. "What I didn't realize at the time was that I had also recorded Peter Hopper arguing in the next room with his assistant, Jenny Seaton."

Peter froze. He'd thought it was Max's recording and Max's alone. He had no idea that all four of us had heard it. I very much doubt he'd have let us on the stage if he'd suspected we had.

It was so bright under all those lights. I passed the mic to Asha. This was a joint statement, after all, and I was literally shaking. It was a relief to let her take over, as we'd discussed.

"We listened to the recording together: me, Keira, Ephram, and Max." There was an eagerness to her tone, and I was glad she'd volunteered to explain the important bit. I was still trembling, and Peter was staring at us now, mouth open. I glanced at the TV camera on the right. The lights were on, and the woman behind it was staring intently at the screen on her side. I hoped that meant she was broadcasting live or at least recording.

"We heard Peter and Jenny discussing their relationship, and Jenny saying she had 'got rid of' Peter's baby. Jenny Seaton is telling the truth. Peter Hopper is a liar."

There. She'd said it. We couldn't take it back now.

She passed the mic to Ephram and he spoke, his voice carrying well. "The recording was lost, probably destroyed by Maxwell de Jong, who tried to convince us not to come forward with this information. But the three of us are witnesses to what we heard."

More flashes of light. Peter looked lost beside us on the stage. At the back of the room, I saw the shine of Jules's silver dress as she ran out of the double doors. How much had she known? How much had she suspected? I remembered her, sitting by Peter's side and nodding as he blamed "both sides" for the library attack. Any sympathy I might have had evaporated.

My mother looked stricken, and I felt her shock, her pain. I hadn't told her about our plan. She might have tried to talk me out of it. She might have succeeded.

It was hard to meet her gaze, but I tried to give her a reassuring smile as Ephram handed the mic back to me.

"And that's not the only reason I'm refusing the scholarship," I said. "We learned a lot working at Camp 43, including how the Nazis tried to destroy anything that did not fit their narrow definition of what a German should be. Their genocide against the Jewish people is rightfully remembered, but their attempts to exterminate 2SLGBTQ+ people are often forgotten. Never again means never again for everyone."

The other guests stared, obviously wondering what they should do, how they should react. I felt sorry for them, worrying if this would impact their children and their scholarships.

"Pulling books from libraries because you don't like the people in them is the first step in trying to erase them altogether, just as it was in Nazi Germany."

Mom watched too, shock still etched on her face.

I could see what she was thinking. I was thinking the same thing myself: goodbye to the perfect future we'd planned at the university that my dad literally built.

I still had a future, of course, but it was unlikely to contain ballrooms like this. I might be sued into permanent poverty. It was hopefully a future without Peter Hopper in power, but with politics, you could never be sure. I was under no illusions that the end of the Hoppers would be the end of their kind of intolerance.

But I wouldn't be complicit in any of it, no matter what it cost me.

When I continued, I spoke to Mom alone.

"Perhaps, if people had stood up then, it could have been stopped. That's why I can't take the Hoppers' money. That's why the three of us are doing what we can now. We can't be a part of this. We spent the summer learning where it leads. This is us, trying to stop it."

Mom's eyes shone, but she nodded.

The lights of the cameras were still on us, but I'd said my bit. Asha, Ephram, and I looked at each other, and I was so glad I had them there, standing with me. I fumbled the mic back into the stand, and we made it to the edge of the stage. Mom ran over and up the stairs to intercept me. She hugged me so tightly it was a moment before I could speak.

"Someone told me Dalhousie is nice," I managed.

I felt the huff of her laugh against my cheek.

"I wasn't ready for you to move out anyway." She let go and stepped back, smiling.

"You okay?" Asha took my hand and squeezed it. I nodded, even though I felt super dizzy.

Ephram smiled. "Then let's go."

We stepped off the stage and into our future together.

Acknowledgements

If you are the kind of person who reads the acknowledgements in books, and it seems you are, you will be well aware that writing a book is not a solitary pursuit. I have a lot of people to thank for getting this book to the point where you hold it in your hands (or on your ereader).

I would like to thank the Toronto Arts Council, for giving me a grant to write this. This book would literally not exist without their encouragement. I had honestly given up on it when I heard they had awarded me the grant. But the fact that they saw something in it made me pick it back up again and finish writing the thing.

The staff at the Toronto Reference Library pulled so many books and other documents from the stacks for me during my months of research for this book, and I will always appreciate them and their helpful professionalism.

I have also had wonderful feedback from a number of early readers. So thank you so much to Jill Belcher (my mum), Jo Hope (my sister), my friends Jo Karaplis, Joyce Grant, Danielle Younge-Ullman and James Bow, as well as Steve Wheeler for all his thoughtful and detailed feedback. All the advice is appreciated more than you know.

Thanks also to my dear East End coven: Star Spider, Karen Krossing, Heather Camlot, Maureen McGowan, Caroline Fernandez,

Loretta Garbutt and Mireille Messier. I miss our Friday mornings together.

And of course, this would not be a book without DCB. Thank you so much to Sarah Jensen, Fei Dong, Luckshika Rajaratnam, Sarah Cooper, and especially Barry Jowett, editor and publisher extraordinaire.

And my family, obviously. Matt, thanks so much for your support. Amelia and Rowan, thanks for complicating and enriching my life beyond measure. I am so grateful you are both exactly the way you are.

Thank you, thank you, thank you.

PHOTO CREDIT: JULIETTE CAPDEVIELLE

Kate Blair is an award-nominated author originally from Hayling Island, UK. She has been a finalist for the Manitoba Young Readers' Choice Award and the Saskatchewan Young Readers' Choice Snow Willow Award. Her novels *Transferral* and *Tangled Planet* were both longlisted for the Sunburst Award and *Transferral* was a Starred Selection of the Canadian Children's Book Centre's Best Books for Kids and Teens. Blair currently lives in Toronto, Ontario.

We acknowledge the sacred land on which Cormorant Books operates. It has been a site of human activity for 15,000 years. This land is the territory of the Huron-Wendat and Petun First Nations, the Seneca, and most recently, the Mississaugas of the Credit River. The territory was the subject of the Dish With One Spoon Wampum Belt Covenant, an agreement between the Iroquois Confederacy and Confederacy of the Ojibway and allied nations to peaceably share and steward the resources around the Great Lakes. Today, the meeting place of Toronto is still home to many Indigenous people from across Turtle Island. We are grateful to have the opportunity to work in the community, on this territory.

We are also mindful of broken covenants and the need to strive to make right with all our relations.